ALSO BY PETER JAMES
FROM CLIPPER LARGE PRINT

Dead Letter Drop

Peter James

W F HOWES LTD

This large print edition published in 2014 by
W F Howes Ltd
Unit 4, Rearsby Business Park, Gaddesby Lane,
Rearsby, Leicester LE7 4YH

1 3 5 7 9 10 8 6 4 2

First published in the United Kingdom in 1981
by W. H. Allen

A CIP catalogue record for this book is available
from the British Library

ISBN 978 1 47126 650 8

Typeset by Palimpsest Book Production Limited,
Falkirk, Stirlingshire

Printed and bound in Great Britain
by TJ International Ltd, Padstow, Cornwall

MIX
Paper from
responsible sources
FSC
www.fsc.org   FSC® C013056

To Georgina, my bride of one novel,
for courage, for strength, for patience
and above all for love

Does the Eagle know what is in the pit
Or wilt thou go ask the Mole?

WILLIAM BLAKE

FOREWORD

Welcome to my first published novel, which crept, unseen and unnoticed, onto the bottom shelves at the rear of a handful of bookshops kind enough to stock it back in 1981 – and remained there, mostly unsold. I remember WH Smith, out of the goodness of their hearts, taking a grand total of thirty copies – a far cry from the 30,000 they would take of books that were destined for the bestseller lists! But I am still hugely grateful to them for giving a total unknown the kudos of being able to say, 'Ah, yes, WH Smith stock it, actually!'

It was rejected by the first publisher who read it, New English Library, headed by Nick Webb. Seven years later, in 1988, he was to surprise me by outbidding all other UK publishers for my supernatural thriller *Possession*. The second publisher, to my joy and delight, bought it. WH Allen paid a princely £2,000 – not a lot of money even in those days.

It was not the first novel that I had written – I wrote three between 1967 and 1970 which, luckily, were never published at all, much to my dismay back then. The first was titled *Ride Down a Roller Coaster* and it was inspired by my hero at the time, a young writer called Adam Diment who wrote three massively successful, racy, spy thrillers – *The Dolly Dolly Spy, The Great Spy Race* and *The Bang Bang Birds* – which enabled him to live a Champagne lifestyle in his mid-twenties and drive an Aston Martin, a car I coveted above all others. *Roller Coaster* wasn't a spy thriller; it was a kind of rake's progress to disaster through the pop and drug world of my own teen era, the 1960s.

Unlike Adam Diment's first book, mine was turned down by an endless succession of UK agents and publishers. A friend who read it told me it might appeal more to American tastes than British. I bought a copy of *The Writers' and Artists' Year Book* and singled out a New York agent, Kurt Hellmer, who had one of the largest entries. Ever hopeful, I dutifully photocopied the manuscript and airmailed it to him. Imagine my surprise when six weeks later I received an airmail letter (this was in the days before that wonderful technology called fax) containing eight pages of effusive praise telling me I was a wonderful writer, but the book needed some editorial work, after which he was confident it would be published – and listing his thoughts with copious notes. But by then, now at film school, I was nearly at the end of my second novel *Atom Bomb Angel* (a title I was to use again over a decade later for my second published novel).

I sent him the new manuscript, but he replied

that he didn't like it as much as *Roller Coaster* and please would I consider his notes. However, I had then started work on my third novel, a zany comedy titled *Bethlehem Where Are You?* Kurt hated this book with a vengeance and told me to go back to *Roller Coaster*. By now I had graduated from film school and emigrated to Canada, where I got a job, through a stroke of luck, at a Toronto television station, writing a daily programme for pre-school children called *Polka Dot Door*. I wrote proudly to Hellmer telling him the news. Within days I had a very snarky letter back from him, telling me to quit this job if I was serious about a career as a novelist, as I would never write a novel if I was writing for a day job. He advised me to get a job in a library or a factory.

I ignored his advice, *Roller Coaster* remained an unfinished project and instead I turned my energies to making films – starting with writing and producing a series of low-budget horrors, and then a comedy called *Spanish Fly,* starring Terry-Thomas and Leslie Phillips, which came out in 1976 to disastrous reviews. Barry Norman, then the doyen of all film critics, called it 'The worst British film since the Second World War and the least funny British funny film ever made.' I have the framed review hanging proudly in my office today!

Spanish Fly, in which I had invested myself heavily, wiped me out financially, and I was unsure what to do to recover. At this time my father and mother were running our successful family business, Cornelia James, Glovemakers to the Queen, with a factory in Brighton. My father became ill with heart trouble and they were thinking of selling the business. I realized that, having not made it as a writer, and being in a parlous financial state, it would be sensible to go into the business, which would at least give me a decent living. So I went to work in the factory, dimly remembering the advice of my agent, the lovely, patient Kurt Hellmer.

My then wife, and several friends who knew of my novel-writing ambitions, kept asking me if I was still going to try to achieve my dream of getting a book published. I was twenty-eight and it was a wake-up call. But what to write? Then, by chance, I read an article in *The Times* saying that with Adam Diment having stopped writing, and with Ian Fleming long dead, there was now an acute shortage of racy spy thrillers. It was a light-bulb moment for me!

I knew one person who had worked in the security services, Vanessa Gebbie, now a successful novelist in her own right, who had once been a secretary in MI5. Although restricted in what she could tell me, I gleaned enough from her, and from reading a raft of fiction and non-fiction about MI5 and MI6, to have some idea of the world of spooks. I also had, buzzing in my head, an idea for an opening scene for a novel – but no idea where to take it from there.

So I wrote the scene – a man and a girl wake in his New York apartment, after a raunchy night, to find someone breaking into the room, who then, immediately and inexplicably, commits suicide. Unlike my Roy Grace novels, which I plot meticulously and always know the ending I want to arrive at, I had no idea what would happen next. So I just kept writing and writing and writing. Finally, in 1979, I finished the book. I titled it *A Pink Envelope with a Bright Blue Bow*.

I photocopied it and airmailed it to my agent, Kurt Hellmer, who I had not spoken to since 1971. Two months went by without hearing a word from him. I finally phoned his number and got a dead line tone. After several more phone calls, I learned that he had died six years earlier. I guess dead agents aren't a lot of use . . .!

I was recommended, through a brilliant entertainments industry lawyer, Bob Storer of Harbottle and Lewes, two agents. One was Debbie Owen, totally delightful, but clearly not that hungry as she was Jeffrey Archer's agent. The other, Jon Thurley, was just starting out on his own, and I was told he was hungry. Four days after I mailed him the book he phoned me to say he wanted to represent me, but I needed to change the title. Two months later I had the publishing deal I had always dreamed of, but never dared to believe would actually happen.

One of the strangest – and nicest – things about my writing career is that I have so often found

myself writing about subjects that subsequently –
entirely coincidentally – become major news, as
with my fifth Roy Grace novel, *Dead Tomorrow*,
which is about the murky world of the international trafficking of human organs. *Dead Letter
Drop* is about the discovery of a mole deep within
MI5. Within days of signing my publishing deal,
the scandal of Anthony Blunt broke. A senior
member of MI5, he had been exposed as a spy
for Russia.

I hope you have as much fun reading *Dead Letter
Drop* as I did writing it. Take it with a pinch of
salt and please don't judge me too harshly!

Peter James
Sussex

CHAPTER 1

There is a strange sensation you get when you know someone has entered your room but you haven't yet seen or heard him. You just feel him there. I got that feeling in my bedroom late one night. It was very late and very dark.

I had had the same chill before on a thousand different occasions, in a thousand different circumstances; a car breaking its grip on a wet road, an aeroplane dropping 5,000 feet in an air pocket, a shadow coming from a dark alley.

There was definitely someone in the room. He wasn't a friend. Friends don't drop by into my bedroom at 2.30 in the morning – not on the thirty-second floor of a building where the elevator has been switched off, and the key is in my jacket pocket, hanging on a chair near the bed, where there are 3 Ingersoll ten-lever deadlocks, 2 Chubb two-bolt upright mortices, a Yale No. 1, and a double safety chain, not to mention a 24-hour armed door surveillance, making entry to this building harder than the exit from most jails. He was no friend. I didn't move. He didn't move. I had an advantage over him: he thought I was

1

asleep. He had a better advantage over me: he'd probably been in the dark for a long time and his eyes would be well accustomed to it. He had one bigger advantage still: he wasn't sprawled, stark naked, dripping in baby oil, with one foot manacled to the bedstead, and he didn't have a quietly sleeping naked bird occupying the 5 feet 11½ inches that separated an extremely greasy hand from an uncocked Beretta.

I spent the next several tenths of a second debating what to do. My visitor obviously wasn't going to hang about for the rest of the evening – he'd have to have been a very dedicated voyeur to go to such lengths. He certainly wasn't any kind of cat burglar out to steal anything – the place didn't have any valuables, neither the Fort Knox nor the National Gallery variety; there was nothing in it that a colour-blind midget with an IQ of 24 couldn't have bought from a Bloomingdale's sale in half an hour flat for a couple of thousand dollars – and in fact probably had. What there was could best be described as embryonic Jewish Renaissance, and constituted the equivalent amount of personal effects you are likely to encounter walking into a room of a half-built Holiday Inn.

My visitor didn't seem like he wanted to chat. If he did, he'd probably have opened the dialogue by now. No, the most likely reason for his visit, I concluded in the two-tenths of a second it took me to weigh up the alternatives, was to do some killing.

On account of lack of choice the most likely victims seemed to be either Sumpy or me. Sumpy is a variation of 'sump' – a nickname I gave her for her fascination with Johnson's Baby Oil – at the procreation end, which is what she seemed to think it was for, rather than at the end product of same for which it was originally intended. If the visitor was for her it could only have been some jilted lover; since Houdini had died before she was born I ruled out the possibility of the caller being for her.

All of a sudden I felt lonely. Our house guest must have just about figured out who was who by now; a 9-millimetre silenced parabellum slug for me and a razor for her so she wouldn't be waking the neighbours with any hollering.

There was no way I could make it to my gun in time. There was no way I could swing my right foot high into the air and bring that bedstead crashing down on his head prior to having to retrieve my brains and most of my skull from my neighbour's apartment. It was equally unlikely that if I remained still he might go away.

The bang came. Not a quiet, silenced plug sound but a great, hefty, high-velocity, 200-grain magnum .44 explosion, and death descended on me. It was a hot, dark thump; a huge, great weight that crushed my bone and shot the wind out of me, shot all the wind out of me. It was damp and bloody and hurt like hell. It was the son-of-a-bitch visitor himself.

3

He lay there, sprawled over the top of me, revolver sticking in his mouth and most of the back of his skull deposited out onto Park Avenue.

I sat up, managed to get the lights on. There were shouts. There were yells and footsteps and bells and sirens and pounding sounds, and Sumpy woke up without even opening her eyes and asked if I had gone mad and went back to sleep again.

I disentangled my foot and staggered to the kitchen to put the kettle on – it didn't look as if I was going to get much more sleep that night. I cracked my head on a cupboard door because I was confused. Reckon I had a right to be. Someone had gone to a lot of trouble to commit suicide.

CHAPTER 2

What a hell of a night it had been. I wanted to spend the morning forgetting it for a few hours. It was a glorious, cold, November Sunday morning and Manhattan looked just great. Only a few factories and few exhaust pipes were chucking their excrement into the sky. The World Trade Centre and the Chrysler Building and the Empire State Building and all the rest of Manhattan's fantastic skyline stood crisp and clear against and into the sky, just as all its creators had ever envisioned it should.

Sumpy and I stood wrapped in our coats on the open deck of the Staten Island ferry with the water of the Hudson river churning past us. I took a large bite from the still-warm potato knish I had been carrying in a paper bag in my pocket, and hoped it would mop up some of the pints and pints of coffee that swilled in my insides and take the taste of the Marlboros and Winstons and Salems and Tareyton Lights and Camel Lights and Cools and Mores and Chesterfields and all the other cigarettes I had been able to scrounge during the night, out of my mouth and throat and lungs and everywhere else.

That knish tasted good. It came from Yonah Schimmel's. The Yonah Schimmel Knish Bakery is one of the great eating establishments of the world; if the Michelin gastronomic guide extended to the US it would surely mention it as 'worthy of a detour'. Anybody who hasn't been there has to go. It is spectacularly insignificant in appearance; it sits in one of the dirtiest, dreariest, grungiest places on God's earth, deep in the heart of Manhattan, on the forlorn border between the East Village and Lower East Side, a bottle cap's flick from the Bowery; a solitary five-storey brownstone with a yellow facia board that stands next to the yard of Blevitzky Bros Monuments, where two elderly vans sit, sagging on their suspension, behind collapsing wire-fencing. The street in front is a dismal dual carriageway with odd bits of barren shrubbery; there are morose and grubby people wandering around, and bits of garbage rolling along in the wind. It could pass with no difficulty as a suburb of any of a hundred American cities.

The inside isn't much of an improvement. A sign behind a high counter invites the clientele to 'Try our new cherry cheesecake knish!' and looks at least 10 years old. Behind the counter stands a short elderly man in a white apron with the burden of the world on his shoulders. The restaurant is empty except for two men in battered leather jackets deep in discussion but he still doesn't have much time to spare to take orders. He marches over to a dumb waiter, a real one with a rope pull, and barks down the shaft, then stands on guard beside it with the hapless look of a sentry on a winter's night.

What comes up from that dumb waiter, however, is pure gold; busting with every conceivable filling – large, heavy, lovingly misshapen, immensely fattening and doubtlessly knee-deep in cholesterol.

Early on that Sunday morning, paradise was a warm Yonah Schimmel potato knish, eaten with the salted breeze of the Hudson and the warm perfume of Sumpy.

I'd kept the truth from her so far. What she thought was simply that we'd had an intruder and I had shot him. I decided that for the time being, and probably for ever, it was best to leave it that way. She thought I'd done something brave and heroic in saving both our lives. I'd no desire to take false credit, but on the other hand she was a bright girl and I didn't want to set her thinking too much in case she came to the realisation that there might be more to my job in the plastic box manufacturing business than met the ordinary long, short or squint-sighted naked eye. And that wouldn't be any good at all.

So Mr Big Hero took another bite of his potato knish and stared out at the badlands and goodlands of sleepy-time Staten Island, where 328,000 Americans were waking to a bright, sunny, all-American Sunday morning, to the *New York*

Sunday Times crossword, and waffles, syrup and bacon, and a gentle screw, and toothpaste, and coffee, and no clatter of the garbage trucks today.

'It's cold,' she said, and she was right; it was cold, damn cold and it felt good, for in the warm a soft slunky feeling would have crept straight up my body and put me in the land of nod, and there wasn't going to be any nod for a long time yet, because when we got back to Manhattan I was going to have to go into the police station at West 54th and spend most of this beautiful day inside its dismal grey walls, answering questions and filling out forms and watching the dregs and misfits and victims of humanity be dragged interminably in and out, for speeding, murder, pickpocketing, mugging, knifing, raping, and reporting lost tabby cats and black widow spiders.

There was no shortage of forms, and carbon copies to go under the forms, and columns to be filled in on the forms. I could have done it all myself in about ten minutes flat, with the aid of a couple of IBM computers and three dozen secretaries; unfortunately the only equipment that the city of New York could offer me was a battered, old, manual Olivetti, with a lower-case 't' that had broken off, and a pair of index fingers attached to 18 stone of fatted flesh in a uniform grubby enough to give anorexia to a clothes moth. His dexterity at extricating his breakfast from his teeth with one finger, picking his nose with another, his

8

ear with a third and typing at the same time was remarkable; but it was the typing that suffered the most.

Relays of coffee arrived in receptacles that made British Rail's plastic beakers seem like Crown Derby. There were no knishes and doughnuts weren't available on this block on a Sunday; none others were worth eating, the resident doughnut expert informed me, but there was a Puerto Rican topless go-go dancer who did blow jobs in the men's room of a coke den up in Harlem Sunday lunchtime, if I was interested in taking a ride. But it didn't particularly appeal.

The keys clacked intermittently, punctuated by the odd curse as he filled in the lower-case 't's by hand, and I began, gratefully, to drift into a few minutes of sleep. When I woke, Supertypist had an added burden to his bogeys and his breakfast and his Olivetti: some idiot had given him a carton of honey-barbecued spare ribs.

Several hours later the last rib hit the waste bin and the last sheet of the forms was wrenched out of the machine. I read through it and put my signature on it, and he read through it and put his 'X' on it and smudged it. My hand was shaken and my back patted. I had been a good boy. I had grappled fearlessly with an intruder, seized his weapon, shot him, and then had the good sense to call the police and fill out their forms for them, and there would be no need for me to attend the inquest, and if I would care to step outside it would be nothing short of a pleasure for the City of New York to provide me with a freebie ride home in a patrol car.

I was tired – dog, dog tired – and wanted out of that police station and into bed. I went outside and breathed the chill air, and watched the steam pouring out of a subway vent in the road, and listened to the distant hum of cars and far-off sirens. Peace. It was growing dark; some street-lamps were on, the rest were flickering to get on. Sumpy would be at her apartment by now, back from lunch with her brother and sister-in-law and their three kids in their house by the sea down in Mamaroneck; just the normal routine of a normal life.

The car pulled up for me, four great burly cops inside. They all looked reasonably alert – it's strange how you can tell something like that just from shadows or silhouettes, but you can. One in the back stepped out to hold the door for me and then climbed in after me; I sat in the middle of the back seat, snugly wedged between two uniformed hulks. They were big, comfortingly big. I lounged back into the greasy vinyl and inhaled the smell of plastic and stale cigarettes that most American cars smell of, and listened to the tramp, tramp noise of the tyres that all American cars make. I felt relaxed and was about to start up some friendly chatter when I felt a hard thin object slide in between my thighs and come firmly to rest against my right ball.

'Don troi nuttin.'

I don't know what the hell they expected me to try. Even if they were all unconscious the only way I could have got out of that car would have been to have drilled a hole in the roof. All of a sudden I felt very awake again. I felt very awake, but I knew I was tired, overtired, dangerously overtired, and that's not good.

CHAPTER 3

One half of me was sorely tempted not to bother to find out who they were, or where they were taking me, or what they planned to do, but just to crash out, let them take me wherever they planned and let the chips fall where they might.

The other half of me that had kept me out of the long wooden box for over three decades wasn't going to have any of it. Secretly I was glad about that.

'Know thine enemy,' says the Good Book. On my 18 months' intensive training in the Highlands six years back I'd been told much the same. I studied them, listening to their chatter: not a great deal to listen to – scrambled eggs for brains in their dialogue department; the highlight of their conversation was whether it would be better to take the first, second or third left to get to the Henry Hudson Parkway. They could count to three.

They were goons, four big rented goons, and I had an ominous feeling that they hadn't got the wrong man; I could almost hear a cement-mixer grinding away in the trunk, making the quick-drying concrete for a pair of snug-fitting size 9½ boots.

I stared through the hairs in the goon on my right's nostrils at the far-away lights of the Bronx as we cruised up the west bank of the Hudson, along the scenic Palisades Parkway past the neatly mown grass and the neatly trimmed hedges and the neatly painted signs to the neatly laid-out beauty spots – all carefully done to show how wealthy and prosperous the State of New Jersey was compared to its shabby neighbour on the other side of that deep, deep river. And tonight it looked deeper than ever.

There was an acute pain in my backside. What had felt like a small lump at the beginning of the ride was hurting more and more at each bump we went over. It was something I was sitting on. The pain, combined with the jabs from the shooter in my private parts every time we jolted, was beginning to make me feel irritable.

The two-way radio suddenly crackled into life. 'Bravo Delta, are you on time for the wedding?'

One of the goons in the front replied, 'Bravo Delta picked up the groom.'

There was a pause while the usual squawks and screeches came through the speaker, then, 'Roger, Bravo Delta, we're on our way to collect the bride. See you at the church.'

'You got it,' said the goon.

It didn't tax my brain a great deal to work out

who the bride might be, but just to help me out the goon in the front passenger seat, whose teeth looked like they had suffered a bad attack from termites, and whose breath smelt like he'd been drinking from a rain-tub full of dead bats, turned the ghastly assembly of scars, dents, spots and boils, perched above his neck and below his hat, that passed as his head. 'Means your broad, sweetheart.'

If nothing else, this gem of English syntax annihilated the remainder of my fears about them having the wrong man. However, it didn't make the pain in my backside any better, and it didn't make me feel any happier. Nor did it give me any better clue as to who they were or what they wanted: a corpse, or a source of information – at the end of it all, probably both. I wasn't overly inclined towards letting them have either; however, in light of the current situation, unless I did something pretty smart, and pretty quickly, it didn't seem that my opinion was going to amount to a hill of beans.

We turned off the Parkway onto 9 West, curving round and underneath the Parkway onto a thickly wooded two-lane road. It was starting to rain; it was light rain, but it hit the car with a distinct slashing sound – a sound I had heard before when it rained in temperatures as cold as it was today: freezing rain – one of the most lethal of all driving hazards. To the driver it looks like ordinary rain, and it is, except that the moment it touches the surface it turns to ice; within moments of freezing rain starting, the road turns into an ice rink. It is not an uncommon phenomenon in the north eastern seaboard states during the winter. It is very difficult and very frightening to drive on. Muttered curses from the front seat, and the motion of the speed of the car easing slightly, indicated that the driver had recognised the hazard; whilst this rain lasted, and it wouldn't last for long, I didn't have to worry about the driver.

I tried in the gloom to study as best I could the shooter that was wedged between my legs; it was either a Smith and Wesson .44 revolver or a cheap copy cranked out by some back-street supplier. Either way it would be about the nearest thing to a hand-held Howitzer, well capable of carrying my crown jewels down through the seat and out through the bottom of the car. If it was a copy then I needed to worry about the trigger mechanism since it probably would be unreliable and more than a little sensitive to the slightest movement – ideal for the type of gorilla holding it, since his breed were not the type to discriminate too much about when or where their shooters went off just as long as they went off long enough and often enough to keep them on someone's payroll.

The goon on my right was gazing out the window, off guard. The one in the passenger seat in front was wiping condensation off the windshield. Through the windshield, a long way ahead, was a green traffic light. Between us and the traffic

15

light was the battery of tail lights of a large truck, probably a tractor-trailer. We were travelling downhill, and too quickly for the surface.

The goon in the front passenger seat switched on the ordinary radio; a commercial jingle blared out. The music stopped and a jolly voice told us all what rotten, lousy, stinking husbands we'd all be if we didn't rush out instantly and make arrangements to have Whamtrash drainage systems installed in our homes and make life for our wives one whole lot easier. From the silence of the goons I could only think they were contemplating the advantages of a Whamtrash system.

'One of your friends came into my apartment last night and shot the wrong guy,' I announced.

The goon with the halitosis swivelled his head around. 'Shaddup.' He turned his head back to watch the road.

The traffic light was turning red. The radio told us of amazing bargains to be had at a local Pontiac dealer. All we had to do was go there and ask for Elmer Hyams. Elmer Hyams would do us real good. We would do our family unit a lot of good by buying a brand new Pontiac. We couldn't buy a brand new Pontiac anywhere else in the United States of America cheaper than by dropping in and saying 'Hi!' to Elmer Hyams.

I rammed my left thumb down hard, real hard, into the trigger mechanism of the goon's 44 and felt the hammer hit my thumb, hit it hard; my right hand smashed down on the reflex nerve of

16

his gun hand, the gun jerked up and I jerked my thumb out; the hammer carried on down to the shell, hit the shell good and hard; the bullet blew out and took a chunk out of the roof; another bullet blew out and took another chunk out of the roof; another bullet blew out and took off most of the roof of the goon on my right's head; another bullet blew out and went in between the goon in the front seat's shoulder blades, and came out of his chest carrying most of his heart with it, and took most of his heart out through the windshield and into the New Jersey countryside.

I now had the gun. The driver had both hands on the wheel and was trying to see what was going on in the back. He forgot for a moment about the red light and the truck that had stopped, then remembered. He stamped on the anchors on the iced-up road and was turning the wheel this way and that. I thumped the goon on my left's balls so hard he jumped up in the air. I had the door handle down and shoved him hard before he came back down in his seat, shoved him out into the road, and I was rolling out there with him. Another bullet blew out and went through his Adam's apple. I thumped into the grass verge and rolled over. I saw the big black car do one complete circle and then slide, nose first, straight under the long, long tailgate of that big, big truck, and that tailgate swallowed up the big black car as it went further and further under, slicing through the windshield, and through the steering wheel, and clean through the necks of the driver and his passenger, depositing their heads in the lap of the goon in the rear seat; it carried right on, slicing through the neck of the goon in the rear seat and depositing what was left of his head out through the rear windshield, so it rolled down the trunk of the car, bounced off the rear fender, and came to a rest a little way up the road.

The stabbing pain in my ass was still there. I gingerly felt my behind and found a big lump, a big, sharp lump. I pulled, and it came away from my trousers, and I held it up in the gloom: it was a set of false teeth.

I sat down, took some gulps of air and carbon monoxide. The highway had gone very quiet. Away up, I could hear the sounds of the truck driver retching. It was the only sound and it went on for a long time.

CHAPTER 4

I was working in New York for the Intercontinental Plastics Corporation. The company occupied seven of the thirty-two floors of the modern high-rise office block at 355 Park Avenue. Six of the floors were lumped together, the fourteenth to the nineteenth; the seventh was the penthouse floor, containing two private apartments for visiting clients or executives. No doubt in order to spare the expense of renting me lodgings during my lengthy stay over here. I was billeted in one of these apartments.

The company looked smart and successful. Its offices were plush, the receptionist and secretaries were pretty, and the facade of the building, with its brown steel and smoked glass, oozed the aura of money.

Intercontinental Plastics Corporation started life under a less grand name: the Idaho Wooden Box Company. It was founded by an out-of-work chicken sexer midway through the Depression. His name was Leo Zlimvaier. A Russian by birth, his father had emigrated with his family to the United States early in the twentieth century.

It was a familiar story. Leo was one of nine children who found themselves uprooted from their home, herded under the decks of an over-crowded boat and thrown around the ocean for weeks on end, amid sweat and vomit and a hundred other discomforts. Eventually young Leo and his family were disgorged into the full glory of the USA, and found themselves at the focal point of Western civilisation: in New York Central Station.

There was a choice open to them of five different railroad tickets. Leo Zlimvaier's father picked the one that, unknown to him at the time, assured him and his family of the bleakest of the five futures on offer. Two and a half days later they emerged, blinking and stupefied, into the bowels of God's country: Boise, Idaho. The first blinding realisation to hit Zlimvaier Senior as he stepped down onto the soil was this: they were in the middle of absolutely nowhere.

Zlimvaier struggled hard, and managed to feed and clothe his family. One by one, as soon as the children became old enough, he gave them as many dollars as he could spare and sent them off into the world to fend for themselves.

Leo's turn came as the Depression was starting. He was armed only with a few dollars and a working knowledge of his father's own profession: chicken sexing. Handicapped by poverty, but no idiot, he came to the rapid conclusion that nobody in the spring of 1930 in Boise, Idaho, or its

20

environs, stood much chance of getting rich out of chicken sexing.

There was, he was soon to discover, an acute shortage of fruit boxes since, owing to the general shortage of jobs, much of the populace had taken to selling apples and other fruit in the streets. Wood, he found out, came cheap, in the form of millions upon millions of trees that no one seemed to be interested in.

Leo Zlimvaier set to work, with the simplest of tools and sheer sweat, turning trees into fruit boxes. There was no shortage of customers for his boxes and he rapidly discovered that with money in his pocket it was easy to find others willing to make the fruit boxes for him. Within 12 months he had built a very large shed and had 75 people working in it. Although he wasn't as yet fully aware of it he was on his way to ranking alongside Charles Darrow, the inventor of Monopoly, and Leo Burnett, founder of the massive advertising agency, and many others who founded vast fortunes during the Depression years.

As the profits piled up, Zlimvaier started investing in machinery that could make fruit boxes very much quicker than the out-of-work engineers and stockbrokers and taxi drivers and insurance salesmen and such like, that were his workforce. Soon his shed was 3 times its original size, contained only 30 men, and churned out 100 times as many fruit boxes as before. At the very height of the Depression Zlimvaier bought his first Cadillac.

He married and produced a son, Dwight, but neither wife nor child really interested him. He was obsessed by boxes. Daily, people were writing to him, asking if he could produce other types of boxes. He started producing boxes for companies instead of farmers. He found the companies would pay higher prices and not quibble, so long as they got their deliveries.

A second factory was started, and the name of the company was changed to the National Business Box Company. Soon Zlimvaier was manufacturing everything from medicine chests to filing cabinets to safes. When the Second World War arrived Zlimvaier changed the name of the company again, this time to the National Munitions Box Corporation. One in every three packing cases and one in every three boxes containing ammunition used by the United States forces during the entire war was made by Leo Zlimvaier's factories.

After the war he started experimenting with plastics. Soon he was producing plastic drink-dispensers, plastic filing cabinets, plastic golf-bags: he produced, in plastic, anything into which something else could be put. He changed the name yet again, now to the National Plastic Box Corporation.

Computers started to appear in general usage in business. At that time they were unsightly piles of spaghetti wiring, searing valves, sheets of raw welded metal, whirring tapes, sprawling over a considerable acreage of floor space in what had once been neat and efficient-looking offices. The

National Plastic Box Corporation managed to produce smart cabinets for them so that all became concealed behind grey or blue boxes with a few impressive rows of switches and blinking lights.

Leo Zlimvaier went international and opened his first factory abroad, on an industrial estate between Slough and London's Heathrow Airport. He once again changed the name of the company. It became the Intercontinental Plastics Corporation. Six months later Zlimvaier keeled over with a massive heart attack and died. His widow inherited the lot. She had no idea the business had ever expanded from the one original shed, which still churned out fruit boxes. She made their 19-year-old son chairman and chief executive. It was the second biggest mistake of her life; her first was marrying Zlimvaier.

As far as the Intercontinental Plastics Corporation was concerned, Dwight Zlimvaier was not his father's son by any stretch of the imagination. He was not interested in plastic and he was not inter-ested in business. His sole consuming passion in life was collecting butterflies. It was only with the greatest reluctance that he dragged himself away from the slaughter, framing and cataloguing of these creatures to sign cheques and approve major decisions. Within four years of his father's death the profits of Intercontinental had slumped to an all-time low. Five factories were closing down through lack of work. The company was easy prey for the take-over brigade.

In an extremely complex and carefully planned succession of transactions the Intercontinental Plastics Corporation was bought by a consortium in England. This consortium needed a legitimate front under which to operate in the United States. Only a handful of Englishmen knew the true identity of this consortium: it was M15.

CHAPTER 5

There was little traffic coming down the highway and what there was travelled slowly past me, only just starting to pick up speed after having gawped at the smash.

I had to try and get to Sumpy before the rest of this mob, and I knew if I had any time at all that it was precious little. My chances of thumbing a ride were slim. Nobody stops for hitchhikers on a dark New Jersey road except the odd rapist for a solitary female. They certainly weren't going to stop for me, bleary-eyed, unwashed and with 36 hours of beard; if I was going to get myself a ride, I was going to have to dispense with the customary niceties.

A short way back, where we'd driven off the Parkway, we'd doubled back round and underneath it. I walked back there and up onto the Parkway, and stood looking down onto 9 West. It was a perfect vantage point; any car turning onto the Parkway would have to slow down to walking pace to make that turn.

I forced my adrenalin to start pumping, as I had been trained to be able to do, forced every muscle and blood vessel and nerve ending in my body into full alert by clenching and relaxing, clenching and relaxing, hyperventilating my lungs; my whole body began to tingle with energy; I was racing; the 25-foot drop to the road started looking easy, dangerously easy.

I crouched, poised, wound up like a spring; every factor of timing and movement that had been rammed into my skull during my training I yanked to the front of my brain's memory banks. I waited.

A truck passed, grinding up through the gears. Another. A giant tractor-trailer, its diesel firing staccato cracks into the evening sky through the exhaust that rose up from the massive hood in front of the windshield. A station wagon, loaded with kids whose heads were swivelled round at the wreck behind them down the road. The siren of the first police car heading for the wreck cut through the air like a cheese knife. A Ferrari howled off up the road, pressed down on its suspension by the force of acceleration like some powerful jungle cat. A motorbike accelerated after it in a hopeless attempt to pace it. A beat-up Ford full of greasers, radio blaring out music through the walls of the car. And then my mark: a large, soft-top Chevrolet going slowly, right-turn indicator flashing.

I stared carefully through the windshield as the car approached; the driver was definitely on his own. I planted my feet firmly on the ground, made sure my right foot was rock firm, then my left foot;

I bent my knees so that they were almost touching the ground, left knee slightly forward. I was going to have one chance and one chance only: if I landed awkwardly I would seriously injure myself; if I missed there was no way I'd get off the road before being hit by the next car, and what would be left of me by several more after that.

I froze the Chevrolet's progress down into fraction of a second by fraction of a second movement. I could see the driver's face clearly: thin, nervous, concentrating for all he was worth on the act of keeping his car travelling in a straight line down the dead straight road. I'd left it too late. No I hadn't. Yes I had; better to wait for the next car. Maybe not get another convertible for some time, not for a long time perhaps, empty like this, travelling so slowly, so close in to the bank. Jump!

I sprang, feet thrust out in front of me; air rushed past. The car was moving one hell of a lot faster from here than it had seemed to be from the bridge. I aimed the metal tips of my heels at the middle panel of the roof, worried about the PVC – it could be damn tough – then felt them slice through; then a thump, a horrendous ripping rending sound, a winding crack of my back on a metal strut, followed by a searing pain on my arm as another metal strut sliced off the skin. I crashed down onto the plastic cover of the back seat, felt the springs flatten and snap beneath me, then bounced up like some clumsy elephant on a trampoline, crashed down again, thumping violently into the seat back, kicked out my feet against the side of the car, and sank them hard into the cushioning on the panel. As my ass crashed back down onto the seat I was already reaching into my breast pocket for my Beretta.

My method of entry into the car had done something terrible to the driver's nerves. We did a sharp swerve across the approach lane and over both lanes of the Parkway; swerved back across the three lanes and onto the hard shoulder; back across the three lanes, this time with the tail end swiping a chunk of itself off against the central barrier. We swung back across the entire three lanes, then the approach lane ended and we swung back across the two remaining lanes, zigzagged wildly three times in succession, miraculously missing the central divider and the verge. My driver was getting the hang of things. We swerved back across only one and a half lanes this time, and then the idiot went and slammed on the anchors for all he was worth.

'Don't brake – accelerate!' I yelled. 'For Chrissake accelerate!' But it was too late; there was a scream of tyres from behind and I turned to see the headlamps of a saloon pointing almost vertically down at the tarmac. I tried to relax against the impact. He hit us with a wallop that lifted us in the air and spun us half round, flung me up in the air cracking my head on a roof spar, flung my driver up against his seat belting. Then he bashed us again, this time more gently, just behind the

28

driver's door. There was a rapid succession of screeching tyres, the banging of metal on metal and the smashing of metal on glass, that trailed on way back into the distance as most of the southbound Parkway drivers behind us tailgated each other.

'Shift it!' I said. 'Shift it!'

'I . . . but . . . I . . .'

'Move this goddam car, move it!'

'Accident. Must stop. Police. Insurance. Must stop.'

'Move it, you jerk, I'm telling you. Drive on!'

'But . . . my car . . .'

'Stamp on that accelerator – gas pedal – goddam stamp on it, or I'll blow your fucking head and balls off.'

'It won't go.' He started frantically to turn the ignition key; each time he did there was a horrible metallic grating sound. 'It won't go!' he repeated.

'It's already going,' I said.

He turned his head with a pathetic, pleading look, to find himself staring down the receiving end of an extremely unsympathetic and very deter-minedly held Beretta.

Something must have got through for he tramped on the gas pedal and the tyres, grinding themselves away against the wheel arches that had been rammed against them, spun protestingly round. As we grated forward there was a clattering, followed by a thunderous roar, as the exhaust parted company with us. Sounding like a cross between a tugboat and an iron foundry, we started to pick up speed.

'Just keep it going, nice and easy and as fast as you can, my friend.'

He gave a tiny nod. He was welded to the steering wheel and sitting bolt upright in his seat, like a rabbit with premature rigor mortis. 'Yes, er, sir.' Unfortunately he was one of those people who find it impossible to hold a car on a completely straight course and he continually sawed at the steering wheel with his hands. Up to about 50 it was tolerable. As the needle started to flicker up to the 65-mark we started to sway in an uncomfortable manner, his sawing movements became bigger and we began to feel very unstable.

'Slow down to 50 and hold it there. Hang a left onto the George Washington Bridge when we get to it.'

'Yes, sir.'

He was a natty little man, spick and span and dainty. A Chopin waltz was playing on his tape deck. He wore his hair short and it was slicked with hair cream. He had on a rather loud, brown checked jacket, with a bright red shirt and pale-blue polyester tie. He reeked of several different brands of after-shave and cologne and talcum powder and face lotion and under-arm spray and in-between-toes spray. He looked like a prime candidate for one of Elmer Hyams's Pontiac bargains.

'What's your name?'

'Henry, er, Timbuck – er, Henry Timbuck – er, Henry C. Timbuck, sir.'

'Glad to know you, Henry C. Timbuck.'

'Thank you, sir.'

He had a cute lisp. His whole voice in fact was cute. It was the typical nasally high-pitched accent of New York gays. He gave his words a little mince as he spoke, and minced his body at the same time. He relaxed, just a trifle, which was a mistake as he nearly put us up the back of a bus.

Henry C. Timbuck looked like he'd been all set for a Sunday night on the Manhattan tiles. I wondered vaguely whether he was off to some bar to sit on his own and try for a pick-up, or off to have dinner with his boyfriend, or off to that loneliest of all pastimes – cruising.

A hurricane was raging in through what was left of the roof, and I climbed over into the front seat to get the protection of the windshield. The stink of perfumes was even stronger.

'What do you do?' I asked him. I have no idea why I asked him; I didn't give a monkey's what he did, and I didn't hear his reply. There were a lot of matters I had to sort out fast, and for me they all took priority over Henry C. Timbuck's career. I churned over the events of today, trying to see where any of it fitted, if any of it fitted at all.

I was shivering with cold. 'Got a heater in this thing?'

Timbuck fiddled with some knobs on the dash

and the car went once more into a violent swerve. Fortunately there was nothing trying to pass us. A stream of roasting air poured onto my feet and a blast of freezing air shot into the centre of my stomach, accompanied by a noise from behind the dash not unlike that of an asthmatic bulldog.

I hit the button on what appeared outwardly to be a standard Seiko digital watch but inside contained the full technical treatment from MI5. Its level of accuracy was so high that it would not gain or lose more than a hundredth of a second in two years, either on the moon, on land, or five miles underwater. Not a lot of point in it, to my thinking, unless one is going in for inter-galactic travelling in a big way. Which I wasn't. Today's date beamed up on the dial. I shouldn't have gotten the date – the button I pushed was for the time. I pushed it again and the date appeared once more, dark purple against the cream background. So I pushed the button for the date. That also gave me the date. I pushed the button for the time again and got my precise height above sea level. I made a mental note to strangle two gentlemen, one named Trout, the other Trumbull, on my return to England. I pushed the time button again, losing patience, and got the temperature, first in Celsius, then in Fahrenheit, followed by a baro-metric read-out. I patiently and gently pushed the button once more. It gave me the time in Japan, followed by the time in Iceland, Libya, Romania and Argentina, then a rapid-fire sequential coded print-out of all emergency dialling codes to Control in London from almost anywhere in the world. Finally the contraption took complete leave of its senses and began to spew out gibberish at an ever increasing speed until the face became a blur of blinking lights that made it look like the entrance to a rather smart strip club.

The car clock read 8.25. 'That clock correct?'

'Er – no, sir . . . usually keep it half an hour fast, but right now it's stopped altogether . . . couple of months now . . .'

'Got a watch?'

'No – I, er, don't carry one . . . you know, muggings . . . I don't take any valuables with me when I go out.'

'What do you do with your nuts – leave them in a glass of water?'

If Henry C. Timbuck had a sense of humour he was doing a good job of concealing it. He ignored my remark, gritting his teeth and pursing his lips; half his face said that no way was he going to lower himself to laughing with a hijacker; the other half said that he was having the most exciting time of his life.

I looked around for the radio. Couldn't see it. There was just the tape deck, tinkling out the Chopin. It was getting on my nerves. I ejected the cartridge. 'Where's the radio?'

'Oh – I had it taken out; gets me down; so much bad news – all the time, whenever you turn the radio on; listen to a nice programme, nice music, nice talking, nice show – on comes the news: murder, rape, air crash, bombs. Why do they go and put nice programmes on then spoil them with the news?'

I didn't have the time right then to explain to Henry C. Timbuck how the world worked. I quietly cursed my luck in picking what must have been the only automobile in the United States of America that didn't have a radio in it.

I reckoned it was a good fifteen minutes since my exit from the bogus police car. I had been with Timbuck for about five minutes. If the crew that had been sent to grab Sumpy weren't already at her flat they couldn't be far away. I had to get to her before they did.

'Sir, I don't exactly know who you are,' said Timbuck, 'and I'll go along with anything you want. You can have all my money – I don't have much on me, but I'll gladly write you out a cheque . . .'

He was silenced by an appalling clatter that started somewhere at the back of the car. He started slowing down.

'Don't slow down!'

'But that noise –'

'It's nothing.'

'It sounds like something's falling off.'

'Accelerate.'

Reluctantly but obediently he obeyed me. 'I'm, er, very fond of this car – it's the first car I've ever had.'

His voice was beginning to drive me crazy.

'You're from England, aren't you? I can tell. I, er, had a friend from England once, used to come and stay with me – mostly at Christmas; he had a dry-cleaning business in Cardiff – guess that's not really England.'

The more he talked the slower and more erratic his driving became. I finally couldn't stand it any more. 'Pull over and stop – we'll have a look at the rear end.'

'Thank you, sir.'

We swerved over onto the hard shoulder and came to a violent halt. He pushed the gear shift up into park. 'I won't be a second, really I won't.'

Henry C. Timbuck hopped out of his car and ran off round to the back. Before my ass had even hit the seat his had vacated, I had that shift down into Drive and the gas pedal flat on the floor; I left poor old Timbuck behind in a shower of gravel and rubber. I got behind the wheel, and the seat-belt buzzer screeched, and the warning lamp flashed on and off. Keeping my foot flat on the floor I grappled with the harness for a few moments before giving it up. I needed a call-box in a hurry. One came up at a gas station a couple of miles on.

It rang. Once. Twice. A third time, fourth, fifth, hell. Then, 'Hallo?' It was Sumpy's voice. She sounded anxious. 'Where are you, Max?'

'Are you okay?'

'Yes, I'm okay. I'm fine. I've had a nice time.'

'Can you talk?'

'What do you mean. Max? Of course I can talk. Are you okay? You really sound terrible.'

I was slightly relieved. She didn't sound as if there was any large goon holding a gun at her head – at the moment. And yet there was something in her voice, something that was different to the normal Sumpy, the sweet soft girl with the deliciously rude mind. I couldn't figure out what it was. Roadside call boxes are not the best places for conducting voice analyses.

I was dead worried. Any moment someone was likely to come bursting into her apartment. I had to gain some time to get over there. 'Sweetheart, listen to me closely and do exactly what I say. Lock and bolt your front door, take off all your clothes, take your handbag into the bathroom, lock the bathroom door, get in the shower and don't come out to anybody, nobody, until you hear me.'

'Are you feeling horny, Max?'

'I'll keep you guessing; but do as I say – you must – and do it now. Okay?'

'Okay.' She sounded dubious.

'You sound like you don't want to.'

'No. I will . . . it's just that, er, the police are sending someone around . . . want me to make a statement . . . something like that . . . about last night.'

Her words shot through my body like a bolt of lightning. It was just possible the police did want a statement but Supertypist had assured

36

me when we had finished at the station that as far as they were concerned the matter was closed. Whoever was going to Sumpy's apartment wasn't from the police, however good his connections in the station at the Midtown Precinct North.

'Just get in the shower. I'll be with you in five minutes and I'll let them in.'

'Okay, Max.'

'Bye.'

I flung myself out of the booth and back into the car. The rear tyre had gone flat and the shape of the rear end wasn't going to put much joy into Timbuck's life when he got to take a closer look at it.

In spite of that flat tyre and the Sunday evening traffic I covered the George Washington Bridge, half the length and the entire width of Manhattan in twelve minutes flat, and abandoned the wreck a block away from Sumpy's Sutton Place apartment building. I ran down and round towards the front of the building. There was a large Chrysler parked right by the entrance with two large hulks in the front. Even from a fair distance they looked like close cousins of the goons to whom I'd so recently taken such a dislike.

I ducked into the building through a side door which was open and ran round to the elevators. All four of them were progressing upwards from fairly low floors. The elevators in this building weren't fast and I decided to get up by foot. I wanted to beat them up to Sumpy's floor in case

37

she was about to be put in one and brought down. I started sprinting up the forty-two flights to Sumpy's floor, wishing to hell more New Yorkers would copy Londoners and live in basements. Fit though I was, my tiredness was getting to me, my heart was banging, and my lungs searing; I seemed to be eternally snatching at the rail, rounding the sharp corners, running up more steps; I was never going to reach the top.

There was a terrible screech, a thump, and I was sprawling up the stairs, completely entangled in an elderly couple that I'd bowled over backwards like skittles – he with his astrakhan coat over his dinner jacket, she dressed to kill in her finery – and a brace of Pekinese dogs, one yelping, the other barking and snapping. I disengaged myself, muttering winded apologies, and continued my onslaught up the staircase.

Finally I saw the number 42 painted on the wall. I stopped to try and gather my breath, then cautiously looked out into the corridor. It was rich-looking, with mock Persian broadloom and thick, dark, handsome wood doors to the apartments. Hovering between the elevators and Sumpy's closed door was an extremely large goon. He was trying, extremely unsuccessfully, to look nonchalant, as though he were waiting for the elevator – but the elevator button wasn't lit.

He turned and faced away from me. Using the thick carpeting to maximum advantage, I got right up behind him. 'Excuse me, is this the forty-first floor?' I asked.

He spun round and laid his chin down, straight on top of my fast rising fist. I didn't hit him too hard in case he was a cop, but just hard enough so he wouldn't be a nuisance to me for the next few minutes. As he crumpled I whipped his gun out. One look at the shoddily made weapon was enough to tell me he was no cop. There was a door right behind him appropriately labelled 'Garbage' and I shoved him through it.

I put my ear against Sumpy's door. I heard the sound of the shower but nothing else. I wanted to surprise the garbage collector's friends and I didn't think walking in through Sumpy's front door would be the best way of doing it. I slid open the lock of the next-door apartment and marched straight in, my gun out in front of me; but there wasn't anyone to point it at. There rarely seemed to be anyone in this apartment – I reckoned it was a knocking shop for some well-off businessman. I knew my way around it pretty well.

High-rise apartments can be nasty traps – they often have walk-out balconies but rarely actual fire escapes, so there is only one way out: via the door. When I had found myself visiting Sumpy on a pretty regular basis – since she preferred her place to mine, mostly – I decided to build myself a second exit, never knowing when it might come in handy.

There was one wall panel that I had fixed,

unknown even to Sumpy. It was in the wall between the shower in Sumpy's apartment and the shower in her neighbour's apartment. I pulled out my knife and inserted the blade between two elegant tiles, which depicted a motley assortment of Etruscans enjoying a gang bang. These tiles, together with several more, came away easily and I was then able to lift out the 3-foot high section of panel. Before Sumpy knew what was happening I was inside that shower beside her, hand over her mouth, getting drenched to the skin with water that was a damn sight too hot for my liking.

CHAPTER 6

I hoisted Sumpy out into the next-door apartment, then went back for her bag. Her eyelids pulsated open and shut, her eyes were wide with shock. I put her down on a sofa and draped some thick velour towels, from lover-boy's closet, around her.

'How many are in there?'

'How many in there? What are you talking about?'

'I'm talking about the policemen you said were coming round.'

'I didn't let anybody in. I did what you said. I got straight in the shower – I've never been cleaner in my life. I heard the door ring but I didn't answer it. What the hell's going on, Max?'

'I'll explain it to you later, not right now. Just do exactly as I say. Whoever rang your doorbell was no policeman.' I replaced the panel and the tiles, then started rummaging in more of the closets. I found a smart Calvin Klein dress and a pile of silk Cornelia James headsquares. Either he kept them for his mistress or he liked dressing up himself. Either way he had damn good taste.

I got Sumpy into the dress and tied a scarf around her soaking hair, then got her over to the door. I looked out. The corridor was empty. We walked smartly out and I pressed the button for the elevator. My eyes were riveted to her apartment door. My right hand was inside my jacket clamped firmly round my gun, with the safety catch off and the rate of fire control switched to the notch with three white dots – indicating that one squeeze of the trigger would unleash three short, round-nosed chunks of very hot lead to be delivered at 375 metres per second in the direction of my choice. I was certain someone had gone in there whilst she was in the shower and was waiting for her to come out. It wasn't going to take too long before whoever it was discovered that Sumpy had vanished down the plug hole.

The lift arrived and the doors opened. As we stepped in, her door flew open and two hefty goons almost tripped over themselves in their rush to get out. The one in front, toting an automatic, saw us. 'Hey you, stop!' He levelled the gun at us at the exact moment the elevator doors closed on us, sparing us from any dialogue. I hit the button for the basement and we started, mercifully, to descend.

'I think we should have stopped, Max.'

'Sure we should – and had our heads blown off. Believe me, Sumpy, just believe me. Those guys are not cops. I'll explain it all to you but not right

42

now. Right now we've got to try and get out of here in one piece.'

I wondered whether the goons were running down the stairs or waiting for the next elevator. The lift wasn't quick but however fast they ran, with the head start we had I reckoned we should get down and out of the lift a short way ahead of them.

The doors opened at the basement onto a gaggle of people waiting to go up, and no sign of the goons. I ushered Sumpy out into the underground parking lot. Her conspicuous red Jensen was parked about four aisles down but I didn't want her to take that – she'd never get past the posse outside.

Apartment building parking lots are always spooky places and this was no exception: dim lighting, smell of warm oil, clicking sounds from warm radiators, faint heavy breathing of extractors. I had my gun out now and was watching the door behind me carefully. Sumpy still seemed very shocked but there was no way I could explain anything to her right now. She was alive, with a fair chance of remaining so if she followed my instructions, and for the time being she would have to be content with that.

There was a green Buick right beside us. I tugged a key off my ring, shoved it in the door lock, and the catch popped up first try. I jumped into the driver's seat and pushed the key into the ignition. It took some fiddling and jiggling with the steering wheel; then the wheel movement came free, the ignition light came on, the gas needle moved up around its dial. I floored the pedal and pushed the key hard over. The engine fired first time. I jumped out and shovelled Sumpy in. 'Drive out, right now. Don't stop for anyone or anything. Drive fifteen blocks, dump the car, get a cab straight to the Travelodge at Kennedy Airport, take a double room in the name of Mr and Mrs John Webb, and I'll join you as soon as I can.'

She looked at me and opened her mouth to speak.

'Go!' I said.

She went.

I stood watching the doorway as she drove around, hit the electric door beam, and the corrugated metal door clanked up; she drove up, out and off. I pulled another silk headsquare from my pocket and tied it around my head. Seated in her car, at a distance I might just fool someone, I hoped.

I ran over to the Jensen, put the key in the lock, and was about to open the door when there was a cracking sound that reverberated round the whole parking lot, closely followed by a volley of whining noises as a bullet scorched itself down the side of a metal girder by my head, then ricochetted off a succession of parked cars. I flattened myself as another bullet followed closely in its wake. I eased myself along on my stomach and poked my head around the massive fender of a

Lincoln. Standing crouched in the doorway was one of the goons who had come out of Sumpy's apartment. He was holding his pistol out in front of him with just one arm, which explained why his aim hadn't been any better – since I was within accurate shooting range of him. He was looking anxiously around for me, pointing the gun here, there. I decided to indicate my whereabouts to him. Placing both elbows firmly on the ground, I gripped my Beretta with both hands, flicked down the front grip, switched to single fire, aimed at the centre of his body, and pulled the trigger twice in rapid succession. Once would have been enough; by the time the second bullet had travelled the 15-odd feet to where he had been standing it must have found itself spinning through empty space, since the first one had caught him full square in the centre of his chest and carried him out backwards through the door into the corridor to the elevators.

There was a sudden clattering sound from the other end of the lot. It was the electric gate shutting again. I lifted myself up onto my knees and carefully looked around. I couldn't see anyone. I closed the front grip on the Beretta and switched back to automatic fire. Crouching low, I dived into the Jensen, rammed the ignition key in, and prayed it would start. Its hefty V8 turned slowly and lazily over, once, twice – come on – three times – come on, come on – then on the fifth turnover all eight cylinders burbled into life, the rev counter whipped up to 1,500, the exhaust gave off an even powerful throbbing. I pulled the gearshift into drive and the car surged forward several inches; I released the handbrake and gently eased out into the aisle.

The car felt deliciously powerful – the slatted hood rising out ahead of me; the precise, firm, leather-bound wheel; the rich smell of Connelly hide rising up all around me from the seats and the panelling. She exuded a sensation of pent-up power waiting to be unleashed.

I was scanning every shape, every shadow; there were two more aisles to go before the gate. Suddenly a beam of light flooded in through the pedestrian entrance by the gate and two figures darted through. They stopped as they saw me and levelled pistols at me in unison. I dived below the dash just as darts of flame shot out of both the barrels. One bullet scored noisily along the roof, the other bored a neat hole in the passenger side of the windshield then bounced around inside the car, striking me on the ear like a wasp sting on about the sixth bounce.

Switching back to automatic fire, I opened the door, stuck my arm out and loosed off three shots in their general direction. I had little chance of hitting them but I wanted to gain myself a few seconds' breathing space. Another bullet whanged into the body of the car just behind me; there was a third gunman. He must have come in the same door by the elevator that his punctured friend had used. The only option open to me was to get the hell out of there.

Still crouched below the dash level, I yanked the gear shift into low and booted the gas pedal down onto the floorboards. I stuck my head up above the dash just long enough to get the hang of the general directions. The engine gave a massive growl, the tyres screeched down the concrete for 50 feet as they clawed away at it for a grip. I wrenched at the wheel as the tail snaked this way then that, trying to keep her pointing in a straight line; then the rubber took, the car flattened its rear springs, the nose lifted up, my stomach was thrust into the seat back, and we catapulted forward. I stamped on the brakes as we howled round the right-hander to the exit ramp. Bullets cracked and clanged and blew out chunks of glass. Then I booted the car for all she was worth, bracing myself against the shock of hitting the ramp. The front wheels passed over the rubber bar for the automatic gate but the gate scarcely had time to lift more than a few inches before we smashed into it and through it with a terrible racket of tearing metal, the nose of the car tossing it aside as though it were cardboard; we came up to the top of the ramp doing close on 70 miles an hour. I stamped on the brakes as hard as I possibly could but we parted company with the ground, travelled several feet through the air, and came down with a thumping crash to find the goons' Chrysler, which I'd seen earlier parked outside the main entrance to the block, had been backed up and was now broadside across my exit path. There was one luckless goon sitting in it and he had a full tenth of a second to realise his luck was out before we slammed straight into the passenger section of the car.

It caved in, like a tin hit with a karate chop, almost certainly killing him instantly; then, in a continuous movement on from this, the car was lifted a few feet up in the air, came down on its side, and started rolling over and over across to the other side of the road, where it flattened a mail box, slammed up against a wall and burst into flames. I was still heading towards it at a good 50 miles an hour. I spun the steering wheel as hard as I could round to the right and pulled on the handbrake with all my strength. The tail of the car came howling round; a car coming down the road swerved onto the pavement to avoid me. and I just clipped his wing. I threw the handbrake off and flattened the gas pedal again; the rev counter whipped into the red as we rocketed down the road. I flicked the gear shift out of low and we surged forward even more. We crossed the first intersection at 80, the second at over 100, then I slammed the brakes on and power-slid us into a quieter street.

I slowed down, not wanting to attract too much attention to myself, particularly not any passing cop car since bullet holes would require more than a cursory explanation. Sumpy was not going to be too happy with me when she saw the car – she was madly in love with it – but I couldn't think about that now. I came out down the other end of the side street into 2nd Avenue and turned into the maze of lights of Manhattan's fast-building Sunday traffic. I passed two or three blocks, then saw a very dark street and turned into it.

The street was deserted. I slid the Jensen in between two parked cars, got out and walked away from it as quickly as I could. I walked on down the street and emerged into the bright of 3rd Avenue. All the time I walked I looked carefully behind me. I didn't think I was being tailed but I wasn't going to take any chances.

I hailed a cab and climbed in. 'Plaza Hotel.' The driver cranked his meter lever, scribbled down the destination and we tramp-tramped off. The cab was filthy even by New York standards and the interior gave the impression that when it wasn't being used to ferry passengers it was loaned out to Central Park Zoo as a monkey house.

After five blocks I spoke. 'I'll get out here.'

'Nowhere near the Plaza, buddy.' Then the driver turned to look at me and the expression on his face told me that, in spite of the fact that the interior needed a good hosing down, he was only too glad that the dripping wet wreck of humanity in the back was getting out. 'Dollar forty.'

I shoved two sopping dollar bills into his hand. 'Keep the change.'

'Hey, what I meant to do with this – put 'em on the washing line?'

'No. Buy a new cab with them.'

He drove off angrily, muttering a string of expletives peculiar to the idiom of the New York cab-driving fraternity.

I walked a block and hailed another cab going the opposite direction. I took another careful look around me and got in. 'Travelodge, Kennedy.' I relaxed deep into the seat, and in half an hour was standing inside the room of Mr and Mrs Webb.

Sumpy was angry, really angry. I'd never seen her angry before. 'You're crazy, that's what you are. Fucking crazy. Or you're a criminal on the run. Personally I think you're just fucking crazy.'

I decided that now was probably not the best time to break the news to her about the car. 'Calm down,' I said.

'Calm down? Calm down? You expect me to fucking calm down?'

There was a thick and very heavy telephone directory near where she was standing. It was neatly bound in simulated leather and had 'Travelodge' printed in gold letters on the outside. Sumpy flung it at me. There were also two glass ashtrays with 'Travelodge' printed on them. She flung those at me. 'Fucking madman.' There was a waste bin. It was in white plastic. It didn't have 'Travelodge' on it. She flung that at me. Then she flung her handbag at me. I'd managed to duck everything else but the handbag got me in the stomach and a shower of keys, loose tampax, a diary, address book, lipstick, mirror, powder, roll-on deodorant, a clutch of parking tickets, and a mousetrap flew out.

'What's this?'

'It's a fucking mousetrap.'

'What's it for?'

'What's it for? It's for trapping mice – you know, little things, long tails, eeeek, eeeek – they come out of holes in the wall, run around, eat cheese.'

I picked up the bag, rummaged in it, found a pack of Marlboro and her Zippo lighter in its engraved platinum case. I took out a cigarette, flared the lighter and gratefully inhaled a long deep lungful of sweet smoke and petrol fumes. I sat down on the bed. I must have looked pretty damn frightful.

'I'm sorry,' she said. She came over, put an arm around me and sat down. 'You're all wet. You're going to catch a chill like that. You don't want to catch a chill.'

No. She was right. I didn't want to catch a chill. I didn't want to catch anything. She helped me pull my wet clothes off, and I crawled in between the snug clean sheets and shut my eyes. I was going to have a long, long sleep.

'Pickpockets,' she said.

'Huh?'

'Pickpockets. That's what the mousetrap is for. Pickpockets.'

'What do pickpockets want mousetraps for?'

'Dummy. I set the mousetrap, put it in my purse, pickpocket puts his hand in, and snap – got his fingers.'

'Who gave you that bright idea?'

'Friend of mine. She's been doing it for years.'

'What happens if you forget – catch your own fingers?'

There was a long silence. I drifted off towards sleep. I never heard her reply.

CHAPTER 7

It all started one morning in Paris a little over six years ago. It was the first really hot day of the year. Spring had been turning to summer for some weeks and that day it had finally turned. That day the whole of Paris felt good, you could sense it in the air. Cars moved a little slower, windows that had been closed for months were now flung open, beautifully fresh summer clothes appeared on their first outings. The cafes once more spilled out onto the sidewalks, with their Pernod ashtrays and shirt-sleeved waiters in black waistcoats.

I sat basking in it all at a table on the Champs Elysées. The coffee tasted good, the Marlboro tasted good, and of the girls walking down the street nine out of ten looked pretty damn good. A bit further down, in the parking lane between the sidewalk and the road, sat my car. She was an elderly but very fit Jaguar XK120. She was looking somewhat dusty but even so, crouched by the kerb with her roof open, more passing eyes stared down her 14½ feet of midnight blue bodywork than at either the 308 GTB Ferrari in front or the Turbo Porsche two cars behind.

She needed a lot of work on her to restore her to the full glory of her youth. She needed a complete respray and her bumpers and radiator grille needed rechroming. She looked smarter with her roof off, as the roof itself was a tatty patchwork of taped holes and rips. The engine needed a decoke, the tyres would have to be changed before next winter, and the interior needed a great deal of elbow grease. One day I hoped I would have enough money to afford it; for the time being she was going to have to stay as she was. Money was tight at the moment but I was confident something would turn up. It usually did, in odd shapes and places – but at least it usually did.

It was seven months since the British army had decided it could get along without me, a decision it had taken a shade under three years to reach. If it could have tolerated me for just a few months longer I could at least have left with a decent lump sum in my pocket. My parents had divorced early in my childhood and then, in rapid succession, got themselves killed in separate accidents in different parts of the world, leaving me in the charge of a not particularly interested, retired brigadier, who resided in Paris. He had one standing rule: that all male nephews, god-children, and any others, such as me, who came under what he considered to be his domain, who could success-fully pass out of the British army officer's training school, Sandhurst, his old stomping ground, would receive a cheque for £100,000 on passing-out day. He had also agreed to support me financially whilst I was at Sandhurst, which support had now been angrily withdrawn.

The army had taught me how to look after myself and how to kill people. Practical, perhaps, but not the best grounding for a business career, although some pundits might say otherwise. I decided to toss myself out to fate and see where she flung me. I had started advertising myself in the personal column of *The Times* in the following manner: 'Young man. Ex-army. Willing to undertake any jobs of a personal bodyguard, investigative or security nature. Own car. Pilot licence. To be found weekday mornings between 11.00 and 1.00 at the Lido Cafe, Champs Elysées, Paris.'

The ad was starting into its second month and the response so far had been encouraging. I had escorted a couple on their skiing holiday; I had delivered some paintings to Dallas; I had for several days followed a woman suspected of having an affair who turned out to be doing nothing more than visiting a shrink in secret; I had delivered a couple's Doberman Pinschers to their villa in the south; and there was one nervous British businessman, resident in Paris, whom once a week I had to escort to the doorway of a cheap prostitute in Rue St Denis – I then had to wait outside the door until they had finished as he was scared of being robbed by her pimp.

I sat back, holding up *The Times* conspicuously, and took another drag on my cigarette. Business had been slack for the last couple of days but I wasn't worried. I had a fancy that a slender, tanned, gorgeous divorcee, loaded with money and in need of a no-strings-attached playmate to accompany her to her villa in Sardinia for a couple of weeks of fun, might take my bait.

The character who pulled up the other chair at the table and sat down didn't exactly fit that bill: he was wearing an old fawn mac fraying at the edges, a heavy bottle-green wool-worsted suit, with a thick woollen Vyella shirt and a club tie I didn't recognise, in a particularly nasty shade of green.

His first action was to pull a filthy handkerchief from his trouser pocket and mop beads of perspiration from his brow. He was breathing heavily, not as a result of having done a sudden sprint for a bus, or anything like that, but in the manner of someone who regards his body as a handicap rather than a useful machine, of someone so unfit and overweight that the mere act of transporting it across a sidewalk on its own legs requires a special effort, of someone who has to strain to heave a forkful of food into his mouth or to raise a glass to his lips. His flesh was sallow, hung limply around his face, gave him a flabby treble chin. His eyes were dark and piggish in their fattened sockets; his hair, thinning and greasy, was plastered unevenly about his head. He obviously didn't enjoy the heat.

I put him in his early fifties. He certainly wasn't anyone's idea of a fairy godmother. The act of getting to this table and sitting down at it had rendered him temporarily speechless. The way he looked, no self-respecting doctor could ever advise him to go out and buy a long-playing record.

'Read your ad,' he said after a long pause. 'Name's Wetherby.' He proffered a hand and gave a surprisingly strong handshake. With the other hand he summoned the waiter and ordered a white coffee and a cognac.

He had an amiable voice: crisp, educated, old-school English. 'Do you want to earn £500 for a morning's work? Cash. No questions asked.'

'What do I have to do?' Quite frankly I didn't care what I had to do. For that kind of money it would have taken a lot to deter me – even more than what he had to say next.

'It's in the boot of your car. Everything. Including the money.' His coffee and his cognac arrived and he took a gulp of each, swilling the mixture in his mouth with about as much delicacy as if he were gargling. He swallowed, smacked his lips and looked up around him. 'Weather's nice.' He made the remark in such a way that it appeared to be directed at no one in particular. 'Very nice. Paris is good this time of year.'

I was surprised he had noticed.

'Yes,' he carried on, 'Paris is very good this time of year.' He took another swig of his mixture. I stared at him curiously. I tried to figure out who he was, what he was. I couldn't think of anything at all to say to him. I felt like a helpless little schoolboy seated in the headmaster's study. 'Like Paris?'

'Yes,' I said. I felt he was about to say something of enormous importance; a monumental revelation of some kind; something that would make me gasp in sheer wonder, that would slot everything into place. I waited expectantly.

'Good. Glad about that. Paris is a nice place. Jolly nice. Well, must be going.' He finished off his brew and stood up. Gave me another firm hand-shake. 'Nice car. Open roof. Good weather for an open roof.'

I tried to read something in his face, in his eyes. There was nothing. Whatever might have been there a few moments ago had gone, snapped shut like a book and sealed in a plain brown wrapper. He melted away among the beautiful girls, the straggling tourists, the smart young men, the limping war-veterans, the chic middle-aged women, and the whirring of 2CVs and the hooting of horns.

The bastard hadn't even left anything for the bill.

I paid the waiter and drove off into the traffic, heading out in the general direction of Versailles and the forests beyond, where I wanted to find a quiet spot and take a look at Santa's stocking.

I'd gone about a quarter of a mile when I was flagged down by a police motorcyclist – an unusual occurrence in a city where speed, and a general wholesale disregard for traffic regulations, are the law of the motorist's jungle.

The cop was elegantly turned out with immaculately blancoed webbing – and halitosis that would drop a skunk in its tracks at 50 feet.

I was scared stiff. I had no idea what that maniac Wetherby had put in the boot and I had an uncomfortable feeling it might be something of more than cursory interest to Monsieur Spick-et-Span here.

'Licence. Carte verte. Passeport.'

'Je n'ai pas le passeport avec moi.'

'Vous restez à Paris?'

'Oui, monsieur.'

'Où?'

'Seize. Rue de la Reine, Passy.'

'Depuis combien des jours?'

'Cinq jours, monsieur.' I lied. I didn't want them to know I was living here and have to go through the hassle of having French plates put on the car.

His bulging revolver holster and bulging baton holster swung from the belt. 'Licence et carte.'

I rummaged through my wallet and through the glove locker and produced my English driving licence, international driving licence and green card insurance docket. He read through them, then walked around the car, studying it closely. He didn't seem to take much notice of the fact that I was sheet-white and trembling. He was probably used to people going sheet-white and trembling when stopped.

59

He handed me back the documents. 'C'est une belle voiture. Ça va. Merci, monsieur. Allez.' He ushered me off, and walked back to his motorbike.

I drove off, gently changing through the gears, letting the revs climb very slowly. I scrabbled in my pocket for my cigarettes. I was shaking like a leaf. I half-lit the cigarette, and smoke and bits of flaring paper whipped away into the slipstream. Maybe it was just a routine stolen car check. Coincidence. And yet . . . The cop hadn't looked the sort that would miss a single point but he hadn't made any comment at all about my papers. I took a drag on my cigarette. Both my insurance and my international driving licence had expired five weeks ago. I wanted to find out what was in that boot. Fast.

I accelerated to a reckless speed, snaking in and out of the traffic. I had a feeling I might be being tailed. I shot a red light, missing the front wheels of a truck by inches, but nothing came over the lights after me and I relaxed a little.

Half an hour later I was thundering down a narrow, twisting country road, the tyres protesting on the warm tarmac. I passed through a couple of sleepy villages, both containing restaurants well praised by the Michelin, and out into the country again. I turned off onto a track into the woods, drove a good distance in from the road, stopped and switched the engine off.

I felt calmer now. A good deep warmth came

through the shade of the fir trees and the air smelt good. I listened carefully. All was quiet. I went round and lifted the boot lid, wondering what I was going to find – a chopped-up corpse perhaps; a midget Russian agent – I just didn't have any idea. It turned out to be a brown Jiffy package, about 18 inches long, 1 foot wide, and several inches thick. It bore no label and no writing but was very heavy.

I opened one end and tipped out the contents: first a parcel in silver gift-wrap and a tag which said, 'To Elaine. Happy birthday. With fondest love' – there was no signature; then a Webley .38 revolver, loaded, with the safety catch on; and an envelope. The envelope contained £500 in used £10 notes, and a note which read, 'Deliver birthday gift to Mme Elaine de Vouvrey, Apt 5, 91 Rue Notre Dame de Bonne Nouvelle, Paris 2, Friday 29 May at 11.00 am. Keep the popgun and the change.'

My first thought was that this was Wetherby's mistress, and she had a husband he was scared of. But £500 seemed to me to be paying rather more than necessary if it was that simple.

There was the sound of a vehicle. I whipped the envelope into my pocket and slammed the boot shut. It was just a tractor towing an old trailer; at the helm was a wizened old farmer with blue beret and obligatory yellow Gauloise stump protruding from his mouth. He gave me a wide berth, churning through some bushes, nodded in a courteous but uninterested manner, and rattled along on his way.

I opened the silver-wrapped box. It contained a soft white powder. I didn't need a chemistry set to tell me it wasn't Yves St Laurent talc.

There must have been about 5 pounds weight of the stuff. Sold in a lump amount in a hurry, it must have been worth about £200,000 – a great deal more if broken down into street deals of 1 gramme, and even more still if broken down into individual fixes.

The little knowledge I had about the French mafia quickly dispelled any aspirations that leapt into my head about heading for the hills with the booty.

Instinct told me from the start that this deal stank, stank worse than a Billingsgate garbage can in a heat wave. Instinct told me right now to go find Wetherby and chuck the whole lot back at him; and if I couldn't find him to go straight to the British Consulate and tell them the story. Sometimes, when I'm cold and lonely, I wish that maybe I'd stuck to that instinct. Luckily it's only sometimes.

I turned up early at 91 Rue Notre Dame de Bonne Nouvelle. I'd decided that if there was going to be anything unpleasant lying in wait for me I should try and catch it on the hop. I'd taken a taxi and wasted several valuable minutes arguing with the driver outside the entrance. I wanted him to wait but he didn't want to wait because it was a no-waiting zone, and in my reasonably competent French I was trying to drum into his stubborn Gallic skull the fact that if he wasn't prepared to wait in this no-waiting zone he was going to find it was also a no-paying zone.

The message got through and I got out, leaving the door open; he left his engine running. I felt good about that open door and that running engine because I had a feeling I might be needing them both in a hurry.

It was the third day of the heat wave and the sun streamed down on me, seemed to be floodlighting me as I paused for a moment on the doorstep, reading the name plates and apartment numbers, feeling very apprehensive and not much comforted by the sagging weight in my jacket pocket of the loaded Colt with its safety catch now off.

It was a tall old building, a four-storey walk-up; I didn't bother to ring the bell but marched straight in and began climbing the stone stairs. It was a spooky building, quiet, dusty. From the outside it looked smart; inside it was shabby. Unusual for France, where it is usually the reverse. Apartment 5 was at the end of the third-floor landing. I rang the bell and then, for no particular reason, stepped aside.

In the event it proved to be a wise move: the door was ripped to shreds by a torrent of submachine gun bullets and, with the gun still firing, the lovely Madame de Vouvrey came crashing through it, blazing off in every direction except – fortunately for me, unfortunately for her – mine. I cracked the Webley off twice. Madame de Vouvrey, if it was indeed Madame de Vouvrey who had this engaging manner of answering the doorbell, was 6½ feet of very vicious-looking bloke with oily black hair and a dark, oily complexion. He recoiled against the door post, looking decidedly like he wished he hadn't got out of bed today; blood shot out of the centre of his forehead and out the top of his chest. The sten gun dropped to the floor and clattered down the stairs, loosing off bursts of fire on its own as it went.

A second gorilla appeared in the doorway, brandishing an ugly-looking piece of lead-firing ironmongery. I cracked off a bullet into him, and he slammed over backwards. Then my left arm suddenly felt like it had been hit with a red-hot sledge hammer, and it flew up and cracked against the wall; there was a whining, splitting sound past my right ear, and bits of wall showered out at me. I spun around and saw another man, thin, small with a goatee beard, about to loose another shot off at me from a small automatic. I took the only course of evasion: a headlong dive down onto him, pumping the Webley's trigger for all I was worth. I heard it crack and crack and crack and then click, and then I head-over-heeled and landed on top of his very fresh corpse.

I lay there for a few moments, my arm in agony,

waiting for the next bullet to come at me. The Colt was empty and I felt around with my right arm for the bearded man's gun. No bullets did come at me, and after a few moments more my hand closed over the automatic.

The silence continued but I waited a full couple of minutes before daring to stand up. In agony though my left arm was, I was still clutching the silver parcel. I staggered to my feet and then, bursting in from the street, came France's answer to Knacker of the Yard with his troupe of boys in blue, and for a glorious moment I'd never been so damn glad to see the fuzz in all my life, until I suddenly realised I was standing among three dead men, holding a smoking automatic in one hand and 5 pounds of heroin in the other. I must have looked pretty damn cute.

CHAPTER 8

The only courtesy I had from the French police during that entire following week was a choice of bunks in the cell: top bunk or bottom bunk. I'd taken the top and was glad of my decision, for sometime during every night they brought in a drunk who collapsed into the bottom bunk and would spend the night alternating between grunting and throwing up. Every morning they'd take him away again. I never got to see the faces of the drunks clearly; for all I knew, it could have been the same one every night.

The week had been pure hell and I was nearing the end of my tether. My arm hurt like hell from where the bullet had been removed, but I hadn't been afforded the luxury of a single night in a hospital bed – they stitched my arm up, bandaged it, and put me straight into the cell. I was sore all over, damn bloody sore.

It was hot, airless and gloomy in the cell; a few streaks of sunlight occasionally managed to find their way in through the maze of bars in a small grille high up in the wall, but all they did was to heighten the gloom below. The police had not permitted me to make any telephone calls and had firmly indicated I was not going to be allowed to make any: not to the consulate, not to a lawyer, not to anywhere. Monsieur was not going to receive any aid from anyone until he had fully divulged the identity of the entire drugs ring.

The ad in *The Times*, the visit from Wetherby did not seem to interest them. They insisted they wanted the truth. For seven days they had dragged me in and out of that cell, into another window-less room but with very bright lighting, where they had interrogated me. Soon I was going to start yelling at them, those mean sods that stank of yesterday's garlic. There was nothing more I could do. I didn't know any more, unless they wanted me to start inventing things, which I didn't think would do me very much good in the long run.

I cursed every night, through the long nights, at having been so stupid, having landed myself in this for a lousy £500, which I probably no longer even had. If I ever got out of here I knew what I was going to do. I was going to find Wetherby and knock his block off.

But he saved me the trouble.

The warder came as usual to take me to the first session of the day and took me into the room that I by now knew only too well. I sat on the wooden chair and waited for my interrogators to show up. Instead, Wetherby came in.

He didn't shake my hand this time but lowered himself with considerable effort into a chair near me. He was still wearing the same mac, the same thick suit, the same green tie. His shirt was of a more lightweight nature. The beads of perspiration were in place on his head and he mopped them off with what looked like the same filthy handkerchief. He puffed a couple of times, and then patted his thighs. He looked cheerful.

'Well, old boy, you're in a spot of trouble.'

'Oh really?'

'Spot of trouble all right; oh dear, oh dear.'

He did not give me the impression of being a man under arrest. 'What are you doing here?' I said.

'Me? Heard you were in a spot of bother – just popped in – see how you're getting on.'

'Who the hell are you?'

'Hot in here,' he said. 'Bad on air-conditioning, the French. Can't understand it – always hot summers, always no air-conditioning. Not much in England either. No. Americans have it. They all have it.'

Wetherby was looking smug. In fact he was looking pretty damn pleased with himself. His arrival in this room placed an extremely odd complexion on things. Extremely odd. He looked decidedly as though he knew something, and I was more than mildly curious to find out what. 'Will you tell me who the hell you are?'

'Long sentences, drugs, in France. Very long. Hard labour. Nasty prisons. No remissions. Heroin – minimum of five years. Yes, minimum of five years.

Never usually get that. Fourteen, fifteen, maybe less; twelve, perhaps. Not good, heroin.' He patted his thighs again; it was an irritating habit. 'Murder's very bad. Very bad. Still got the guillotine; rarely used, though. Usually life. Long time, life, in France. Twenty years. Maybe thirty. Not good.'

There was a long silence – very long. Oddly I felt calmer. I wasn't so scared now, scared the way I had been during the past week. There was something about this peculiar man that was comforting.

Then I felt it all welling up inside me again, churning my stomach inside out. I was in here for real. This was a real prison. I was a real criminal. I wasn't at school any more, about to be gated or caned for a misdemeanour. I wasn't at Sandhurst, about to get a right dressing down for blowing up a dummy tank half an hour before the Field Marshal came to inspect the exercise. I was a heroin-runner and a murderer. A court of justice would dictate my future and they were going to put me behind bars until well into my middle age. I felt myself quivering, and started hating and loving and hating and loving Wetherby; hating him because he had been responsible for putting me here, loving him because – somehow, somewhere, someplace along the line – he had to represent hope. He had to. 'Help me.'

He shoved his hands into his mac pockets. He drew his cheeks in and then opened his lips with a popping sound. 'Not a good place for a young man,' he said. 'Not good at all.'

There was another long silence. I waited.

'You got there early. Very early. Unfortunate. Might have missed the whole thing if you'd arrived there on time. Eleven o'clock you were told. Might have missed the whole thing if you'd gone at eleven. On the other hand, you might not. Lot of shooting. Lot of bullets.' He pulled a crumpled white paper bag from his pocket and proffered it to me: it contained monkey nuts. I declined. He took one, and started shelling it, slowly. 'Lot of shooting. Must have handled yourself very well. Very well.' He paused to munch his nuts. 'They can't all have been rotten shots.' He started to attack another shell. 'You're in big trouble, I'm afraid. Don't need me to tell you. Interpol's been after this lot for a long time. Long time. Big ring. Big trouble. Heroin. Gun-running. Other things too. Not much in your defence. Judges could be lenient. Twenty years for the lot. That'd be light. You'd be lucky for that.'

'What's the way out? Or did you just come to tell me the bad news?'

'Expensive. Very expensive.'

'I don't have a lot of money.'

He broke another shell in half, and shook his head. 'Money's no good. Don't want that. No. Don't want that at all.'

'What do you want?'

There was another interminable pause. Wetherby sat back in his chair with a whole handful of nuts to shell. He worked on them one by one. When

70

he had finished he stared me straight in the face. 'You,' he said.

'Pardon?'

Suddenly Wetherby ceased to be an overweight peanut-guzzling slob; his face sprang alive; it was intelligent and tough as iron. 'We want you to come and join the British civil service.'

'The civil service? Are you joking?'

'No, Mr Flynn, I am not joking.'

'You want me to come and push a pen in Whitehall?' I was stunned.

'Not exactly, old boy.'

'But what do you mean. For how long?'

'No idea, old boy. But it'll be better than this. And damn well paid.'

'What do I get: local planning or child welfare?'

'Neither, old boy. The Home Office; in the department which deals with security – and I don't mean locks or pensions – The British Security Service, originally Department 5 of Military Intelligence and better known by its abbreviation: MI5. You've heard of it, I'm sure?'

I nodded weakly.

'We think you'd be a good chap to have on board; need young fellows with drive, initiative. Of course, there's no obligation on you.' He reached for another shell. 'No obligation at all. But I personally think you'll find it worth a try.'

'I don't seem to have much choice.'

'Well. We'll see. Put you through the training. If you make the grade, good.'

71

'And if I don't?'

'France has no statute of limitation for murder, old boy.'

'What do you mean?'

'In some countries if a crime is committed and the police don't prosecute within a certain period of time – maybe five years, ten, fifteen – then the criminal goes scot free. In France they don't have that. They can go for you tomorrow, or in six months . . . or in forty years' time.'

I stared at Wetherby a long, long time. His face had slackened again and his interest was once more turned to his nuts. If this was a standard procedure the British Secret Service had a pretty damn strange method of recruiting.

CHAPTER 9

I awoke to the strange heavy-breathing sound of the wall-to-wall underfloor heating ducts pumping in a dosage of hot air to keep the temperature up at its present level. Whoever had set it must have suffered from low blood pressure. It was boiling.

I didn't stir for several moments as I didn't want to wake Sumpy, then I heard the sharp flick of the page of a paperback book and realised she was already awake and reading, filling her mind at this early hour of the day with the drivelling dialogue of yet another modern romantic novel: 'Oh Rodney, darling, why don't you tell Mary about us today?' 'I can't, my angel, it's the kids' first day home for the summer vacation.'

For a bright girl, she really read rubbish. Maybe she found it therapeutic, an escape from the pressure of her work. She was an authority on Impressionist painting: a consultant to Sotheby Parke Bernet, on retainer, but she worked mainly freelance, valuing pictures for prospective purchasers. It had its own strains and stresses. Nobody would be too thrilled with her if they forked out a couple of hundred thousand dollars on a painting of a bowl of apples only to later discover it had been done by an unknown child of 4.

'Morning!' I said, turning and looking up at her; she really did look terrific in the morning – a great virtue in my book.

She tore herself away from the page to give me a quick peck on the cheek. 'How about some coffee?' she said.

'Sure; and some eggs, bacon, tomato, sausage, fried bread, beans, mushrooms, toast, marmalade and cornflakes to go with it.' I slid out of the bed and waded through the warm shag broadloom over to the window. I drew back the curtains and stared through the treble-glazing onto a mid-December New York morning. The sky was a stark red; some sleet was falling and there was a thick white frost on the grass below and on the windows of the parked cars. Out over on the Van Wyck Expressway a solid queue of cars crept along towards Manhattan, narrowing to a sausage to squeeze past some obstruction – an accident, probably – that was marked by the twin, intermittent, flashing red lights on the roof of a patrol car.

I got back into bed, lay against the pillows, and started to gather my wits and my thoughts; the more I gathered them, the more I wished I hadn't woken up at all. They say that problems look different after a good night's sleep, and they're right; mine certainly did – they looked one whole lot worse.

Sumpy got out of bed to go to the washroom. As soon as the door had closed behind her I leaned over for her handbag. I poured out the contents then pulled up the bottom liner, which I'd carefully glued down the night before last, and removed an envelope from under it, then replaced the liner and the contents and put the bag back on the floor.

The envelope wasn't addressed to me but to my boss, Sir Charles Cunningham-Hope, better known to all by his code name, Fifeshire. I was sure he would not mind my opening it, since he was currently out of any active service.

I held the envelope out in front of me, thankful that nothing had happened to it. It was a soft pink colour, and round the middle of it was a bright blue ribbon, neatly tied into a bow.

Fifeshire was the Director-General of MI5, and was directly answerable to the Home Secretary, currently Anthony Lines. I first met him six years ago shortly after my press-ganging by Wetherby, as he insisted on meeting all new recruits personally and expounding to them his view of the role of MI5, his role, and how the recruit's role was to fit into the overall scheme of things.

For reasons that one cannot define – some call it chemistry, some vibrations – we hit it off immediately and he took me under his direct wing. I was lucky. Most of his agents had a thankless task. They had rotten jobs – rotten, stinking lousy jobs. They had to grub around the surface of the earth, furrowing and burrowing like maggots and weevils and moles and voles; they froze and hurt and hid, pretended and lied and twisted and turned; they inhabited cheap hotel rooms and expensive hotel rooms; they never had friends and never had wives and children, and were frequently dead within ten years.

My assignments were no different from anyone else's; they were equally foul. But Fifeshire did at least thank me at the end of each one and dole out generous portions of whisky or sherry, or anything that took the fancy, in his cavernous, oak-panelled, sound-deadened office in Carlton House Terrace, overlooking the Mall and the stone pillbox-shaped and ivy-camouflaged building that had covered the Admiralty communications head-quarters, deep in the vaults below, during the Second World War.

But in spite of the cheery reception he gave, Fifeshire always kept a distance. Most agents he called only by their numbers and referred to them only by their numbers, not that he referred to them much. He believed in isolation; that agents should never meet one another; that they should train in isolation, work in isolation and, when necessary, die in isolation.

Fifeshire had a country estate in Gloucestershire and a flat in Wimpole Street. He had never married, to anyone's knowledge, and worked continuously, never stopping, whether he was in the office, or pacing the floors of his flat, or leading a bucolic weekend as the country squire. He had a missionary zeal for his work, to try and maintain the credibility of British Intelligence, to try and hold it together and build it stronger and stronger.

At his core he was tough as steel, quicker-thinking than any calculator, and ruthlessly hard. At the start of the Second World War he had joined the army and shot through the ranks to Major-General. Before his luck ran out and a German shell removed the head that contained his outstanding mind, the talent was spotted; he was airlifted out of the front into Whitehall and had remained there ever since.

Bombs had ceased to rain from the sky; the war passed and truces were made, but for Fifeshire the war went on, and would go on for ever. Cold war, warm war, bloody war, silent war – it made no difference, it all boiled down to the same thing: survival. He intended to survive, and for that to happen his world had to survive; and for the world to survive on terms he could accept, his country had to survive and be able to stand up and be counted. And so he fought – day in, day out.

In the post-war period, a number of events, highlighted by such major fiascos as Philby, and Eden's stunning lack of foresight in the Suez crisis, had a devastating effect in the United States on the credibility of British Intelligence; Fifeshire therefore had an unenviable task.

And yet he was succeeding. Since he took command in 1957 all the major Western powers had come to look to him as one of their most reliable sources of information. Whatever they might have thought of the governments and the politicians that comprised them, Fifeshire, and the outfit he had honed and ground and sculpted and built, they listened to.

Facts were what Fifeshire sought to acquire during all his waking hours. He believed implicity in facts. Like Dickens's Gradgrind, he instilled the message in his pupils; 'What I want is Facts . . . Facts alone are wanted in life.' Fifeshire lusted after facts. They were the life-blood of British Intelligence. His agents were merely tools for obtaining them. He wanted to know everything about everyone; no one was to be left to chance, no one to be trusted, not even those who worked for him – especially those who worked for him. 'What good is the whole of British Intelligence,' he would say, 'if there's one damn spy in it?'

I was deployed to spy on the staff of MI5. For the last six years I had followed various members of staff to shops, to cinemas, to the lavatory, to hookers and massage parlours and mistresses, to holidays in Bognor and Tenerife and Nassau and Moscow; I had seen husbands hanging from chandeliers while their wives beat them with willow canes, and a 60-year-old spinster secretary roller-skate naked around her living room; I had recorded a thousand meetings on sound-tape, video-tape, celluloid, hung around a thousand windswept street corners, eaten a thousand miserable ham sandwiches in ten seconds flat, and I hadn't yet found a single damn traitor.

But there was one. I was sure of it. Fifeshire was sure of it. And he knew that if he kept on looking, and I kept on looking, and the others he deployed kept on looking, sooner or later, whoever it was would make a mistake.

It was in the fourth year of my work that I ran foul of Scatliffe. He had a hawk-nosed, skinny, wrinkly tartar of a secretary, who looked like a giant eagle that had escaped from its cage. She was one of those very meticulous people who keep everything carefully in its place and a careful record of the place it's kept in. She was also, I discovered, an incredible hoarder.

She had a large flat in a decaying Georgian terraced house in Westbourne Terrace, off the Bayswater Road. It was packed to the gills with the most incredible rubbish: cartons upon cartons of tights reduced in a Debenham's sale; hundreds of empty plastic powder puffs; piles of men's nylon socks, reduced in another sale; rows and rows of different-sized shoes; magazines and newspapers dating back decades; empty food tins washed out and stored away. She had evidently seen the boom in old bric-à-brac and was determined not to miss out next time around.

Under every single object she had carefully placed a hair. By checking the positions of the hairs she could tell if anything had been moved. It had taken me days to search through it all and

I hadn't noticed the hairs. She arrived home early one day, having left work with a migraine, and spotted me leaving the building. She checked the position of the hairs and put two and two together. She reported to Scatliffe that I had been spying on her.

Commander Clive Scatliffe was second in command to Fifeshire. He was a waspish man in his late forties, short, thin and wiry, with greying hair swept back in a rakish manner that didn't suit him, and made him look like a cross between a concert pianist and a second-hand car dealer. He had small, penetrating, ice-cold eyes, that forever darted around, never looking anyone straight for long; a small thin mouth that pursed tight, spat out words, then pursed tight again. His skin was pasty white, looking like it never saw sunshine, and his hands were small and bony, and rarely stopped clenching each other. He exuded a constant atmosphere of high pressure.

Scatliffe had come up through the ranks from out of left field. Three years ago no one had heard of him. But he worked like a demon, was extremely intelligent, kissed every ass that was attached to anyone of importance, then followed them round as they turned to say thank you and stabbed them in the back. He had been a close friend of the previous Home Secretary and now had Anthony Lines eating out of his pocket. Few people liked him, including Fifeshire, who never openly declared his hostility towards Scatliffe, but I could tell. The one undeniable fact was that Scatliffe was heading for the hot seat. Even Fifeshire declared that he was his most likely successor. He was professional enough to admire the man's capabilities, though he made no secret of the fact that his personal choice was Victor Hattan, the well-liked director of Security for SIS.

Scatliffe was mad as hell that I had been spying on his secretary. He hauled me into his office and screamed at me for a full ten minutes. He didn't care if God himself had instructed me, his personal staff were beyond scrutiny; for them to have to undergo surveillance was a slight on his judgement. He kicked up such a stink in the department that in the interests of peace and harmony the normally unshakeable Fifeshire was forced to soft-pedal and leave Scatliffe and his staff to their own devices for a while.

Some months after the dust had settled Fifeshire told me he felt I should try and make peace with Scatliffe. Ever since the incident Scatliffe had had the boot in for me, unfairly, as Fifeshire agreed, blaming me rather than Fifeshire for the incident. Fifeshire said that he would one day be stepping down – not for a while, but within a few years – and that when he did, Scatliffe would replace him; unless his vitriolic attitude towards me could be softened before then, I would be in for a rough ride.

I told Fifeshire it wasn't possible for anyone to give me a rougher ride than he himself did. He assured me it was. The way he said it was such that I didn't bother to argue the point. He'd convinced me.

I was assigned to Scatliffe for a twelve-month period. He was a man with less warmth than a cryogenically preserved corpse. He likened agents to insects, referring to them as common or garden spies, and treated us with as much respect as a gardener tending greenfly with a spray can of DDT.

Weekends he spent with his wife at their house in Surrey, but during the week he lived alone in London; like Fifeshire, rising early and working late. His workday would begin in a peculiar manner, when a nubile black hooker would come round to his Campden Hill apartment, punctually at 6.15 every morning, and jerk him off, before the Home Office Rover collected him at 7.00 to whisk him to the office.

Fifeshire enjoyed the photographs enormously. They were the only bright spot that year. It was a rotten year. I got the lousiest jobs going, and in the extra efforts I made to do them well I invariably buggered them up. At the end of it I was beginning to feel that I might be having a better time inside a French slammer.

Fifeshire went so far as to try and get me transferred out of MI5 altogether and into MI6, or some other department of the Secret Intelligence Service, but somehow Scatliffe had gotten his claws into every area and hadn't spread much good news about me in any of those quarters.

Then early in May Fifeshire summoned me to his office. I entered the ante-room, and his secretary, Margaret, a smart, divorced woman in her early forties, sprang up from her desk. 'Good morning, Max,' she said brightly, 'I'll just tell Sir Charles that you're here.'

'Thanks.'

A few moments later I was ushered through into Mastermind's blockhouse.

'Good morning, young fellow,' he said.

'Good morning, sir.'

'You look well.'

I presumed he must have been looking at a photograph of me; I'd gone to bed at half past five that morning, having spent most of the night standing in a doorway in Wandsworth while a new junior in the department, named Rodney Tweed, rogered a window-dresser named Derek, who'd picked him up in the Drayton Arms pub in the Old Brompton Road. I was white and shaking, my eyes bright red, and I was coughing and spluttering from too many cigarettes. 'Thank you,' I said.

Seven fifteen in the morning is a very uncivilised hour to hold a meeting, but Fifeshire looked bright-eyed and well settled into his day's work. He was a powerfully built man, not particularly tall, but striking all the same. He had a thick neck, with a bullet-shaped head, and a nose that was long but did not protrude much from his face; it was the type of nose that, if punched, would be more likely to inflict damage to the fist than to be damaged itself. The hair on his head was a mixture of dark greys, with the occasional black, and the silver streaks on either side of his temples gave him a very distinguished appearance. His eyebrows were very bushy, forming an awning over his penetrating brown eyes. The bags under his eyes were heavy and wrinkled; they were the only feature on his face which showed his age; he was 66. When he had finished speaking he never completely closed his mouth, his lips were always slightly parted; it gave one a reassuring feeling that he was always concentrating intently on what one was saying.

'I'm sending you to America,' he said. 'It'll be the toughest job you've ever had, and you'll be walking a tightrope in a political minefield. If you fall off you'll be landing me personally in a lot of stick, to say nothing of putting the kibosh on a couple of centuries of fairly friendly Anglo-American relations.'

He paused, staring at me hard, then continued. 'As you may be aware we spy on friendly nations as much as we spy on hostile nations, since all nations have, historically, a habit of changing their allegiances from time to time. For our national security we must have detailed inside knowledge of what every single country in the world is up to, both internally and in its foreign policies.

'When British agents are caught in hostile nations it does little to impair relations, since such countries accept spying as par for the course; but when our allies catch us spying on them they get very, very upset – not that they don't all do it themselves, because they do, but because it invariably opens up a hornet's nest of embarrassing questions from the media. So rule one, young fellow, is don't get caught.'

'I thought the United States was MI6's domain?'

'It is; and it has far more autonomy than is good for it. When I took over MI5, we actually had to report to MI6. But not any more. He smiled. It has always been my view that to do my job effectively I must keep an eye on MI6, and to do this I arranged some years ago the establishment of MI5 cover operation in all countries where enemy penetration of MI6 could be seriously damaging to us. The United States is one such place: MI6 operations there are based at the British Embassy in Washington, but our base is, for a number of reasons, in New York.

'Apart from the Prime Minister and myself, there is only a handful of people who know of this. We operate through a very legitimate front, a large company specialising in the manufacture of computer and calculator cabinets; it has branch offices throughout the United States, a head office in New York, and a factory and offices here in England, from which the company is now actually controlled. It is called the Intercontinental Plastics Corporation, and it is one of the market leaders in its field. The advantages of a company in the computer field are obvious: we get to know of virtually every new development in the computer field in the United States, without having to go and look for them: Intercontinental is asked to tender for the manufacture of the cabinets.

'You are being sent over by the English parent firm in order to study and report back on the company's production control methods, a role which will give you complete autonomy to go anywhere, talk to anyone, look at anything, without arousing any degree of suspicion.

'I have a strong feeling, for reasons I shan't bother you with, that when we acquired Intercontinental, we may have acquired more than we realised. I want you to go through its staff with the finest toothcomb you can lay your hands on, and to miss out nothing, absolutely nothing. Now, before I go on, do you have any questions?'

'I do, sir: I don't know the first thing about computers.'

'You will, before you start your job, young fellow, you will.'

On 12 August, barely three months later, I was riding the elevator up to Intercontinental Plastic Corporation's Park Avenue offices to start my first morning's work as the whizz-kid production control analyst from London.

For three months I'd eaten, drunk, woken, slept, breathed and belched computers and plastics, 24 hours a day. I'd attended America's elite Massachusetts Institute of Technology, I'd visited the leading electronics firms of Japan, Germany

86

and England, and I'd been despatched to the furthest reaches of the globe to see examples of Intercontinental's work in operation. God alone knew how much of it had rubbed off on me; riding up in that elevator I had a horrible feeling it wasn't enough.

Three days later, on 15 August, Fifeshire was in hospital, fighting for his life, with six bullets in him and most of his essential internal wiring in shreds. He'd been riding in a car with President Battanga of the Mwoaba Isles, who was over for a conference of the Non-Aligned Countries. Two hooded motorcyclists had riddled the car with machine-gun fire, at a traffic light, killing Battanga and the chauffeur, and critically wounding Fifeshire. An outfit calling itself the Mwoaban Liberation Army later claimed responsibility, although the Mwoaban Government angrily denied the existence of any such organisation and vehemently accused the British Government of plotting unrest in the Mwoaba Isles; it didn't state why Britain should wish to cause unrest, but hinted strongly that the Mwoabans might be about to discover a major oil-field.

CHAPTER 10

I heard Sumpy start the shower. I untied the blue ribbon, and ripped open the envelope: it contained a letter and a small wafer-thin object about an inch long and a third of an inch wide. It was mostly the colour of white marble but on the top side it had a small metal box with a circle of hard clear plastic in the middle, through which one could see a tiny grey rectangle that had minute shiny wires all around it like a spider's web. On the reverse side it looked like a member of the centipede family, with twenty-four tiny metal legs bent under it. Stamped on the underneath was the word 'Malaysia' and a serial number. If nothing else, my three months of training in the computer business had taught me to be able to recognise what this object was: a silicon chip. Doubtless it was programmed to do something, but not having a computer in which to insert it handy, I had no idea what.

I read the letter. It was short and didn't provide a great deal of enlightenment. It said:

'Dear Sir Charles,
The number that matters is 14B. When

we meet, and I add my own information to the enclosed, I think you will agree that my credentials are satisfactory. As you may already be aware, the colour scheme of this missive is not irrelevant.'

It was signed Doctor Yuri Orchnev. On the back of the envelope was some scribbling: the name Charlie Harrison, and an address: Coconut Grove, Duneway Avenue, Fire Island.

Fire Island is a sand-bar, over 30 miles long but only a few hundred yards wide at its widest point, a short way off the south coast of Long Island. It's treasured by the islanders to a point of jingoism seldom encountered since the heyday of the British Empire. Untypically of most of the North American continent, cars are strictly banned – not that they'd be much use, since there are no roads. The island is famed as being a gay paradise, although in fact its largely vacation-only population is drawn from a wide cross-section of well-off New York City dwellers, who spread out into the independent communities of summer houses, shops and trendy friendly restaurants strung out along its length, and live out their summer weekends in a state of chic bohemia.

It struck me as being unlikely that the late Dr Yuri Orchnev, if it was the writer himself from whom I had obtained this letter as he lay dead on my apartment floor the night before last, was either en route to, or returning from, a holiday on this island. Mid-December down this part of the world is not prime beach time.

I studied the writing on the back of the envelope carefully. I knew the name Charlie Harrison all right; he was a computer operator, in charge of Intercontinental's own computer system.

I read through the letter again. There was no date, no address. Why did the man who came into my apartment at half past two in the morning and shot himself have this letter in his pocket? I'd searched him thoroughly at the time, but he had no identification on him whatsoever; nothing; all he had was this letter.

I wanted to find out what that chip contained, and I wanted to find out what went on at Coconut Grove, Fire Island, and where Charlie Harrison slotted into the scheme of things. It was Wednesday today. If there was anything going on at Fire Island, it would most likely be at the weekend. It became a toss-up for Charlie Harrison or the chip first. I decided on the chip. Harrison would take longer to crack; surveillance of people was an arduous task. In the four months so far I'd worked through less than a quarter of Intercontinental's staff; I'd cleared them all except for a secretary who was having an affair, because I hadn't yet found out with whom, and a programmer called Howie Kottle, whom I thought might be gay.

My thoughts were shattered by Sumpy, who had emerged from the shower and was repeating the breakfast order for the third time to a slow-witted and apparently hard-of-hearing room-service operator.

I was worried about what to do with Sumpy. I had a feeling that if she went back to her apartment she would find the goons had taken it apart with a meat cleaver, and they'd probably still be hanging around, waiting to take her apart with the same meat cleaver. I wanted to keep her out of harm's way until I'd got rid of the harm. Hiding her 5 feet 11½ inch blonde-haired, sun-tanned, highly volatile frame was not going to be an easy task.

'How do you fancy a holiday?' I said.

'Before I do anything, Mr Maxwell Flynn –'

'Maximilian,' I interrupted, 'it comes from the Latin, not from the instant coffee.'

'I don't care if you're named after a Nigerian greenfoot monkey,' she said ever so sweetly. 'I want to know where you come from and where you plan to go, because I've just about had it up to here.' She swung her hand to the top of her forehead. 'And if you were the short-assed midget you're acting like, you'd know that was one hell of a long way.'

I sat and looked at her for a long pause as she stomped up and down the room. Finally I spoke. 'What do you want me to tell you?'

'What do I want you to tell me? What do I want you to tell me? I'll tell you what I want you to tell me: I want you to tell me why you shoot a man dead in your room in the middle of the night; why

91

you tell me not to let cops into my apartment; why you dig a hole through my apartment wall while I'm taking a shower, and kidnap me; why you don't stop when the cops point a gun at you; why you make me steal a car and come out and check into a hotel under a false name; that okay for openers?' She stood and glared at me.

Had I been in her position, I'd probably have felt the same way. But I wasn't in her position. And I couldn't explain anything to her. I just didn't want her to go back to her apartment.

'Do you want to come to Boston with me today?'

'I can't. I'm having lunch with Lynn. Then I have to catch the three o'clock flight to Rome – I have to go look at some pictures. I'm not even going to have time to go home and pack, and I'm going to be away several days.'

Lynn, whoever she was, had just done us both a great favour.

A couple of hours later, and wishing to hell I'd been sensible and got on that plane to Rome with Sumpy, I was peering through the misting windshield of a rented Buick, slipping and sliding her through a blizzard of snow that was fast covering the Connecticut Turnpike. The snow had already started to fall when I dropped Sumpy off at the restaurant to meet her friend. It would be stretching the truth to say we'd parted on amicable terms. The muck that was now tumbling out of the sky did nothing to lift my cheerless mood.

An endless convoy of tractor-trailers thrashed past, chucking crate-load upon crate-load of slush, grit, salt and general gunge onto the windshield, while the wipers struggled to turn the combination into a translucent smear, through which I could vaguely make out the darkening road ahead. It was three o'clock and dark was falling very quickly.

I turned on the radio for some cheerful music, and was boomingly exhorted to turn off at the next junction, find the nearest church, and rush in and pray to the Lord God Almighty for the salvation of my soul and the souls of millions of others, all of which were, apparently, in imminent peril due to a multitude of sins too long for the Reverend Doctor Lonsdale Forrester, the Motorists' Pastor, to relate in the air time he had available between commercials. 'And while you're driving, looking for the next church, give thanks to the Lord, yeah, give thanks to the Lord, for the gas in your tanks, for the tyres on your wheels, for your axles, for your transmissions, for the pistons in your cylinders . . .'

I turned the tuner and an immensely cheery voice was halfway through telling us about how an entire family of five had just been wiped out in an automobile accident. I tuned again: 'Get your children ULTRA-DEATH this Christmas, the great new family game; draw a card, throw the dice – and you might get to choose euthanasia for your favourite aunt . . .'; I tuned again and a voice told me that if my journey wasn't essential, not to start it as it was going to snow shortly. He evidently needed either a new set of glasses or windows in his studio. I turned off the radio and lit a cigarette. What should have been a four and a half hour run to Boston was going to take a lot longer, and at this rate, I would be lucky to get there this side of midnight.

I could have used Intercontinental's own computer to prise the secrets out of my little plastic friend in my pocket, but I had a feeling right now that staying away from the offices would be the best thing for my health. I'd telephoned Martha, my secretary, and told her I wasn't feeling too hot and was going to take a few days' rest. Having seen Sumpy come into the office to collect me on a couple of occasions, Martha was discreet enough not to ask whether I'd be contactable at home, and merely wished me a quick recovery. I wondered about Martha; about whether she knew who her real employers were. She was a smart girl, and I wouldn't have been surprised to find she was a Fifeshire operative as well. If she was she'd covered her tracks well; since she happened to be extremely attractive, the idea of attempting to get to know her better in the not-too-distant future appealed to me as a pleasant diversion.

The traffic ahead came to an abrupt halt, and I pressed the brake pedal and released it several times in rapid succession to prevent the wheels locking up, and stopped. I thought hard about the layout of the campus at the Massachusetts Institute

94

of Technology. I'd spent only a few weeks there during my computer training and in that time had been shown most of the billions of dollars' worth of equipment that were laid on for the purpose of educating the brightest echelons of America's student scientists in the technical ways of the world. I hoped no one was going to mind a small part of that equipment being put to practical use for a short while.

The weather got worse and the road got longer, and I camped the night on the floor of the Interchange 70 Howard Johnson Motel, in the company of most of the population of the North Eastern seaboard; they all appeared to be commercial travellers with urgent nine o'clock appointments in the furthermost points of the continent, men to whom earnest conversation about inventory control on gearboxes, vacuum packing of anglepoise lamps, weekly call lists and mileage rationalisation were evidently more important than sleep.

In the morning I felt foul, and didn't feel like joining the long queue to the washroom. I went outside to start clearing the snow and ice from my car windows. The storm had been and gone, and left behind it a glorious morning of glistening white ground and stark deep-blue sky basking in the gentle glow of the winter-weak sun. The roads were clear, though wet with the melted snow, and I covered the remaining miles into Boston in time to join in the rush-hour traffic.

I drove down Mass Avenue, over the Harvard Bridge, and then turned right behind the main body of the Institute buildings. I parked the car in an open lot, and walked down to the stunningly graceful embankment, Memorial Drive.

Bearded, tieless, greasy-faced from not having washed this morning, jacket and trousers crumpled, and with the white pallor of a sleepless night, I felt I should easily pass as a post-graduate student.

I crossed over and walked along by the Charles River, and looked over the far side at Boston, with the gold dome of the State House and the John Hancock Tower rising from the snow-covered ground. A horde of 45-year-old joggers nearly mowed me down as I turned to start walking again.

The air was cold and the tiny warmth of the sun felt good. My shoes rapidly turned to pulp in the slush, and I cursed myself for not having any boots.

The Computer Science rooms would, I knew, be busy, but there was an IBM 370 in the Chemistry block that I remembered being told was rarely used, and I made my way to it. The whole place seemed to have shrunk since my first visit, the way places always seem to.

I reached the building and went straight in; a security man was standing in the entrance, which was a new addition since I'd been there.

'I'm going up to the 370.'

'You with the seminar?'

I nodded that I was.

'Up the stairs, second on the right.'

I thanked him, cursing to myself that there was a seminar, walked up and went in through the door. It was a familiar layout of two rooms adjoining, with a large amount of window space in between. Through the window was the operator in the temperature-controlled room where a plethora of shiny blue boxes with winking lights and clumps of wires concealed something considerably more intelligent than the old cash registers upon which Watson founded his International Business Machines.

In the room I was in, the VDU room, were the visual display telescreens, the plotters, the card readers and the printers. There was also a large group of students, ranging from the younger ones in their cords or jeans, track-suit tops or faded jerseys, and mandatory Adidas shoes, to older ones in herringbone sports jackets and flannel trousers. Over half the entire group wore thick rimless glasses; the age group spanned 19 to 50. A tall thin man, with a sallow face and zipped up corduroy jacket, was expounding on some figures on a diagram on one of the visual display screens in the centre of the room. He stopped and looked at me almost apologetically when I walked in. 'Oh – er – are you wanting to run a program?'

'Well, I was – but I can wait.'

'Not the Zee Beta Assignment is it?'

'Er – no!'

'Traffic control?'

'No – it's a new one I'm working out – part of my term paper.'

He peered at me. 'You don't look familiar.'

I wasn't surprised. Fortunately I remembered some names from my previous visit. 'Actually I'm up from Princeton. I'm on a special course under Dr Yass.' I hoped to hell Dr Yass hadn't been hit by a bus during the couple of months since he'd escorted me around Princeton for a morning. I was aware of nineteen of the other twenty faces in the room staring at me. The twentieth was busy plucking the hairs out of his head, one by one. Enlightenment glowed in the lecturer's face; yet again the ancient art of name-dropping had worked.

'Go right ahead, if it's not going to take too long. I'll be taking a while yet. It'll be good for these students here to watch.'

My already overstretched nerves began jangling badly; blind panic was only inches away. My previous experience of actually running computers was very minimal indeed. The knowledge that I had acquired was suitable only for talking, in a seemingly knowledgeable manner, about such machines – not for operating them. I knew just about enough, given time and a fair wind, to perform the most elementary of operations. Given the current climate of this room, even if I could escape the attention of the operator there was no way I was going to achieve anything by plugging my chip into this computer, except perhaps to provide a good few days' employment for an IBM repair team. Furthermore, in the unlikely event of my succeeding in obtaining any satisfactory results, I wouldn't have been over-anxious for the secrets of the chip to be revealed to twenty-one strangers; there were other people, not a million miles from this room, who, had they been aware of my predicament, I am pretty damn sure would have shared that sentiment.

'Thank you, but I've several hours' work to do. It can wait.'

'We'll be through here by 5.00. If there's no name down, it's all yours.' He jerked his head over at a sheet of paper pinned near the door.

'Thank you,' I said. I walked over to the sheet, and the lecture resumed.

'Now, the early analogue machines had . . .'

I looked for today's date. Beside the time of five o'clock there was a name, written in thick, untidy writing: E. Scrutch. I nodded my thanks to the lecturer and left the room. He didn't notice; he was back in the days when computers were bigger than dinosaurs and a lot more ponderous; now they're smaller than guns, and a damn sight more dangerous. The security man wasn't there when I got downstairs; I ducked behind his desk and found a row of keys, all identical and tagged 'Pass – must be signed for'. I pocketed one and left the building.

The name E. Scrutch stuck in my mind. Who was E. Scrutch? Who could possibly christen anyone E. Scrutch? It was one of the most singularly unattractive-sounding names I could remember encountering; I imagined him to be short, thin, with a jutting face, and stubble on both his chin and the top of his head.

I took my usual precaution of scanning the area as I walked away from the building; I didn't feel there was much likelihood of my having a tail, but the scanning process had been so thoroughly drummed into me during my training six years ago, and during the yearly refresher courses, that it had become part of my normal movement. Within a second, and probably quite a bit less, and in one seemingly innocent action, I knew what was going on in the full 360 degrees of area around me, and to the casual observer would have appeared to have done no more than to have straightened some ruffled hairs on the back of my neck.

I carried on across the campus, towards downtown Boston and the hope of dry boots.

Half an hour later I was seated in sublime warmth in a cafe named Uncle Bunny's Incredible Edibles, my feet having a good time inside a thick, dry pair of socks inside a thick, waterproof pair of boots. I had a mug of steaming coffee and a plate somewhere underneath one of Uncle Bunny's smaller sandwiches. It wasn't just the plate that had disappeared but most of the table as well, under a sprawling mountain of turkey, avocado, chips, wholemeal bread, bean sprouts and gherkins.

It was a student hangout cafe – everything this end of town was a student hangout – with orange tables and hard plastic chairs, advertisements in the window and a student staff. The cafe was quiet at the moment, the lunchtime rush hadn't yet begun, and the few young hopes of America that were there sat, in the traditional arched back poise of students, staring mournfully into black holes, which, when they came out of their reveries, they remembered to be mugs of coffee, and they sipped.

In this great land of new awareness, of car-sharing, thought-sharing, experience-sharing, wife-sharing and God-knew-what-else-sharing, I sincerely hoped E. Scrutch would be into computer-sharing.

CHAPTER 11

E. Scrutch came as a shock; the name which had haunted me through a long and slow day belonged to some 20 to 25 stone of very aggressive female. She was completely and utterly enormous, like something out of a comic cartoon book, except that she was real, standing there before my eyes in the computer room.

Her presence in the room diminished it, distorted the perspective like a scene from Alice in Wonderland. She had short dark hair, which served only to accentuate the size of her head, and this, whilst considerably larger than is normal for such an object, looked like an afterthought that had been plucked from the wrong-sized box, before being plonked, like a pimple, on the top of her bull neck.

She wore a badly cut full-length smock, which did nothing to disguise the total shapelessness of her body, and made it quite impossible to identify her breasts, stomach or even knees amid the enormous rolls of flesh that hung about her; were she horizontal, and a couple of hundred miles long, she would have been a geographer's paradise. As she was, standing upright and about 64 inches tall, visions of paradise did not roll immediately into my mind.

She was staring at me with a pair of eyes that could have been glass, except they were bloodshot. 'You want something?' It wasn't a question, it was a military command, barked out with all the softness and femininity of a sergeant major addressing the first parade of a platoon of new recruits.

'No, don't let me bother you.'

'You are bothering me. I've got a lotta work to do and you're the fourth schmuck to bother me in the last ten minutes. I've booked this room, so why doesn't everybody fucking leave me alone?' She stuck a finger in her ear, and twiddled it furiously; she then removed it, and started scraping a lump of wax from under her finger nail. Gaining access to this computer wasn't going to be easy.

I tried the name-dropping trick once more. 'Dr Yass is going to be upset – he's asked me to get some work done for him by this evening.'

'I don't give a shit about that creep; got the worst-run campus in the country and the only way to get a fucking degree out of him is to be 5 foot 7, with blonde hair.' She glared at me. 'Either sex,' she added.

Our heart-to-heart chat was interrupted by the emergence from the computer room of the operator. 'I've fixed that tape drive – won't give any more trouble now. I have to go home; my kid has to go to the hospital. I won't be back for a couple of hours at least. Try not to break anything while I'm gone.' He hurried off.

I felt that a new line of attack was required, since conventional and logical attempts to reason were likely to end in my physical ejection from the room. I didn't say anything for some moments, and she stood blinking at me, like a toad eyeing a fly. I shrugged my shoulders and attempted to put on my 'I'm actually a very nice guy' expression.

'You look like you need a good crap,' she said.

They say that when a girl takes an interest in the condition of your clothes then she's in the marriage stakes; I wondered if the same applied for an interest in the condition of one's bowels. Her sheer size and physical ugliness weren't my major worries; my eyelids were in good working order and in any emergency could be clamped shut. But I hadn't learned how to shut my nostrils, and since I could smell her clearly from here, close up I reckoned she'd be pretty ghastly. But I steeled myself – somehow. 'I like your dress,' I said.

For a moment she looked like she'd been hit by a nuclear bomb. The moment passed and then she looked like she'd been hit by a passing car. That moment passed too, and she then looked like she'd been hit by a pillow-load of feathers. That moment passed too, and she looked like the back door of a Tiffany delivery truck had just burst open in passing her and showered her with one whole load of diamonds. 'My dress?'

'It's very pretty.' If ever, in its entire history, the

104

British Secret Service had expected an agent to make the supreme sacrifice of all time, that moment, I felt, with not a little trepidation, might be about to come.

'You like it?' She was actually reeling in shock. It was probably the first compliment she had received in her 24-odd years on this planet and she was finding it difficult to handle.

'I do. You look lovely when you're angry. Don't start being nice now.'

She just stood and looked at me. Then she put both her hands into her smock pocket and her eyes flooded with tears. I offered her a cigarette and she accepted; I lit it for her and put it in her mouth. Great crocodile tears came down. I waited until they'd subsided, and then laid it on further. 'You look like you've had a rough time just recently.'

'My boyfriend just ran off with someone.'

Now it was my turn to recoil in shock; even girls that looked like this had boyfriends? She began talking: he was 26 years old and had never had a girlfriend before. He was acknowledged as one of the most brilliant pupils MIT had ever seen; he was working on a design that was going to revolutionise the computer world; it was a design so brilliant it would make the current silicon chip micro-processors look as outmoded as the abacus. They'd been having a truly deep and meaningful relationship, and she slaved for him while he worked away. Then suddenly, last

Thursday, he had run off to Ohio with a gay truck driver who'd helped him fix a flat tyre on his car.

Within ten minutes I had my arm around her; she did smell ghastly. Within fifteen minutes Einstein had vanished from her thoughts and we were kissing passionately. Her breath was gruesome, and the only way to avoid it was to clamp my lips so tightly to hers that we made an airlock between our mouths. I kept to the inside of her lips as best I could, since the outsides were covered with rough hair. The only mitigating fact about this poor creature was that the skin on her body was as soft and supple as any could be; I tried to imagine she was someone else, someone stunningly beautiful, but it was hard.

Her smock slipped down, and her bra was soon eased up over her head and tossed out of sight. Her breasts were utterly gigantic, hanging and quivering like water-filled balloons and capped with nipples like ashtrays. She pulled me down onto her, and it was like tumbling into a half-full water bed; she groaned and moaned, clutched at me, clamping fingernails that felt like the jaws of bulldozers into my back. Every now and then she broke her mouth away to make little grunts and squeals that gave me the illusion I was lying in a muddy bog in the middle of a farmyard during an earthquake. Suddenly she started shaking like a road drill, the tempo accelerating by the second; great gulps of air shot out of her mouth with a high-pitched whistle, and she started at the same time to fart vehemently.

To try and remove my mind from this hideous reality, I allowed myself to lapse into a dream that I was strapped to the engine casing of a diesel bus in a traffic jam. She emitted one huge final sigh, released the iron jaws from the small of my back, let out one final cannon volley of a fart, and sank back onto the floor, completely and utterly spent. I leaned forward; she gave me a huge soppy grin, and plunged into sleep.

I got myself dressed, covered her up as best I could, then let myself into the computer room, which the operator had left unlocked. It took me some while to check through the machinery, and even then I wasn't sure if what I was going to do would bring everything to a grinding halt or not. There was only one way to find out; I pulled out a printed circuit board: the computer didn't die on me; I pulled a chip out of it, and replaced it with my own, then put the PCB back in. To my relief there was no perceptible difference in the running of the computer. I went back into the VDU room and settled down to work.

My luck held good, and within a few minutes my little plastic friend was cheerfully telling me all it knew as fast as I could absorb it.

Unfortunately it was less lucid than I had hoped, and at the end I had a vast array of numbers that were completely meaningless to me. Basically there were several sets of numbers, the first being 1 to

105, the second being 1 to 115, the third being 1 to 119. the fourth 1 to 130, and on up to the highest one, 1 to 442. Each number was divided into four, six or eights parts, but I could at first find no common denominator between them.

I had no idea what they might refer to – whether it be the neutrons in particles of some mineral, or the numbers of families in Central Park on any given Sunday, or a new secret formula for reconstructing Noah's Ark. I started to work methodically through each number; 1, A, B, C, D; 2, A . . . My first clue came at the first number 14 I came to: A appeared all right, as did C and D. but there was no B. I discovered the same to be the case with all the other 14Bs. They simply did not register.

A couple of hours had passed, and I had eyeball disease coming on from looking at all the figures. I was anxious to leave before the operator returned, and before Sleeping Beauty awoke; I was going to adopt the cowardly method of ending an affair – by disappearing. If I was going to do it I would have to do it fast, since she was showing signs of stirring. And yet I was loath to tear myself away from the computer; I wanted desperately to unravel the mystery. This little silicon chip that Dr Orchnev, whoever he might be, had seen fit to deliver to me as his last act on earth – it must have meant something to him. One hell of a lot. 14B. I wrote the number down and stared at it; it meant nothing;

I used to see a 14B bus in London; or was it a 44? Went along Piccadilly then up Shaftesbury Avenue; or somewhere like that. I prodded and tapped at the plethora of keys. Maybe there was something I had to do to this computer that I had forgotten; maybe I should wake E. Scrutch and enlist her help. I thought about my salary; it wasn't that great; the hell with it. I collected the chip and slipped out of the room, out of the building and into the bitterly cold night air.

When the cold comes on the Northeastern seaboard it really comes and temperatures of 15 and even 20 below are not uncommon. The temperature must have been down in this region now; the air hurt my lungs and the dew on the ground had frozen hard; the roads were going to be treacherous and I had a long drive ahead.

I reached the car park and found my car door frozen solid. I heated my key with my cigarette lighter; after a few moments' reluctance it slipped into the lock and turned. The windows had half an inch of ice on them; rather than chisel away at them, I took the lazy way, of starting the engine and turning the de-mister on full. In my jacket and shirt it was too cold to sit in the car and wait for the air to warm; I reckoned it would take a good ten minutes. A smoke-shop was open across the road, so I went over to get some cigarettes and something to chew on the journey.

Inside was harsh white lighting but there was a welcoming warmth from an oil heater; a fuzzy baseball game blared noisily from an elderly television in a corner above the counter, whilst the proprietor and a customer struggled to have a conversation above the racket. I stood there while they talked.

'But that wasn't the year for the Bruins.'

'Sure to hell wasn't. Remember when the Maple Leafs came down?'

'Sure I remember –' The proprietor broke off for a moment and turned to me. 'Yeah?'

'Do you have any English cigarettes?'

'Sorry, what d'yer say?'

'Do you have –' I broke off in mid-sentence. There was a vivid flash outside, followed by a sharp, deep explosion not more than a hundred yards away and in the direction from which I'd come.

'English, did yer say?'

The proprietor hadn't noticed.

'Holy Jesus – you see that?' The customer, a short fat man in a battered flying jacket, spun round. Even without his cab parked at the kerbside, one could have guessed his profession.

'See what?' said the proprietor.

'Great damn flash!' He ran out the door.

'Got Players – you want tipped?'

I gave him the money and followed the cabby out. There was a column of flame rising from the parking lot; cars were stopping in the road and people were sprinting towards the flames; there were smaller balls of fire all around, as if blown from a huge firework. It didn't take me more than a second glance to know for sure that the car that was burning was mine.

With people converging onto the parking lot it would have been difficult to have slipped away at this moment, so I moved over too, playing the part of an amazed onlooker; I didn't have to act too hard to look amazed.

'Stop a bus – they got fire extinguishers,' said a voice.

'Little late for that, I reckon,' said another.

'Anyone in there?'

'I sure hope not.'

'What the hell happened to that?' There were voices everywhere.

'Must have been a short in the wiring.'

'Buick isn't it? I had a Buick caught fire once. Damnedest car I ever had.'

'That was no short in the wiring.'

'Hell no – you hear the explosion?'

The car was literally ripped to shreds; the doors had been blown away and the roof was torn from the front pillars and was swaying up and down on the rear pillars like a grotesque drawbridge. The flames roared, vividly illuminating the parking lot.

The fire engines turned up and then the ambulances. Ambulance men rushed around and seemed distressed that there weren't any bodies, mutilated or otherwise, to be found; they spread out and searched the vicinity, like some bizarre game of hunt-the-thimble.

Eventually the crowd started to disperse, and I dispersed with them. I walked and kept on walking. I was feeling very sick indeed, at the thought of the near miss, at not having checked the car, at the knowledge that somehow, someone had followed me here to Boston and I hadn't noticed. I walked into a bar and ordered a large bourbon, straight up.

I leaned against the counter, took a gulp and lit one of my new cigarettes. The bomb must have been attached to the exhaust or part of the engine; with a heat trigger device. I thought hard. I had hired the car on one of my false licences, so no one would be able to trace it back to me. How the hell did anyone know I was in Boston? Nobody knew where I was going – except Sumpy; and no, it just wasn't possible – there was no way she could be involved. And yet . . . nobody could have tailed me, so someone knew, unless by a million to one shot someone had spotted me in Boston. Possible, but unlikely, and then they wouldn't have known my car, unless they'd actually seen me drive into the parking lot. No. It wasn't possible; and yet, equally, it wasn't Sumpy. But someone knew. In Belfast a mistake could have been made, a bomb put under the wrong car; but car bombs weren't a feature of American life and the coincidence was just too much to swallow. No way.

Someone was going to an awful lot of long lengths to get rid of me and I wanted to know who, because when I found out who, then I might be able to find out why, and when I had found out why, I figured I might be able to cure them of this unpleasant craving.

Right now it was ten o'clock at night; I had no change of clothes and I was in an even stranger than usual city; I felt pretty damn uncomfortable. I left the bar and hailed a cab to the airport, and watched out the back window for a long way before I could be sure we weren't being trailed and I could relax a little.

The bourbon began to give me an agreeable lift, and at the airport I discovered that the last flight to La Guardia, New York, had been delayed due to engine trouble and there was a seat available.

CHAPTER 12

As we taxied down the runway I churned over every detail I could remember about Sumpy, from the time I had first met her. I wondered whether that first encounter could have been a set-up: it was at a preview drinks party at the Frick Gallery, to which I had been invited by an old schoolfriend who was working for Sotheby Parke Bernet in New York.

The exhibition was of erotic surrealism; in my view it was the art world's way of having an exhibition of hardcore pornography and calling it respectable. Sumpy had felt much the same way, as we both found ourselves staring at the same set of very overgrown organs. 'Jealousy will get you nowhere,' she had said.

Unless the numerical puzzle of my little plastic friend contained a king's ransom in the form of a computer program for producing perfect original Cezannes, I couldn't think of any reason Sumpy could have for wanting to get rid of me. Right now, as I wondered idly whether the plane would succeed in lifting off the ground and up into the sky, or whether it would plummet into the two-storey housing estates beyond, and as I wondered idly about my myriad of other problems, the one and only certainty I had was that Sumpy was for real.

The seat belt and no smoking sign went off, and the air started filling with cigarette smoke. The plane was full of tired and fed-up-looking businessmen, a few of whom knew each other and held murmured conversations, but most were either reading or sleeping.

I retraced yesterday's procedure of renting the Buick, driving back to the Travelodge, collecting Sumpy and then dropping her off to meet Lynn, and then I realised: it was her goddam lipstick. I'd forgotten all about it. On the way to Lynn, Sumpy was putting on her lipstick; I'd swerved hard to avoid a cab driver who thought he was in a one-way street, and the lipstick had rolled onto the floor and vanished out of sight. She said not to bother after I'd groped under the seats for a couple of minutes, she didn't care for the shade too much anyway.

Whoever was after me had obviously figured that by bugging her, they'd keep a tab on me, since they figured I wouldn't be too far away. It must have been a damn powerful bug for them to have tracked me to Boston, since sure as hell no one had tailed me from New York to there. The lipstick would have been the ideal hiding place for a bug, and the bug could have been planted in it at any time without her knowledge; equally, she could

115

have known all about it, and dropped it deliber-
ately. I didn't know what to believe; in my heart
of hearts I didn't believe Sumpy could be involved,
but at the same time I was sufficiently long in the
tooth to know that in my game anything could
be, and frequently was, possible.

'Can I get you a drink, sir?'

She was gorgeous. She could have got me
anything in the world. It was clear from her
disapproving stare that she didn't feel the same
way about me. I had no idea what I must have
looked like, but I was pretty damn sure that it
wasn't too hot. I ordered another bourbon; she
even took my money in advance.

I lowered my tray, then pushed the button in the
armrest to recline the seat-back. A white plastic
label in front of me told me I was sitting in seat
8B. The empty seat next to me, by the window,
was 8 A. The other side of the aisle, the seats were
8C and 8D. I was in a Boeing 737, one of the
smaller of the passenger jets in general commercial
use. I idled some minutes away working out the
number of passengers the plane could seat. But
my reckoning it was 114, plus a few jump-seats
for the crew. And then the penny dropped.

It dropped making about the same noise as a
truck loaded with plate glass colliding with
a nitroglycerine tanker, during which time the
gorgeous iceberg had come and put my drink
down and gone away again and I hadn't even
noticed. 14B. Airline seats? Rows of four seats;

rows of six seats; rows of eight seats. Small airliners had four seats, like this and the Douglas DC9. Larger ones, like the DC8 and the Boeing 707 had six seats across – three and three – and the Jumbos – the Boeing 747, Tristar, DC10 and Airbus – had ten seats across – three by each window and four in the middle. It did fit but it still didn't make any sense. I wanted to check further and summoned the iceberg back. 'How many seats are there in this plane?'

'One hundred and fifteen, sir.' She was off again down the aisle before I could say anything else. I'd been one out. Not bad.

The iceberg's team-mate wasn't so pretty, but at least she was human. She took my list of questions to the flight deck and came back with the answers. The numbers of seats on every commercial airliner in current service corresponded exactly with the information from my plastic chum.

I took a walk down the aisle and found seat 14B. Its occupant looked like an ex-Harvard law student who was rapidly on his way to becoming a partner in a Manhattan firm. About 32, square tortoise-shell glasses, hair short and neat, good-looking with strong Jewish features, he was talking earnestly and seriously to an awkward-looking man on his left, either a colleague or a client. They were wading their way through a thick pile of photo-copies, which, as I walked back past them again, I could see to be a real estate transaction. The man in 14B looked tough enough to take on any other lawyer, but not tough enough to have killed someone for the seat he was sitting in.

I sat down again. What, I wanted to know, was the significance of airline seats? What, in particular, was significant about 14B? Why had 14B been missing from every set of seats? From Orchnev's brief letter it was apparent that Fifeshire knew the answer.

I began to feel very cold as a chill started to run up and down inside me. Maybe those people who had gone to such lengths to kill me in the last few days had also tried to stop Fifeshire from being able to tell; maybe Battanga, who had been killed in the car, hadn't been the target at all; maybe the Mwoaban Government were right and there was no such thing as the Mwoaban Liberation Army, and it was Fifeshire and not Battanga who had been the target.

I greatly envied Sherlock Holmes his Watson: the sheer comfort of having someone around with whom to talk things over, if only to get it off one's chest and have a good night's sleep, and be rested and have a clear mind for the morning. Holmes also had a clear brief before embarking on each case; I'd had virtually nothing.

I wondered if already I had gone too far; perhaps after Orchnev's suicide I should have reported the facts back to Scatliffe and then awaited his instructions. But, to be fair to myself, I hadn't had much of a chance. I knew now that the sensible thing to do would be to get off this plane in New York and get on the first one out to London. But I had a feeling I had latched onto something important, something that maybe, just maybe, no one except me knew, and I had to follow it through alone. My main problem was going to be to remain alive.

We touched down in La Guardia at half eleven, and I took a cab straight into Manhattan. I got out a couple of blocks from the Intercontinental building and made straight for the car park ramp. I didn't want to go in the front entrance and have to sign the night book, so I settled in the shadows in the hope that someone would drive out soon. The offices operated around the clock, although on a thin shift at night.

I had to wait longer than I thought, and it was a full two hours before the electrically operated door ground up, and a weary computer technician drove out; I ducked under the door just as it started closing again, and walked through the almost deserted parking lot to the service stairway. I climbed fourteen flights, running into no one, and emerged into the dark corridor of the personnel floor. There was little likelihood of anyone being around on this floor at this hour – it was now after 2.00 – but I didn't turn any lights on to be on the safe side.

I went into the file room, shut the door, and switched on the lamp that was built into my watch. I quickly found the file I was looking for. It had the name Charles Harrison neatly typed on a plastic strip on the top, and I started to read the story of his life, as told by the Personnel Officer of Intercontinental Plastics Corporation – not one of the world's most sensational narrators.

Charlie Harrison was born in a suburb of Birmingham, Alabama, educated there at secondary school, graduated to Princeton and gained a first in computer science. He went to IBM, stayed there five years, did a further two years with Honeywell, and joined Intercontinental as head of the computer department six years ago. For someone of his background it seemed odd to me that he should have joined a company like Intercontinental; his leaning was obviously computers, and whilst the company had two massive computers, it only used them for its day-to-day business requirements; it didn't build and develop computers – Harrison's speciality – only their plastic cabinets.

I switched on the photocopier and waited while it warmed up. All was still quiet. I photocopied all Harrison's records, switched the machine off, replaced the file, and left the building again via the car park, this time going out the fire escape door which opened from the inside.

I walked a safe distance from the building and hailed a cab to the Statler Hilton, a suitably anonymous giant of a hotel, where I figured they were unlikely to be bothered by someone checking in at 3.00 in the morning without any luggage, because people did that all the time. The American Express card is a great substitute for a trunk load of baggage.

120

CHAPTER 13

I slept through until 8.30, when I was awoken by a bellhop, bringing me a beautifully cleaned full-length Lurex evening gown. I asked him to try and exchange it for an electric razor, which was something I felt more in need of. But he'd given me an idea.

After a hot bath, a long slow shave and a long slow breakfast, I began to feel a lot more human again.

My first visit was to the Birth and Death register offices in The Health Department on Worth Street. It took me less time than I had expected to find out what I wanted.

My second call was to an army surplus store, to buy some image intensifier field-glasses. My third call was to a medical supply outfit, to buy several pairs of surgical gloves. My fourth call was to Budget Rent-A-Car; I didn't think that Avis would have been too pleased to see me again. I parked the car, a reasonably anonymous Ford, in a lot off 42nd Street, and walked around the Times Square area, until I found a suitable hairdressing salon.

I emerged an hour and a half later, a peroxide

blonde, with a back-combed bouffon hairdo. Less than a block away, I acquired an outfit to match: Chocolate leather trousers, a beige blouson jumper, and a full-length wolf overcoat; all courtesy of the British taxpayer. The first pass was made at me not 15 feet from the shop.

I climbed back into the car with some difficulty, and practised my smile on the car park attendant; he replied with a stare that I interpreted to be a mixture of curiosity and pity. Still, I figured that if I was going to a gay paradise, sticking out like a sore thumb would probably be the best way to pass unnoticed. More important, I felt some sort of a disguise was necessary right now; I wouldn't pass scrutiny from someone who knew me well, but it should put sufficient doubt in most people's minds to give me the advantage of a few valuable seconds in a tight spot. I had a feeling there might be a reception committee waiting on Fire Island, and I wanted at least to go in with a sporting chance.

I drove out of Manhattan over the 59th Street Bridge, to the sound of tyres whining on the gridding, the traffic above on the overhead section thundering like an express train. After the bridge there was a massive concrete viaduct to the left, then a seemingly endless sprawl of gas stations, tyre depots, hamburger drive-ins, diners, punctuated by the eternal barrage of cigarette hoardings booming out the message that it's virile to smoke low tar, and each brand vying with the others as to which will kill you the slowest. I passed the massive blue-and-grey Queens Centre, then a battery of brownstone high-rises, and then the scenery gradually began to change, with massive areas of green appearing, and the towering blocks and sprawl of buildings becoming less frequent.

Past Kennedy Airport the constructions suddenly dropped completely away and we were out in the open countryside of Long Island, with smart wooden crash-barriers and elegant stone bridges, with lush greenery and elegant white timbered houses tucked away behind the trees. I could smell the strong, exhilarating, reassuring cologne of fresh air, wet trees and money.

Most of the snowfall of the night before last had missed this area, although there were a few patches of white here and there. I had that great feeling of relief one has when one leaves any city behind, and the quiet calm of this scenery against the towering, sprawling claws of New York made that feeling all the stronger.

The man in the ticket office at the Fire Island ferry looked me up and down a dozen times, then shrugged; he stood in his fleecy parka, hands wrapped in thick sheepskin mitts which he clapped continuously together, cursing that the stove had run out of heating oil, and looking dubiously at the darkening sky. Yes, the ferry was running; how often it was running, he had no idea; it was off-season now, and the boat was not as regular as in summer time, he informed me. It had last departed over an hour ago, and to his knowledge it hadn't sunk; when it would return was anybody's guess. All he could do was to give me a reasonable degree of hope that, provided the weather did not worsen, I could expect to find myself on Fire Island within the next two to three hours, and he pointed out a white-painted shack, with two windows and a door, and the words Porky's Clam Bar sticking out above its sloping tiled roof, where he suggested I wait.

Inside was a blaze of warmth, with tightly packed, wooden tables and chairs, a wood-beamed ceiling, blue-and-white check cotton curtains, and a full-length bar loaded with trays of blueberry muffins and, as the sign on the wall assured us, home-made belly-busting Lunar donuts. There was a liberal sprinkling of artefacts in keeping with the seafood and seaside atmosphere, including tiffany-style lamps with lobster and clam shell motifs, hanging plants on thick rope cradles, a map of Olde Long Island, and a 28-pound lobster nailed to a wooden board. Handwritten signs on the wall advertised 'The clams that made Long Island famous served here', 'Root beer served in a frozen mug', and what has now become an almost statutory item in every American restaurant with any aspersions to grandeur, Eau Perrier.

I ordered a beer and a bowl of steamers from a small boy in a baseball cap who had been sitting on a bar-stool, practising sticking a knife into a beer mat, and he rushed off through a doorway shouting at the top of his voice, 'There's a lady out there wants serving.'

A good wait later a girl in a sailor-suit uniform placed a massive bundle of silver foil on the table, and opened it up to reveal an enormous pile of whitey-beige shells of varying size, from medium to huge, each with a shrivelled grey protuberance like an elephant's trunk. As far as attractive-looking food goes, Long Island steamer clams must rate in the top 10 most ugly creatures ever to be eaten by mankind; but as far as taste goes, they have few peers.

I glanced up; the girl, and the boy in the base-ball cap, were both looking curiously at me. I turned my attention to my bowl and began to lift out the content of another shell, when I heard a snigger. I saw a second girl in sailor uniform dart her head back behind the doorway, then cautiously look round again at me. For someone who's job it is to pass unnoticed at any time, anywhere, I hadn't begun my trip to Fire Island too successfully.

The weather lifted a little, and in a shorter time than the ticket collector had predicted, I was in the covered downstairs section of the hydrofoil as it pitched through the none-too-gentle swell with a disturbing lack of ease. The pencil silhouette of the island appeared from time to time as the bow dipped. I looked up at the ceiling and wasn't sure whether to be reassured or worried by the fact that it was thick with orange lifejackets.

Other than the pilot, a large bearded man with a fat cigar, who was reminiscent of the man in the John Player advertisement, and a youth with him on the bridge, there was only one other person on the ferry, an elderly woman in a purple mackintosh, who held three miniature poodles on a tangled string of leashes. She discussed with them the finer points of the voyage, pointing out to them landmarks they shouldn't miss, and discussing how they might like their steak cooked for supper. They were called Tootsie, Popsie and Baby.

The arrival of the ferry in Ocean Beach harbour could not be accurately described as a major event for the islanders. A man in a donkey jacket came with evident reluctance out of the long shed that ran the length of the dock, caught the line the youth tossed him and pulled it swiftly down over a bollard.

It was bitterly cold now, and as I stepped ashore I felt the wind and damp gnawing through every inch of my body. It made me thoroughly unenthusiastic for anything. If Ocean Beach had a charm in summer, it had been packed away most efficiently for the winter; the whole place felt morose, like an abandoned film set. The air was full of the flapping of boat tarpaulins and the clacking of halyards as an assortment of power boats and small yachts jerked uncomfortably at their moorings in the tiny marina, on the other side of the George Crohn Senior Wagon Park, where a myriad of rusting four-wheeled kiddy karts sat waiting for their owners to return next spring and load them with their baggage and provisions.

I walked around the town, looking for an open shop. A sign in a window said, 'Have a great winter, see you in the spring. Larry and Don'. Underneath it, two young men in athletic outfits beamed out, one pulling the other in a kiddy kart. A shutter banged in the wind, and some gulls flew screeching overhead. A small group of people sat drinking coffee inside a real estate agency, but I walked past.

A general store was open and I went in. The woman behind the counter was a cheerful old stick and gave the impression of not having had any form of contact with human life for several days as she reeled into a ten-minute monologue about such topics as the weather, the general state of repair of the harbour wall, and the dangerous condition of the lanes on the island due to increasing congestion of bicycles. There was no stopping her, and by the time she had finished talking, I knew everything about the island except the one thing I was interested in: the house in Duneway Avenue called Coconut Grove. On this topic Fire Island's answer to the Doomsday Book was stumped. All she knew was that it was owned by someone she thought lived in New York, who rented it through an agency. Mostly, this summer, she thought it had remained empty, although occasionally a tall fair-haired man, Harriman or Harris she thought his name might be, would visit it. Sometimes he came alone, sometimes with another man; but no one from the house ever came into the shops, nor did they take any interest in the community affairs of the island. She asked me if I was thinking of renting the house, and I told her I had heard it might be coming on the market and I wanted to take a look at it.

She gave me elaborate directions to the house. I thanked her and set off through the tiny town. A notice in the window of the wooden police station warned me not to evade buying a bicycle licence. A large free-standing notice further on made it very plain that there was to be no eating or drinking nor changing of clothes on the beach, that the use of radios was regulated, and that I was to pick up my dog's droppings. The population of Fire Island was evidently big licks on notices.

I walked past a massive water recycling plant and was suddenly out of the town. A long concrete path stretched out in front of me, lined with thick evergreen vegetation – pines, firs, holly; anyone planning to ambush me would have it all his own way with this high shrubbery. I was glad of my disguise, but knew, as anyone lying in wait for me would know, that not too many people would be out walking around this island for their health right now.

I had my hand sunk deep into my coat pocket, and clamped firmly and reassuringly around the handle and trigger of my gun. I know of agents who don't like to carry guns; I'm not one of them. There are many agents who prefer to carry small unobtrusive guns; I prefer to wear a jacket that's one size too large than a gun that's one size too small.

We're allowed to choose whatever gun we want, and my current companion is a Beretta 93 R – one of the most up-to-date weapons on the market. It holds magazines of 15 or 20 rounds of 9 mm parabellum bullets, and can be made to fire them either as a semi-automatic, one round at a time, or as a machine pistol, firing bursts of three at a time. If one happens to have sufficient ammunition about one's person, it is capable of firing off 110 rounds per minute – which is more than adequate for the average tight corner. An additional little gadget it has is a handle in front of the trigger which can be folded down for two-handed shooting – much the most accurate way to use a hand-gun. It's about as accurate and powerful a hand-gun as it is possible to have, and it fits into a clever holster under my left arm-pit: The holster can easily be taken apart and re-assembled around the gun to make the whole thing look like a pistol-grip cine camera – very simple, blindingly obvious, and it never fails to fool airline security inspectors.

I passed a succession of old and modern timber

houses and bungalows, mostly shuttered up against the winter, all looking bleak and uninviting in the fast fading twilight. Knowing the logical route to the house, I worked out a different route of my own, which I hoped would bring me out around the far side of the house. Being a complete stranger to the island was no help, but since all paths went either lengthways or width ways, navigation wasn't too difficult; I cut across the width of the island, keeping as close to the hedges as I could. At one intersection I was nearly run down by an old man on a bicycle, fishing rod trailing out over his shoulder behind him; it was good just to see human life.

I hit Duneway Avenue at what, provided the woman's directions were correct, was the furthest point away from Coconut Grove. It was a concrete path, like all the others, with houses fairly evenly spaced down it; I calculated that Coconut Grove was about 300 yards from where I stood. The sky was still a little light for comfort, and I ducked into the porch of a boarded-up house to wait for dark.

The night was falling rapidly, and in little over half an hour, I emerged, crossed over Duneway Avenue and walked down to the next intersection; there I paced 300 yards, which brought me to the back of a tall house of almost futuristic design, topped with an attic studio. A bizarre fire escape, made from statues of naked men standing on each other's shoulders, went right up to this attic. I

130

climbed it, and at the top, using the window ledge as a foothold, hauled myself up onto the roof. It was pitch dark now, and I crawled carefully over to the far side. Less than 50 feet in front was a bungalow with a light shining behind its drawn curtains. I pulled out of my pocket the night-vision binoculars I had bought in New York that morning, and studied the bungalow closely. It was the only building around that had any lights on, and I figured that it must be Coconut Grove. The curtains this side were all fully drawn. I scanned the area around the bungalow; everything appeared in ghostly clarity, and whilst it was dim the detail was so good I could have seen a rabbit move. It didn't take me long to find my mark: a great hulk in a mackintosh, spreadeagled over a rooftop, about two houses closer to the harbour than the bungalow. I could see a rifle, with telescopic sights, by the man's right hand. Poor sod, whoever he was, must have been half-frozen to death. He was taking a gulp from a thermos flask, his head transfixed in the direction down which he would have expected me to come.

I decided to tackle Harrison first and let the night watchman carry on freezing a while. I climbed back down to the ground, cut straight through to the bungalow, and went up to the curtained window where the light came from. Close up, there was a slight chink and I peered through it. The sight was not a particularly pretty one: a tall fair-haired man that I immediately

131

recognised as Charlie Harrison was sprawled, stark naked, on what looked like a doctor's couch. A shorter, dark-haired man, who I put in his early thirties, also naked, was gently squeezing the contents of a tube of lubricating jelly down the small of Harrison's back, and rubbing it in with slow caresses. He squeezed more over Harrison's buttocks, rubbing that in too, then sweeping his hand down inside Harrison's crutch and along the inside of his thighs; Harrison squirmed in apparent ecstasy at every movement.

There was a door a few feet from where I stood, and I carefully tried it. It was the typical wood-framed wire-mesh door for keeping insects out of North American houses. It swung open, revealing a second, Yale-locked door. I carry about my person a small flat device with a choice of bevelled edges; it is particularly suited to Yale locks and this one was no exception. The door opened, and with my gun out I stepped through into a kitchen, securing the door behind me. There was a closed door on my right, which presumably led through to where the party was. Provided nothing had changed, both occupants should have their backs to this door; I pulled it open, very slowly, and heard their voices.

'Oh, Howie, ooohhh, oh, fantastic, shit, wow! Oh wow! Come inside me, man!'

I could see them clearly now; the sight was even less attractive from here.

'I'll get more jelly.'

'Yeah, wow!'

Howie turned and walked straight towards the kitchen. I ducked behind the door, and as he came through I gently pushed it to behind him, clamped my left hand around his mouth, and slammed my right arm into the base of his neck; he folded up without a murmur, and I lowered him gently onto the floor. I'd never seen him before. I opened the door again; Harrison was still lying face down, clenching and opening his hands in anticipation. I marched straight up to him, and thrust my gun the full length of its barrel up his welcoming anus.

He screamed out a strange, deep howl, a mixture of pain and sublime ecstasy. 'Ooohhh! Wow! Howie!'

'I'm not Howie, and this isn't his cock,' I said.

He froze for a moment, then spun his head round towards me. I pushed harder on the gun, and with a groan his head fell forward into the pillow; goose-pimples of fear sprang across his body. 'You're hurting – ohhh – you're hurting.'

'It wasn't hurting a moment ago, and Howie's got three inches on this.'

'Ohhh – for God's sake take it out – ohhh – who are you – ohhh – what do you want?'

'I'll do the questions, you do the answers.' I pressed my point home a little further. He let out another fairly genuine-sounding moan. 'Firstly, who's your friend – the fiddler on the roof?'

'You what?'

'You heard – your buddy in the mac, with the

pop gun – he's not looking for grouse, and if he is, he's about three and a half thousand miles too far West right now.'

'Take – please take out – oww – take out – oww – take that out –' He was whimpering and starting to shake.

'Talk.'

'I don't know out there. I don't know who's out there. I don't. I really don't.'

'There's a man on a rooftop with a rifle, other side of the lane. He's not up there for his damn health – who the hell is he?'

'I don't know. I really don't know. Ohhhh – please – take it out. I don't know who he is and I never saw him.'

'All right, my friend, let's change the subject. Tell me what the number 14B means to you?'

'14B?'

'You heard right. Tell me all about it?' This time I pushed the gun very hard, and he screamed very hard. 'You'd better understand I've come a long way to have a chat with you, and I'm not going back home till either you're dead or I have the answers to a lot of questions, and it's going to be a whole lot more pleasant for you if you give the right answers, because each time you don't, you're going to get another one of these.' I jabbed the gun again, and he screamed piercingly. It didn't sound to me that it was all pain. 'Got it?'

'I've got it.'

'Right. Let's begin at the top: Your name's Charles Moreton Harrison?'

He emitted an affirmative grunt.

'Born Charlottesville, Virginia, 14 October 1937?'

Another similar grunt.

'Both your parents, your two brothers and your sister were killed in an air crash in Acapulco on 20 December 1958?'

He grunted again. This time I gave him a hard prod. It caused him to cough for several moments. 'What's that for?'

'It's for lying.'

'I'm telling the truth.'

'Charles Moreton Harrison, born in Charlottesville, Virginia, 14 October 1937, whose family was wiped out in Acapulco on 20 December 1958 was drafted into the US Army on 12 January 1966. On May 10th of that year he was sent to Vietnam. On June 2nd he went out in a six-man patrol which walked into a Vietcong ambush. The six men between them stopped 290 bullets; what was left of their bodies was found that afternoon. So who the hell are you?'

CHAPTER 14

His name was Boris Karavenoff and he worked for the KGB. He'd been planted as a mole fourteen years back, assuming the dead Harrison's identity. The Russians had been looking for someone in the computer field, with no living relatives to be able to positively identify him. When Harrison had been killed in Vietnam, Karavenoff, chosen for his similar appearance, had been neatly planted in the US with all mention of military service deleted from his records. I allowed myself a smile; in the language of the Americans, I'd got to first base.

Karavenoff blurted it out with a peculiar tone in his voice – there was an element of relief, a sense of shedding off all the years of deception and anxiety, of ecstasy at being freed of the shackles, yet also of regret, as if in casting off Charlie Harrison he was parting company with an old friend. His head sank down into the pillow and his body went limp; he lay still for several moments, then he lifted his head slightly and looked towards me. 'Please take the gun out and I'll tell you everything I know.'

I believed him. I took the gun out and he started to talk. He had been studying computer programming at the Leningrad Institute when the KGB approached him with the offer to go to America. In one year, at an academy in Izhevsk, he was meticulously converted into an American. He was taught how to be a good American, a nice American, a nasty American, what he should know about American history and what he shouldn't know, how to talk about football and baseball, about Yogi Berra and the other great names of his youth, how to walk, how to talk, when to buy a battered Chevvy and when to change it for a slightly less battered Chevvy and why he shouldn't change it for a Lincoln Continental, what to watch on the box, how to chew gum and how to eat hamburgers. They even taught him how to fart the American way.

Boris Karavenoff's role was that of the last man in the line of Russian Intelligence inside the United States; he was the person that actually physically sent to Moscow the information that the KGB network in the US managed to acquire. He also received from Moscow any instructions for the network and was responsible for passing them on. The tools Karavenoff employed for his trade were, not unnaturally, computers.

Most computer owners suffer from the same problem as most car owners: they haven't the faintest clue what goes on under the bonnet. The result is that they have to rely totally on the experts they hire to operate, run and maintain their computers. The scope for crooked operators is, as many have already discovered, enormous. One enterprising programmer for a New York banking concern added several noughts onto his own bank balance, withdrew the money, invested it wisely, earned himself several million dollars, then repaid the money to the bank, with full interest, and restored his balance to its original level, disposing of his profit in a numbered Swiss account. It took this self-made millionaire over a year to persuade his employers to believe what he had done.

There have been several instances of smart computer operators, who, discovering that the computers were capable of more than was required by their owners, have established profitable sidelines renting out space and time to other companies, without the knowledge of their employers. One such operator, who had advised the board of a food wholesaling combine on which computer to buy, ensured they bought one considerably in excess of their needs. Under a separate name, and in offices over a thousand miles away, he rented this same computer to a national car-hire firm, a toy manufacturer, a mining company, a travel agency and a hospital. Everything ran smoothly for over five years, and it was not until after his death in a car accident that his enterprise was discovered.

There is scarcely an airline in the world that is not on a computer system. The video screens are as much a part of airline ticket offices or check-in desks as are the smiles on the girls who sit beside them.

Every airline has a computer installation in each major city, and one master installation. All the installations are connected via telephone lines. Pan Am's master installation is near New York: If Harry Smith, in Tokyo on a business trip, wants to book a seat on a flight from London to Los Angeles, a girl at Pan Am desk in Tokyo types the seat request into her terminal. That request is flashed through the telephone wires to New York, and in a fraction of a second the computer in New York checks the bookings on that flight and flashes back a reply: either the flight is full, or there are vacant seats. If there are vacant seats it says how many there are and which ones they are: first class, clipper or economy. The computer has to work fast because there may be a hundred people at Pan Am desks around the world all wanting information about that particular flight. The moment Harry Smith books his seat, the computer makes note, and tells everyone there is one seat less.

At the same time as making the bookings, the master computer is doing Pan Am's accounts, sending out its bills, making up the payroll, keeping track of how many gallons of fuel each plane is using on each flight, making notes of VIPs, of kosher menus, vegetarian menus, of unaccompanied children, of elderly travellers in need of special assistance, of where the planes are at any given point in time, who is flying which, what the next month's roster is going to be, figuring out who's ordered what from the mail order catalogues on each flight, and sending the goods off. In addition it is linked via telephone lines to all the computers of all the other airlines, so that if Harry Smith is unable to get a flight to New York with Pan Am, Pan Am can maybe book him on either TWA, or British Airways, or Air India, or Japan Airlines, or Singapore Airlines or KLM or Lufthansa or Air France, or any other of the myriad of glittering, silver-bellied birdies that shimmer and thunder through the dawn, midday, dusk and night skies of the world.

It's a busy little fellow.

The international airline business is unique among all other businesses in its worldwide spread of offices. Some travel agencies and car-hire firms are making valiant efforts to join these ranks, but still have nowhere near the spread of the airlines. In every major town and in every airport of the world are offices or desks with computer terminals that have instant access to the flight data of their own and every other international airline in the world.

The data that travels, 24 hours a day, 7 days a week, freely and speedily between the countries and the cities of the world, seems innocuous enough: flight number, starting point, stopover points, destination, day of week, time of day, type of aircraft, number of seats. For most passengers there is no special information and they travel purely as names on a list. But for some there can be many lines of information. The contents of two or three pages of a novel could be stored in the space available in the computer for a single seat.

Boris Karavenoff used the space available for seat numbers 14B for his communications with Moscow. He had, without the slightest difficulty, hooked the Intercontinental computers into the international airlines network, by tapping into the wires running from a branch booking office. Using an identically programmed silicon chip to the one I had in my pocket, he could, whenever he liked, book a seat 14B on any flight of any airline in the world. A short coded signal would inform an Aeroflot ticket desk in Moscow of the relevant flight, and the information, naturally in code, would be recorded; the reservation would then be cancelled, and the information would be gone from the teletype screens and the computer memory banks for ever. The process was reversed if Moscow wished to pass a communication to Karavenoff. The solution to part one of Dr Yuri Orchnev's cryptic puzzle had emerged.

Psychologists say that almost all criminals, petty or major, have a secret desire to confess their crimes, almost as an act of bravado. Under skilful interrogation the criminal can be made to open up like an enthusiastic schoolboy, to cheerfully pour out everything he knows and, while talking, to develop an obsession not to miss out a single

141

detail. Right now Boris Karavenoff was in this frame of mind; provided I could get off this island alive I was going to have one hell of a report to make back to London.

The one subject on which he knew nothing was the man up on the roof; he seemed genuinely surprised that there was someone there and pointed out that it could as easily be himself as me that the man was after. I nodded agreement, although I knew that wasn't true – if it was, Karavenoff and his chum would have been dead long before I'd arrived. I asked him about Sleeping Beauty in the kitchen: he was a computer programmer in the US Defence Bureau; Karavenoff pointed up at the ceiling; in a sunken light socket. I could clearly see a camera lens. 'Automatic,' he said, 'comes on with that light.' He pointed up at one of the bulbs that was glowing brightly – just a little too brightly for normal room lighting. It was a routine blackmail setup.

I broached the subject of the great mystery writer and nocturnal sharpshooter, Dr Yuri Orchnev. Karavenoff didn't know much about him, other than that he was a fairly senior member of the KGB computer technology team in Moscow.

What he did know, however, was something I had spent six years under Fifeshire's instructions trying to verify: that there was a Russian agent in a very senior position in British Intelligence. Orchnev had had communications with him via the British Embassy in Washington on a number of occasions during the last year. His true identity had never been revealed to Karavenoff; he knew of him only by his code name. It was the Pink Envelope.

CHAPTER 15

I was concerned that Karavenoff's friend would wake soon – I hadn't hit him hard; I was also concerned to tackle the fiddler on the roof before he got bored and left his perch, but in Karavenoff I had hit a mine of information and I didn't want to stem the flow. Whether or not everything he told me was true, I did not know, but I had a feeling it was, and since he didn't know what I knew I figured that, lying there stark naked and defenceless, he was unlikely to risk telling many lies.

I cast my mind back to the note from Orchnev to Fifeshire. 'As you may already be aware the colour scheme of this missive is not irrelevant.' I tried to work out to whom it could be referring – perhaps even to Fifeshire himself – although I found that hard to believe. I pumped Karavenoff hard on the Pink Envelope, but he knew little more than what he had already told me: he was based in Whitehall, had been there a long time and was in a very powerful position. I believed Karavenoff – his work concerned America rather than Britain.

There was no reason why he should have known any more.

I brought up Orchnev again. Karavenoff racked his brains, then came up with a piece of information that slotted one enormous piece of the puzzle into shape for me: Orchnev had been under secret observation by the KGB for some time. He had very recently attempted to contact the head of the CIA in Washington. Somehow a Russian agent inside the British Embassy in Washington had intercepted this letter, and for some reason it had been passed over to England to the Pink Envelope. Karavenoff had no idea what it was all about. I, however, was starting to have a damn good idea.

There was a long silence. I offered him a cigarette, and we both smoked. He lay there, lanky, skinny, covered in goose pimples, his small penis shrivelled in its skin; he looked vulnerable and lost.

'What are you going to do now?' he asked suddenly. 'Kill me?'

He'd asked a damn good question. I had no intention of killing him but right now I wasn't going to let him know that. I decided to see if he had any bright ideas before putting mine forward. I carried on smoking in silence.

'I guess what I've told you this evening is the end of Charlie Harrison, whatever happens.' He looked at me nervously, his eyes crystal clear with fright.

I didn't want to put any ideas into his head by telling him what he was saying assumed rather optimistically that I would be getting off this island alive.

'I'll get fifteen, maybe twenty years in penitentiary,' he continued, 'All for what? Nothing, that's what. You rob a bank, you take a few hundred grand. You get ten years, five off for good behaviour. You do five years inside, you come out, you got half a million bucks stashed away to make up for it. What do I get? Fuck all. After twenty years I come out, get deported back to Russia. I'll get tried over there for failure, then slung out to the back of beyond to spend the rest of my days doing something that uses my technical knowledge to the minimum – probably make me a telephone repair man.' He gave a wry grin.

I looked at him. 'If they want you back they'll get you back quicker than that; they'll trade you for some American they have.' It had the right effect. It made him look even more nervous still.

'Why would they want me back?'

'It wouldn't be to make a national hero out of you, that's for sure.'

'I came over to do a job; nobody told me it was going to take fourteen years. Hell, that's a big chunk of anyone's life. A goddam big chunk.' There appeared to me to be a distinct lack of enthusiasm for Soviet ideology in the tone of his voice. 'I've grown fond of this place; truth be known, I always had a hankering to come to

America. When the job came up I jumped at it. I figured if I was smart, I'd get to stay here for ever; everything was just pretty damn fine – until you walked in through the door.' He looked as though he were about to burst into tears.

'There's another way,' I said.

'I know,' he said. We looked very straight at each other for the first time. 'Would they accept me?'

'I don't know. I don't work for the CIA. I don't work for the Americans at all.'

'You got a British accent. I thought it was strange. You work for the Brits?'

'Yes,' I said.

At least he had the decency to smile. 'As the Americans say, sometimes it just ain't one's day.'

I looked at the floor and stubbed out my cigarette thoughtfully. 'Not necessarily. Our love for the US isn't that high at the moment.'

His eyes opened a little.

'If you want to play ball with me, I'm not going to be in any hurry to turn you over – not now and maybe not ever.' For the first time since our brief association had begun, the cloud of abject misery lifted, a little, from his face.

When I finally left the bungalow it was fast closing on midnight and the last ferry out before morning. I had trussed up and gagged Karavenoff and the Sleeping Beauty, and turned the place upside down to make it look like a burglary, to give Sleeping Beauty an explanation for the unpleasant headache he would have in the morning.

I switched off all the lights and stayed in the house for some while to accustom my eyes to the dark; before finally stepping out I scoured the area with my binoculars, but could see no sign of anyone watching. The wind was now blowing very strong and that, combined with the roar of the sea, was more than adequate cover for any noise I might make. I went around to the side of the bungalow, checking every few steps with the binoculars. I didn't have to worry about Karavenoff; in spite of my favourable views about his sincerity I had still done a good job on his ropes and it would be several hours before he wriggled free.

As I reached the side of the bungalow I lifted the binoculars up to the roof of the house opposite; the figure was still up there, mac fluttering in the wind. I envied him his job even less than mine; I knew how he must be feeling, not that I felt a lot of sympathy. I'd had to do something similar; it had been colder than this and I'd had to stay put for near on three days.

I crept up closer and took cover behind the garden hedge; I was within 20 feet of him. I transferred my gun to my left hand and gripped the small rock I had scooped up from the ground in my right hand. I took careful aim, knowing I wasn't going to have a second opportunity, and flung it very hard at him. It struck right in the small of his back; even above the wind and the sea I heard the thump, followed immediately by a gasp that was a mixture of pain and surprise. There was a clattering sound of the rifle sliding down the tiles, closely followed by the scream of the man sliding down the tiles after it, a small thump as the rifle hit the ground, and a positively loud thump as the man hit the ground. My gun was back in my right hand as I looked on from behind the bush. The man lay in a still heap; I waited a while but there was no sign of any movement.

I walked over to the man; he was unconscious but not dead. He looked familiar, even in this dark garden. I looked closer. There was no mistaking his identity. I was shocked to the core. It was six years since we had last met, in a cell in Paris, but there was no doubt at all: it was MI5's peanut-munching recruiter, Wetherby.

I ran my hand into his breast pocket, and pulled out a wallet containing some credit cards and a driving licence identifying him as one Arnold Edward Rolls, insurance loss adjuster, of Leeds, England. However, in his mackintosh pocket I found all the identification I needed: an old crumpled paper bag full of unshelled peanuts.

What on earth, I wondered, was this strange man, who had gone to such extraordinary and devious lengths to pressgang me into the service, now doing going to such extraordinary lengths to get rid of me; at least I presumed it was me he had been waiting for.

A fury welled up inside me but I told myself to calm down; there were so many peculiar happenings right now that one more wasn't going to make any difference. It was possible that his visit to this island wasn't connected with my own, or possible that he was here to protect me. Unlikely, I felt, but possible. I was damned if I was going to give him the benefit of the doubt, but decided to allow him a small amount of leeway.

There was a thin trickle of blood coming from the back of his head where it had made contact with the ground. I couldn't tell if any bones in his body were broken but his breathing was normal and I reckoned he probably had concussion and a lot of bruises. I looked at my watch; I had about thirty-five minutes to the last ferry – it had taken less time to topple him than I'd thought. We were on the Atlantic side of the island, and the wind was blowing offshore. There was a small catamaran lying at the top of the beach only a short distance away – I'd noticed it earlier in the evening through my glasses. I heaved Wetherby's nut-nourished hulk onto my shoulders and staggered down onto the beach with him, dumping him on the sand. I heaved the boat down to the water's edge, then dragged Wetherby down to it and pushed him underneath the tarpaulin into the cockpit.

He was going to have one hell of a time figuring out what was happening when he came too. At worst, the craft would get sliced in half by a tanker. At best, Wetherby would be off my back for a day or two and, provided he was off my back for a day or two, I didn't give a damn what happened to him. I heaved the boat into the water, the icy water clamming my trousers to my legs, my shoes filling with wet sand, and then suddenly the boat was afloat and without my having to give it even a parting push, it surged away from the shore; turning first this way, then that, it headed off at a steady drift in the general direction of Nantucket. Beyond Nantucket was the whole Atlantic Ocean. It was with no small grin that I thought to myself that if Wetherby missed Nantucket, he was going to find himself up something one whole lot bigger than the proverbial Shit Creek.

I got back to my car at a quarter to one and headed off through the night up towards Canada. I wasn't sure how good my knot-tying was, nor whether Karavenoff really could be trusted, nor whether Sleeping Beauty would go blurting the story of the break-in to the police. If the police were to start looking for a burglar, right now I would be their most likely candidate for openers. I wanted to get back to England, and I wanted to get back quickly, before anyone found out I was coming. I had an uneasy feeling that a certain person or persons not unconnected with an outfit in London that Wetherby worked for, might be keeping more than a casual eye on the Kennedy Airport departure lounge.

I crossed the Canadian border at half-nine in the morning, pulled into the first service station I came to and slept for half an hour in the car. I felt a little refreshed, but not much, when I awoke and downed a plateful of eggs and bacon and several cups of black coffee in a cafe before heading on to Toronto.

I reached the airport at half-eleven and booked a seat on the first available flight to London. It was the Air Canada 7.00 pm flight. I asked for seat 14B, and the girl told me she was sorry, it was reserved, she could give me A or C. I smiled and took A.

On an empty row of seats in the lounge I crashed out for a few hours. I slept fitfully, assembling all the events of the past few days, then pulling them apart and reassembling them again. Fifeshire wasn't involved. Nor Sumpy. Karavenoff was telling the truth. Where did Wetherby fit in and why was he suddenly playing the role of hit man? Why had these attempts been made on me? Was it my knowledge of the way Orchnev had died, or of the contents of his letter or of the plastic chip? Nobody except me knew how Orchnev had died, so it must be because of the letter or the chip or, most likely, both. But the letter was addressed to Fifeshire. Why did anyone want to kill me for it – particularly, as it now seemed, my own side? Because they knew I had stumbled into something major and didn't want me to screw it up? Unlikely. Could Fifeshire be the Pink Envelope? Was Orchnev trying to warn him that his cover was blown? Did my own side, knowing this, believe I was in this too and want to stop me getting away? It fitted, fitted perfectly. But I didn't believe it.

CHAPTER 16

There was a uniformed policeman on guard outside Fifeshire's room at the London Clinic, who informed me that no one was allowed in. I scribbled a note and asked him to take it to Fifeshire. He agreed, and was back within moments, ushering me in.

I had never seen Sir Charles Cunningham-Hope anywhere other than behind a desk before, and it was quite a shock to see him sitting, in a paisley silk dressing gown, in a small chair by the window, looking weak and vulnerable. There was an ugly mark on his neck, just below his left ear, and turning his head was evidently uncomfortable for him. There were piles of war history books all over the room, and sheaths of notes, but no despatch boxes or any other sign of official work papers.

He rose from his chair, and we shook hands warmly; he pointed me to the chair opposite. 'What a surprise! It's good of you to come and see me.' He seemed genuinely pleased I had come. 'How are you keeping?'

'Healthy,' I said, 'in spite of your colleagues.'

He laughed. 'My former colleagues,' he said.

'Former?' He must have felt the shock in my voice. 'What do you mean, sir? You haven't resigned?'

There was a long and awkward silence. He turned and looked out of the window at the busy Marylebone Road and the Regent's Park gates opposite. 'Not exactly,' he said, 'not exactly.' There was a long pause, then he changed the subject abruptly. 'How's the Department?'

'I don't know – I've been in New York since I last saw you.'

'Still on the same assignment?'

'Yes. Nobody's taken me off it.'

'Good,' he said. 'Hagget still in charge over there?'

'Yes. What do you mean "not exactly"?' I said, swinging the subject back.

There was another long pause. 'There seem to be one or two people who, ah, feel this, ah – um, mishap, ah, might be a good opportunity for my, ah, retirement; I think they could be right. This fellow Scatliffe's temporarily in my seat – as you no doubt know, he's a, ah, an, um, a competent man, and from all accounts he's doing his job ably. I know you and he haven't in the past, ah, seen eye to eye on certain matters, but I'm sure time will heal those wounds, I think you have the ability to eventually win him around. He's younger than me – a good deal younger, and maybe more in touch. This is important, to be in touch with the world; I don't think I can be any more; I've grown too old.'

'More in touch? Maybe today's agents do go roller-discoing, but it doesn't mean their bosses have to!'

Fifeshire smiled. 'It'll be a good six months before I can walk without a stick. You can't have a cripple for a chief; that's hardly going to inspire a team of action men! I'll be shunted off to a nice quiet office, given a pleasant title, and my salary will be upped; but I won't know what's going on any more than the cleaning ladies will. This is a good time for me to bow out – there's plenty of books I want to write; and I do feel I should step down, give the young a chance of promotion – I know you don't want to stay in the field all your life – well, if us old ones didn't go occasionally, there wouldn't be any room in the building for the likes of you.'

'I have some information that's going to make you change your mind.'

Fifeshire smiled. 'You've a good future, young fellow. Maybe you weren't too happy about joining us in the first place, but Wetherby was right – the man's no fool you know – when he picked you. Hear he's been transferred to MI6 and been posted to Washington; controller of operatives in the US. Good stepping stone to the hot seat, that post.'

Fifeshire's words slotted another piece of the puzzle into place, although I still couldn't yet see the picture. I refrained, with considerable difficulty, from telling Fifeshire about the boating trip that this man he rated so highly was currently enjoying.

155

'My mind is made up,' he continued, 'I was just starting my letter to the Minister, when you arrived.'

'With respect, sir, you won't be continuing it when I've gone.'

His face hardened visibly; suddenly, for a moment, his steel showed once more; he stared that hard cold stare that must in his lifetime have destroyed a million weak ideas long before they were ever presented to him. I returned the stare as unflinchingly as I could. I concentrated with all my might, staring deep into the centre of his eyes. 'I have a letter for you from Dr Yuri Orchnev.' He didn't blink. He didn't flinch. He didn't move one fraction, or change one shade of colour. The name meant absolutely nothing to him. I handed the letter to him. He read it quickly, then through again, slowly.

'What was enclosed?'

I handed him the chip. He looked at it.

'It looks like a micro-processor chip,' he said, 'am I right?'

I nodded.

'What's its speciality?'

'Airline seats.'

The expression on his face indicated his brain was searching for some significance. After a few moments the expression changed to one that indicated no significance had been found.

'Does it build airline seats?'

'No, it books them.'

He lifted the chip up in his fingers. 'That's more than I could do when I was that size.'

I smiled.

'What exactly does it book?'

I told him, in detail. While I talked he leaned forward and proffered a box of Havanas; I refused politely; he took one of the massive cigars and started to examine it.

'How did you get hold of this chip?' he asked when I had finished.

'Room service delivered it to my apartment.'

He started running the Havana along a course between his index finger and his thumb, a short way from his right ear. 'Did room service say where it came from?'

'Room service wasn't in a very talkative mood.'

He appeared to hear something interesting in his Havana, and put it closer to his ear. 'Airline seats,' he said, 'Orchnev . . .' He laid the cigar down on the table and picked up the letter, studying it closely. 'This letter – the tone of it – it's as if he's had previous correspondence, or at least communication, with me. But I've never heard of the man. Orchnev. Orchnev.' He repeated the name to himself a number of times but it evidently rang no bells. From his dressing-gown pocket he produced a cigar cutter; it was an old silver one with a sliding blade. He extricated the blade, then tested its sharpness with his finger. 'What do you know of Orchnev?'

'Not much, but enough to feel I had to come and speak to you right away.'

Fifeshire began, very carefully and very precisely, to circumcise his cigar. He nodded at me to continue.

'Orchnev was in a fairly senior position in the computer technology division of the KGB—'

'Was?' Fifeshire interrupted.

'He's dead – been dead about a week. For the past six months he'd been in communication on a number of occasions with a man in a very senior position in British Intelligence in London.'

Fifeshire stopped his surgery. 'Who?'

'I don't know his real name, I know him only by a code name the Russians have for him; and the name is a trifle curious; they call him the Pink Envelope.'

'The Pink Envelope?' He frowned hard.

'I know it sounds odd, but I'm certain it's true.'

'Perhaps the name means something very significant in Russian.'

'Or else its a poor translation of the Scarlet Pimpernel.'

He resumed his surgery. I related to him what Karavenoff had told me; he listened silently. His interest in his cigar appeared to wane and he put it down once more. 'How much of this have you told Commander Scatliffe?'

'None.'

'You realise you're breaking orders coming to me? All your reports should be made to the Commander.'

'I'm aware of that, sir.'

158

'For all you know, this, er, Pink Envelope – could be me.'

'It had crossed my mind, sir.'

He had the grace to smile.

'Who do you think it is?' He put the cutter back in his pocket and pulled out a lighter.

'The man who shot Battanga.'

There was a single sharp report; it volleyed around the room, then faded down below the hum of the London traffic. Fifeshire had dropped his lighter onto the table.

'What exactly do you mean?'

'Nobody was out to assassinate Battanga.'

'He had a lot of enemies.'

'I'm sure he did. I'm equally sure none of them were hanging around Mount Street at a quarter to one on Friday 15 August of this year.'

'Why are you so sure?'

'Right now, I don't have proof; give me a few days, and I'll get it for you. Surely you can see that it's possible there's another side to the story? Battanga was an unpopular ruler and by all accounts not a particularly pleasant fellow – you may know better; if anybody wanted to kill you, whilst you were together with him would have been the ideal time: pretend they're assassinating him but actually you were the real target. To the whole world it looks as though it was unfortunate for you that you were in the car with him. The assassin telephones a newspaper, claiming to be a Mwoaban terrorist group – it all sounds perfectly logical to everyone; the assassin, whilst failing to actually kill you, finds things are working out even better than he thought, for that very reason – that he hasn't killed you! You are effectively silenced but because Battanga is dead, and not you, there is no suspicion that you might have been the target.'

'I think you're letting your imagination run away a little,' he smiled.

'I'm not, sir, I'm damn sure I'm not.'

'So whoever it was that shot me was a Pink Envelope and not a Black Lefty?'

I ignored the sudden snideness. 'I'm absolutely certain that it was either the Pink Envelope himself or more likely someone hired by him, or even working with him.'

'It's possible, I must admit. You could be right – but, frankly, I doubt it very much.'

'Let me continue, sir. Since the letter and the chip came into my possession, there have been several attempts to kill me: to give you an example, three nights ago my car was blown to pieces by a bomb; someone is trying very hard to silence me.'

'Probably the Russians themselves,' Fifeshire interrupted.

'It would seem likely,' I agreed, 'but I can't see how that fits in with the attempt made the night before last: I got to the assailant first, before he had a chance to do anything, and I very positively identified him.'

'Who was he?'

'The man you spoke of so highly only a few minutes ago. Wetherby.'

There was a long pause. Fifeshire lit his cigar, slowly and carefully, then took several long puffs on it; he leaned forward. He didn't give the impression of being in a hospital room any more; he was once more at his Whitehall desk. 'Go back to the start,' he said, 'go back to 15 August. I want to hear every single thing that's happened since then, every single detail.'

It was after 2.00 when I finally emerged into the Wimpole Street afternoon. It was late November yet the temperature was pushing 60, and I was sweltering in the heavy gear I had been wearing for over two days. During this same time I hadn't bathed or shaved; I had done all my sleeping either in car, airport or aeroplane seats; and I was suffering a severe bout of everything-lag. I felt revolting; my nerves were jangling, and the 4-hour dialogue with Fifeshire hadn't improved them much.

I'd told him most of what I knew, although I told him I'd shot Orchnev, not that Orchnev had shot himself. Fifeshire himself had disturbing news about the department: Victor Hattan, his personal choice as successor, had drowned in a sailing accident three weeks after the shooting; a further three of his top field men had died on reasonably routine assignments; and his own secretary, Margaret, had jumped to her death from a 9th-floor hotel room

161

while on holiday in Spain – nobody had even bothered to tell him until he had telephoned some weeks later to try and speak to her.

The good news that came out of the session was that Sir Charles Cunningham-Hope had abandoned all thoughts of retiring. My head was crammed to its exhausted gills with instructions. It was comforting to have instructions; they had been singularly lacking during recent times.

As the final coup de grace of whatever evil spirits currently lurked in my charts, my rented car had been towed away. Not that its destination was much out of my way. I removed my wolf coat, and started to walk. I walked among people; among old ladies and mothers with shopping baskets and children indiscriminately slung about their arms; among hurrying men in their work suits; among fruit sellers and Indian-necklace sellers and leather-belt sellers and personalised horoscope-badge sellers; among brightly coloured cars and brightly coloured shop fronts; and among pretty girls going about their day, being pretty girls in a hundred thousand different tantalising ways. I walked mostly among pretty girls.

CHAPTER 17

The nerve centre of British Intelligence consists of just over 3 square miles of atom-bomb proof knowledge. It lies several hundred feet underground, below the vast acreage of greenery in the centre of London that is Hyde Park. It lies deep down beneath the famous underground car park, beneath the lowest reaches of the underground railway network, and is encased in an awesome tonnage of concrete and lead.

Underneath the calm green of the park and the dim gloom of the police car pound – where my rent-a-wreck was no doubt languishing – and the layers upon layers of concrete, are some 5,000 men and women, all with faces pallid from lack of sunlight, from an eternal diet of civil service coffee and civil service ham sandwiches, and made worse by the cold stark glare of the neon strip lighting.

In this weird white-walled, white-lit, white-sound-deadened grotto of corridors and windowless rooms, computers clatter and flash as far away into the distance as the eye can see; people move from department to department on electric tricycles, always clutching wads of files, always in a desperate rush. The casual observer would rapidly form the impression that everyone down here knows exactly what they are doing – much like the impression given to the casual observer of a column of ants – not that there were any casual observers down here; none that British Intelligence knew of, anyway.

When Ian Fleming wrote his Bond books the futuristic headquarters of the lunatic megalomaniacs that adorned the finales of many of his books did not come entirely from his imagination, but in part from his own direct observations of this place during his own service in Intelligence.

Down here everything works; in a matter of seconds one can find out what the weather was like at 3.30 pm on 8 May 1953 in Botswana; or the political affiliation of any professional football-player in the world; or the names of all the owners in England of cars made behind the Iron Curtain, their political affiliations, and probably, if one looked hard enough, the favourite colours and shoe sizes of their grandmothers. At the push of another button the name of the 927th convicted house-breaker in Durham would appear, where he bought his cigarettes from, what his favourite television programme was and what he ate while watching it. Another button would reveal all the known and suspected Communist schoolteachers there were at the present time in Wooton-Under-Edge, or in Ongar, or in Bognor Regis, together with details ranging from their family trees, down, sometimes, to as much as their menstrual cycles or which after-shave their wives gave them for Christmas.

These 3 square miles make Big Brother look like the village idiot. The only thing I wouldn't be able to find out down here would be when the next 2 × 4 would come swinging my way so that I'd know when to duck; on the other hand, it might be able to give me a lot of clues.

Arthur Jephcott was a jolly fellow, tweedy and slightly clumsily built, with a thin bony head, an unkempt beard at the bottom and a short pile of tangled hair on top, sparkling eyes, and a pair of hands he never knew quite where to put. He looked as if he would have been more at home marching country lanes with a stout stick, or buried behind piles of dusty books and yellowing manuscripts, in an office crammed full of curios, in a publishing company in Bloomsbury; behind him should have been a window with a view out over dismal, murky streets, and the office should have had an overriding smell of faded leather, damp and dust.

Instead, the door to Arthur Jephcott's office opened into a precision-honed vacuum of sterility; there was a desk, a chair in front and a chair behind, an extractor fan, a computer terminal built into the top of the desk with a display screen that could be seen from both sides of the desk, two overhead strip lights, and absolutely nothing else; not a picture on the walls, nothing – complete clinical nothingness.

Arthur gave me an odd look, just for a fraction

of a second, as I entered; it was a look I couldn't immediately explain and it vanished as quickly as it appeared. He stood up, and a broad beam sprang across his face. 'Good to see you again, dear fellow. Looking good! Trifle peaky under the gills, perhaps, but good!' His greeting was warm, and he meant it.

'You too,' I said enthusiastically. I liked him. Always had. He often gave me snippets of news that he shouldn't have done, little bits of classified information that gave me insights into the members and activities of the Department. Arthur was one of the best-informed men in British Intelligence, and I knew that what scraps he imparted to me were but tiny raindrops in the ocean, but I nonetheless eagerly and greedily devoured them; they helped give me a rough idea of what some of the other agents, of similar experience to my own, were up to, and generally what was going on; I would have given anything to have taken him out and got him stinking drunk and pumped his head for all it was worth. He knew so damn much because of his job. In effect his job was that of senior librarian for British Intelligence data: he controlled everything in Intelligence that involved computers, which was just about everything; all records, all incidents, all details, however small or large, about England, the British Isles and every other country in the world, anything at all in fact that could remotely be considered as concerning national security would be filed under Arthur's personal supervision, and he would know how to retrieve it – normally within seconds; if it was particularly old or insignificant, it could take as long as one whole minute. Stored down here was every word of newsprint the Soviet Union had ever produced; every word ever printed in any language about any dissident; duplicates of all Scotland Yard's crime records; Interpol's records; personal dossiers on all the members of the US CIA; personal dossiers on everyone in every form of public life in every country of the world. There were dossiers on everyone in the world with a criminal record and on most of those without one who probably deserved one, from the bosses of organised crime down to the last crackpot. If it hadn't been for the invention of the computer, both Arthur and I would have been standing knee-deep in dossiers.

Arthur pointed me into the empty chair, and I sat down. 'So tell me, what have you been up to?' Arthur leaned over, smiling. I smiled back.

'A bit of this and a bit of that.'

'Have you indeed?' He grinned.

'I would have thought you might be able to tell me!'

He looked taken aback. 'What on earth do you mean?'

I waved my arm at the surroundings. 'I thought this lot kept such a close eye on everyone, it knows what they're going to do even before they do it.'

Arthur laughed heartily. 'Heavens, what a

thought. The time it takes before information is handed to us to file . . . **I** often think we'd get it quicker by going out and buying history books.'

I gave him a look which told him that I knew what he'd said was rubbish; he caught the look, but moved away from the subject. 'What can I – or rather, Wotan – do for you?'

Wotan is the nickname given to the computer that is the brain of this entire headquarters.

'How is Wotan?'

'Not too bad, not too bad; like wine, improving with age. The amount of things Wotan doesn't know are getting fewer and fewer; won't be long before there's little left that's not in his brain that will be worth knowing. But the trouble is there's so much happening these days, so much, it's a constant struggle to keep pace. That's why the likes of you are so important to us, damned important. Don't ever forget it.'

I asked him some technical questions about recent increases in Wotan's capacity, which sent him off on a ten-minute eulogy on modern science, leading to a dramatic climax of how all the greatest inventions of man had come together, culminating in one gigantic orgy of knowledge, and the child this orgy produced was Wotan. He was more excited than any child talking about his new train set could ever be. He was beaming as he talked and vibrating in the pauses. Wotan evidently turned him on.

When he finished he leaned forward once again.

'Well, now you know the latest, what would you like us to do for you?'

I pulled out the chip. 'First thing, I want to leave this with you. I need it back tomorrow, and want you to tell me everything you can about its contents.'

He turned it over in his palm. 'A familiar enough face. What do you already know?'

'Not much,' I said, 'I've got a few ideas and I'd like to see if yours tally. It's vital we find out exactly what its purpose is.'

Arthur nodded.

'The next thing,' I said, 'is this.' I produced a letter from Fifeshire and handed it to him.

He looked at it. 'What do you want me to do?' he said after reading it through.

'Carry out the instructions in it.'

Arthur looked quizzically at me. 'Where do you want to begin?'

'Doesn't it say?'

'Haven't you read it?'

'No.'

'Then you'd better.' He handed the letter to me.

I read it. I had asked Fifeshire to authorise Arthur to make certain classified information available to me. Fifeshire had gone one further, and instructed Arthur that he was to make available to me absolutely any information about anyone, however senior they might be, not only in MI5, MI6 and all the other areas of Intelligence but also the Government and the armed forces and anywhere else I wanted to

169

look. I was to be allowed access to any files I cared to see, from the Prime Minister downwards. I read the note with more than a little surprise. 'Where I would like to begin,' I said, 'is with the name and records of everyone employed in British Intelligence.'

Arthur looked staggered. 'Wouldn't you like something simpler,' he said, 'like last year's cup final result?'

I grinned.

'You know what they call you in the Department, Max?'

'No.'

It was Arthur's turn to grin. 'The Digger,' he said.

'The Digger? What's that supposed to mean?'

It was his turn to grin. 'You seem to have a reputation for thoroughness – not leaving stones unturned, digging away until you get to the bottom, never letting go. To tell you the truth I don't think anyone thought you'd make a very good spy. You've changed their minds for them very neatly.'

'Who's "everyone"?'

Arthur smiled. 'Word gets around,' was all he would say. 'Right, shall we make a start?'

'Have you some paper?'

He looked at me ruefully. 'When were you last here? We don't use it any more, not in this office. If all the information that goes in and out of this office went down on paper, England would be 3 feet deep in the stuff in a month.' He tapped the computer terminal. 'Much cleaner. Much kinder on trees too. Any notes you want to make you'd better jot down on whatever you have on you. That's Arthur's Law.' He smiled. 'Anyhow, it's bad for the old brain to write things down. Remember them up here,' he tapped his head. Then he leaned forward and tapped the keyboard. The word R-E-Q-U-E-S-T- followed by a string of meaningless letters appeared, then the word P-E-R-S-O-N-N-E-L appeared. The words disappeared, there was a brief pause, and then the words reappeared again, by themselves, with one additional word: R-E-A-D-Y. It was reassuring to know computers could be so banal.

'Want some tea?' said Arthur.

I nodded, and he gave an order into an intercom on the back of his desk. Then we started. For the next ten minutes a succession of names followed by personal details poured onto the screen. They appeared in a clinical lettering that was oblivious to the fact that human lives was the subject matter: 'Dallyn. June, Sally. Nee Wick. B. 16-3-38. Widow. Late husband: Kevin, Eric. Cause of death: coronary arrest. Place of death: Black Lion Lane, London W1, prostitute's apartment. Prostitute: Nola Kebbit. Children: Daniel Henry Nigel, Susan Margaret Anne, Mary Angela Jennifer . . .'

It was all there; the dates, the schools, the hobbies, the family friends, where they spent their holidays, who they slept with, the charities they supported; all the good and bad and the skeletons in the closets; all the facts not originally entered on the job application forms, that had been gleaned by the team of agents whose sole job, unsavoury but necessary, was much the same as that of ordinary private eyes operating throughout the country: to pry out all the facts. The only difference between these agents and the private eyes was that private eyes mainly worked on jobs concerning marriage fidelity; the agents worked on jobs concerning a different type of fidelity: fidelity to the country.

Tea arrived. It wasn't served by a robot but by a tea lady who looked like she'd been kloned from an original mould, produced by a factory that supplied railway and factory canteens throughout the land. As she opened the door the screen went blank, and would remain blank until after she had departed and Arthur pushed the reset button.

Arthur sat awkwardly, confused by the presence of this lady as she shuffled about, placing first saucers, then cups, then spoons in front of us, then pouring first milk into the cups, then tea, then putting down a plate and then putting biscuits onto the plate. He swivelled his head as if it was on a mechanical pivot, to look at her, at the tray, at me, at the table, then back to her again. For the last hour he had brimmed with information, glowed like a light bulb while Wotan spewed forth, and now, suddenly, he had shrivelled up, as if another coin needed to be put into his meter.

I looked at his bushy face and thought about the extraordinary life he had spent so much of, and would continue to spend a great deal more of, down here in this bright hole, going home at night in his Ford Cortina to another bright hole, to a bright little wife to whom he no doubt waxed lyrical about the latest advances in microprocessor technology, about Josephson junctions and packet switching and finite state theory.

Arthur, with his walking holidays in Snowdonia, and his £12,000 a year pay packet, would no doubt go on for many years to come, waking with a bushy smile in the mornings while I would wake a shaking wreck, diving for my gun, trying to remember where I was each morning; in 30 years' time Arthur would still be waking, smiling, in his own bed, slitting open his mail, reading his papers, and I would probably be long since buried – silently, quietly killed and buried in some far-off lonely land.

A bag was thrust under my nose. It contained Turkish delight: green ones with white icing. It was a crinkly paper bag of the sort sold at any confectioners. Crème-de-menthe-flavoured Turkish delight was his one vice in life, so he had previously told me; he never smoked, never drank, but ate incessant quantities of crème-de-menthe Turkish delight. I took one from the bag, and it laid a little trail of icing sugar across the glistening table-top.

I had a couple more lumps. That little paper bag and the growing trails of icing sugar, the plate of biscuits and the steaming cups on the table were all a welcome intrusion into this strange twilight world that, but for this array of items from the ordinary world outside, could well have been on another planet altogether. Thinking about Wetherby's crinkly bag of peanuts, I idly wondered whether a crinkly bag of goodies was an essential item of equipment for employees of British Intelligence.

We settled back down to work again. We were about a quarter of the way through the A's. Arthur put a Turkish delight and half a gingernut into his mouth, and chewed them happily. 'Curious taste, the two together; mix very well. Did you bring your overnight bag?'

'No, I've taken a 6-year lease on this corner of your office.'

'Well, I hope the lease is renewable, because it's going to take all of that.' He was longing to ask me what it was I was looking for, and then to be able to point me straight to the answer – if it lay in here at all, which I doubted; but he knew it wasn't his job to ask, and I certainly wasn't going to tell him.

An hour and a half later we got to my name. The file was up to date to the start of my assignment in the States. No one had been able to find out very much of interest about me and there was certainly nothing there that upset me. There was nothing under Jephcott that upset him either. He'd probably made sure of that himself, not that there was likely to have been anything much anyway.

We finished that particular job at eleven o'clock.

Arthur looked blearily at me; the hair in the immediate vicinity of his mouth was almost white with icing sugar. I hadn't slept for two nights and right now, as far as I was concerned, another one wasn't going to make much difference. I wanted to get my job done and to be gone from England before anyone else found out I was here, and news didn't travel slowly in my particular company.

Arthur telephoned his wife for the third time. He had missed the cocktail party they had been going to, he'd missed the dinner party she'd decided to go on to and meet him at, and he was becoming resigned to the fact that there was every likelihood he was going to miss breakfast as well. He talked to his wife with all the tenderness of someone dictating a letter to the rates officer. He put the receiver down and looked up at me. 'Let's get it over with.'

'Orchnev,' I said.

He looked thoughtful. 'Rings a bell. Can't place it, though. Does ring a bell.' He stroked his beard. 'Russian. Wanted to flog some secrets. Something like that.' He tapped the keyboards and a short dossier appeared, much as Karavenoff had described, but more detailed. The dossier ended with a written letter to Fifeshire dated 15 July – exactly one month before Fifeshire was shot. The letter was short and to the point. Orchnev introduced himself as being a senior member of the Science Council of the Politburo. He wished to defect and live in England, and would be willing to trade information for cooperation on the part of the British authorities. He stated he would be prepared to provide evidence of the calibre of information he had, and asked Fifeshire to reply to an address in West Germany.

The letter had been delivered by a complicated route; it was brought to the United States by a bribed Aeroflot stewardess, it then went to the British Embassy in Washington, who passed it on in the diplomatic bag. It was marked 'Received' by Whitehall on 12 August – three days before the shooting. It was not the sort of letter Fifeshire would have forgotten, yet he hadn't mentioned it when I saw him, in spite of my showing him the second letter.

'You must have a reply to this letter,' I said.

Arthur shook his head. 'It would be here if there was one. Maybe Sir Charles didn't have time to deal with it before the shooting.'

'Then surely someone else would have . . .' I trailed off. I was saying it to myself as much as to Arthur. Who dealt with whose correspondence wasn't his division. 'Could the reply be in another file?'

'If it was there'd be a copy here too. Everything in Wotan is cross-referenced to everything else. Everything with the name Orchnev in it would be duplicated here.'

'Wotan could be fallible.'

Arthur's tiredness was beginning to show. 'Most unlikely,' he said, almost bitchily, springing to

Wotan's defence. 'And where do you suppose you'd start looking?'

'I don't know, Arthur, I don't know.' I did know, but I too was tiring now, and I had a pretty strong feeling that Wotan probably hadn't made a mistake and I wasn't going to find anything else here. I knew one thing for certain; from the wording of the letter that was in my pocket there must have been a reply to Orchnev and most probably quite a bit of correspondence with him. It wasn't in Wotan because someone hadn't wanted it in Wotan.

CHAPTER 18

Arthur offered me a lift home and I accepted gratefully. The rented car could stay in the police pound; it wasn't my headache. I wondered what condition my mews house in Holland Park would be in, since invariably when I go away for any length of time my cleaning lady falls sick and doesn't turn up, and the fridge, loaded with meat and milk, always breaks down the day after I've left.

There was something Arthur wanted to say to me, to tell me – I more than sensed it, I was sure of it; yet as we left, in the express elevator which took us up to the back of the police car pound, he just made small talk. I climbed sleepily into his bright green Cortina; it smelt of dogs, as I had imagined it might.

I gave him plenty of opportunities to say what he wanted on the way to Holland Park but he just continued with the small talk. I asked him to drop me a couple of blocks from the mews; I felt like some fresh air and I wanted to check the immediate vicinity of the house for any prowlers. I arranged to see Arthur the following afternoon and thanked him for his time.

I walked on down Notting Hill Gate and turned into Holland Street. The past hours with Arthur had given me plenty more to chew on; but whilst the pieces seemed to fit, the puzzle was only getting larger. Fifeshire, I was certain, had told me the truth; but if he hadn't received Orchnev's first letter then it must have been someone in the same department who had intercepted it. Maybe Arthur knew who it was that had prevented the information getting into Wotan; maybe that is what he was trying to bring himself to tell me – a lot of maybes at the moment. Arthur did, for sure, want to tell me something; I had no doubt that one way or another I'd be finding out what before too long.

I turned the corner into the dark. From a house at the end with several cars parked outside and light streaking from behind the curtains, music blared out, punctuated by odd snatches of laughter; it was evidently a good party. There were no other lights on in the rest of the mews.

I turned the key in the lock; it should have been double-locked, but the door opened at the first turn of the key. I pulled out my gun, slipped the safety catch, and went in, snapping on the hall light as I did so, then falling headlong, with my foot trapped in something.

The carpet and floorboards had been removed; I lay there, blinking in amazement at the dust-covered foundations and the timber joists; it was between two joists that I had caught my foot. I picked myself up and started to look around. No cleaning lady would have stood a chance. The place was literally destroyed: every inch of fabric – curtains, carpets, sofa covering, chair coverings – had been systematically torn into strips. The furniture had been dismantled and hacked into little pieces. Light bulbs had been broken open, the plumbing disconnected and all the pipes – water, drainage, sewage, the lot – ripped from out of the bowels of the house and laid on the floors. The walls had been stripped, not only of their paint and wallpaper but also their plaster; even the round brass door handles had been hacksawed out.

Whoever had been here must have been pretty damn sure there was something hidden, or pretty mad at me. The only thing that had been left reasonably intact was the actual shell of the building; other than that, with the exception of a couple of lights, there was nothing that had not been destroyed. Fortunately I'm not too sentimental.

I cleared myself a few feet of space, assembled a pile of shredded fabrics, lay down and slept through until morning. I awoke at about half six, feeling cold, stiff and in need of a night's sleep. I couldn't even make myself a cup of coffee, since someone had been to work on the kettle with a can opener and the stove looked like a child's attempt at building a Meccano battleship.

I'd had a good look round before getting to the house and hadn't seen any sign of either a tail or anyone surveilling the house, but I wanted to remain out of sight and decided not to take any chances. I left via the bathroom skylight and into a garden behind. A short distance away my own car was in a garage, having gone in for a long-overdue service and respray while I was away. The garage would be opening in about an hour's time. I walked down the road to a cafe and had some breakfast. The beard on my face was now into its third day and I was starting to smell horrible. I knew, because I noticed it myself.

I got to the garage at five past eight and a mechanic was just unlocking. He greeted me cheerfully, not appearing to notice my condition, and pointed to my XK 120 Jaguar tucked away in the rear corner of the garage, surrounded by a tightly packed bunch of sick-looking vehicles. 'Lucky yer didn't get back sooner, guv, only dropped th'engine back yisserday. We wozn't expecting yer frannuvver week. She's goin' like a jewel, but don't take 'er more'n three-five in iny gear for a few hunnerd miles – after that she'll be good for any ling yer want. Or'll jus git these out th'away for yir.'

He cleared the space in front of her remarkably quickly, and I walked up to examine her. His grasp of the Queen's English wasn't too hot, but he was God's gift to motor cars. The paint job was superb, and the midnight blue gleamed even in this dimly

181

lit garage. The house and furniture I hadn't ever cared about that much, but if anyone had so much as laid a finger on her I would have been one hell of a lot madder.

When I bought her nearly ten years back, she had been sitting in a barn on an old farm; the farmer had acquired her for his wife in 1953 but after driving her only a couple of times had abandoned the car because it wasn't any good at crossing fields. Fortunately the barn had been dry and it had taken little effort to get her going. The two of us had struck up an immediate and lasting friendship.

I eased myself into the seat now, and put my hands on the black four-spoked steering wheel, stared down the long bonnet, and at the tops of the wheel arches rising on either side. I turned the key and immediately the ignition light came on, the gauges sprang into life, the fuel gauge needle darting across the dial, the ammeter needle flickering nervously in the centre of its dial. I pulled the choke and pushed the starter button, and the starter motor turned the engine slowly, lazily, quietly, like it always did; then with a muffled boom, followed by a sucking sound from the air intakes, then a crackling burble from the exhaust the long needle of the large rev counter heaved itself up from its rest at zero and, after sweeping unsteadily backwards and forwards past the thousand mark, settled firmly at 1,500; the speedometer needle jumped up and down a little on its rest in apparent anticipation; I blipped the accelerator and the rev counter needle swung up to 2,500 beautifully smoothly, then swung back down again to 1,500. I dropped my left hand onto the slim knob of the gear lever and pushed her into first; I tugged the fly-off hand-brake and it fell limply down onto the carpeted floor. My foot came up off the clutch as I pressed the accelerator again, and we surged gently forward, out of the garage and into the street; for a few glorious moments all my problems were a million miles away.

The road was clear; I turned the wheel and accelerated off. She was being beautifully responsive, eager for her run, and sounding sweeter than I had ever remembered. The bonnet in front of me, through the split windscreen, loped through the building traffic, effortlessly pulling the rest of the car along behind it.

The going was easy as we were driving against the flow of the rush hour; we went down Notting Hill Gate, round White City roundabout, down towards Hammersmith, then down over Putney Bridge, through Putney, and out onto the A3. We hooked left at the Robin Hood roundabout, then I opened her up to the maximum 3,500 rev limit the mechanic had advised, and in half a minute was thundering along at a rock steady 90 on the clock. I pushed the side screen open a short distance and the bitter December air thrashed in; I let it continue for several seconds until I was shaking with the cold, and then closed it again. It made me feel a lot better still.

I drove to Guildford, where I bought a battery razor, a sports jacket, trousers, shirt, tie and underclothing, then washed and shaved in a public lavatory under the hawk-eye of an uncommonly wretched attendant who was convinced I was going to try to steal the soap.

I had a couple more cups of coffee in a cafe and actually began to feel like any normal human being once more. It wasn't such a bad feeling.

CHAPTER 19

I drove a few miles out of Guildford, down the bypass, and turned off at a signpost marked Milford. It was a country road, just about two lanes, and every few hundred yards were sets of gateposts, ranging from the ordinary to the baronial, beyond which stretched rhododendron-lined gravel driveways up to hidden houses. There was thinning shrubbery on either side of the road, mostly brown or bare in its winter state, with the occasional splash of evergreens. I drove over a small hump-backed bridge and came to a parade of shops and a village green which was evidently the cricket pitch in summer.

I obtained directions from a newsagent and carried on. After a mile or so I found what I was looking for: Scatliffe's house. It was the type of house any self-respecting stockbroker might have owned. Mock Tudor, built probably in the late twenties, set about 50 yards back from the road, and no shortage of gravel and evergreen shrubbery in front of it; it was by no means a magnificent dwelling but it was smart. There was a mud-spattered Mini Metro in the driveway, and I noticed the front door was ajar.

I drove on past, then turned around, pulled over well into the side of the road and switched off the engine. It looked to me as though Mrs Scatliffe was about to go off shopping, which suited me fine; whilst Scatliffe was now high up the scale he didn't yet rate a police guard on his house, although the local constabulary would no doubt keep a closer watch on it than on most. From the information from Wotan I knew that there were no live-in staff and a char came only three days a week and this wasn't one of her days. There was a part-time gardener but he only came afternoons.

I lit a cigarette and turned on the radio to see what was going on in the world. Radio Four was occupied by a passionate do-it-yourself Christmas-decorations maker; she was explaining how to make paper chains out of cornflake packets. Radio Three was into Brahms. Radio Two had Jimmy Saville holding his own with a heart-transplant surgeon. Radio One was analysing the chart potential of a record called 'I did Dung' by a new group called Filthy. The world was going on as normal.

I thought about Sumpy; she'd be back in New York by now. I thought about Christmas and wondered where I would be. I looked at the dust that had gathered in a hundred places inside the car – above the dashboard, on the steering column, over the dials – and wondered when I'd have the time to give her the spring-clean she needed.

The nose of the Metro appeared out of the drive and amid a cloud of steam and smoke from the choked engine on this cold morning the car turned out onto the road and drove off away from me.

I started up and followed, to make sure she wasn't just going to the shops nearby. She drove down onto the bypass, then turned left towards Guildford. I turned back, drove on past her house out of sight of the drive, pulled over onto the verge, wrote a note stating 'Broken down', stuck it on the windscreen, raised the bonnet, and set off briskly for the house. I reckoned on a good hour before the local bobby would start showing any interest in the car. Parking a car in the countryside is always a problem; in a town, nobody takes any notice but to a dutiful bobby a parked car in the middle of nowhere is as suspicious as a man walking down a street in a black mask, carrying a bag labelled Swag.

Mrs Scatliffe couldn't have been planning to be away long – she hadn't even locked the front door. Just to be sure no one was in I rang the bell, with a spiel ready about a mix-up between the local water board and gas board, resulting in a gas leak in the water pipes, and fingered my identification card from the gas board in my pocket. But the spiel wasn't required and I let myself in.

The house was decorated much as the exterior had hinted; it was comfortable, well carpeted and parqueted, and the furniture was mostly comfortable-looking conservative and reproduction antique. There was a strong bias towards the nautical in the paintings and prints, not surprisingly since Scatliffe had spent a good deal of his life in the navy, although mainly in Admiralty House rather than on ships.

I quickly checked all the rooms in the house to ensure there were no visitors anywhere that I ought to know about. The house was empty.

I settled into Scatliffe's study and started a routine systematic search. The system I used was one Scatliffe himself had devised.

His desk revealed nothing, except that he appeared to support a considerable number of charities, including being a member, for some reason, of the Water Rats. He was a month overdue with his American Express bill, about which a computer had written him a caustic letter; he had just applied for a credit account at Harrods; and he was collecting estimates for a switch from oil-fired central heating to gas. I was amused to discover correspondence in which he had been attempting unsuccessfully to persuade Scotland Yard to intervene on his behalf in cancelling half a dozen parking tickets: an extremely rude letter to him from the Chief Commissioner accused him and his whole department of a cavalier attitude towards yellow lines, and a general wholesale contempt for the motoring laws of the country.

Relationships between the Yard and the Department were frequently less than amicable, with the Yard regarding us as a bunch of privileged thugs who went around doing whatever we wanted, leaving them to clear up the messes we left behind. In a way they had a point. They dealt with the enforcement of the written laws of the land, adhering as closely to the book as possible. Our work had little to do with these laws and we abided much of the time by nothing but the law of the jungle. The police could measure their results by numbers of convictions and annual increases or decreases in the crime rate. We never had yard-sticks; there is little that is black or white in the murky world of espionage and counter-espionage: one is perpetually scrabbling and scratching around in an endless blanket of grey.

Never was this blanket more apparent than today, sitting in Scatliffe's study, searching for God-knew-what – some little scrap of paper that would make my hunch a certainty – listening for the engine of Mrs Scatliffe's Metro – a noise, which, if I missed, would result in my being drummed out of the Department by the seat of my pants, my short and curlies, and anything else remotely grabbable.

I found the safe. Scatliffe had made little effort to hide it; it was behind a leather-bound collection of John Buchan novels, and it opened within 30 seconds. There was nothing in it. Nothing. I stared inside, then felt the base plate. There was a little give and after a few moments of jiggling with my knife blade it came away, revealing a combination dial underneath; it was more than a little crafty.

The dial was harder to crack and it was a full couple of minutes before the door swung up and I pulled out the contents: a sheath of documents and two small heavy boxes.

The documents were uninteresting, mostly share certificates, and the boxes contained Krugerrands; about £10,000 worth at today's prices. I was disappointed and put everything back as I had found it.

I made a brief but reasonably thorough search of the rest of the house and turned up nothing of any interest. I could find no other hidden safe nor hidey-hole and, short of a search that would leave his house in a similar state to that in which I had found my own, there was little further I could do. I let myself out and walked back down the drive; just before I got to the gates I heard a car slowing down and within seconds of my disappearing into a particularly accommodating rhododendron bush, Mrs Scatliffe came sailing into the driveway.

I felt a lot happier when I was back in the Jaguar, cosseted by the smell of old leather and warm engine oil, with the throaty roar of the exhaust as I drove out past the far side of Guildford, past Basil Spence's towering red-brick monstrosity of a cathedral, heading towards the M3 back to London.

I rarely enjoyed poking around other people's houses and I enjoyed poking around Scatliffe's least of any; there would have been a lot to answer

190

for if I'd been caught. As I drove, I began to unwind, my heartbeat slowing down from cerebral haemorrhage level to its more normal coronary arrest level.

I was disappointed my trip down here hadn't been fruitful, but I knew I would have been very lucky if Scatliffe had been careless enough to leave anything lying around. I thought about Charlie Harrison, now better known to me as Boris Karavenoff, and hoped he was doing his stuff. I hoped that Arthur Jephcott was as trustworthy as Fifeshire had assured me he was. I hoped I wasn't making a terrible mistake; I was going to look more than a little foolish if I was wrong. I checked the mirror constantly for signs of a tail but the road behind me was clear.

Until Wetherby had surfaced, I had no idea who was after me; I'd figured it must be the Russians. But the appearance of Wetherby had changed all that, or so it seemed to me; it was my own side that were after me. I didn't yet have any proof, but the facts tallied. Maybe Wetherby was a double agent. Maybe. Maybe he was working under instructions from the Pink Envelope. Maybe he was the Pink Envelope; but Karavenoff had said the Pink Envelope was in a very senior position in Whitehall – Wetherby had been transferred to Washington. My gut-feeling was that it was Scatliffe; but I had no evidence. None at all. But if not Scatliffe, then who?

I churned over all those I had met since joining

MI5. I hadn't met many people – it had been policy, ever since Philby, to discourage socialising and friendships within the Department. But Karavenoff said the Pink Envelope was powerful; I had certainly met all of those who were powerful: Fifeshire; William Carreras, head of MI6; Scatliffe; Euan Wagstaff, deputy head of MI6; Sir Maurice Unwin, head of MI6 Washington; Granville Hicks, his deputy; Sir John Hobart, Chief of the Secret Intelligence Service, Major Sir Nyall Kerr, head of Combined Central Information, the organisation at Hyde Park, with Arthur Jephcott and the quiet boffin Norman Prest directly under him; Guy Cove-Eastden, head of the Armoury, with Leslie Piper, in charge of the dirty tricks department, and Charles Babinger. the ballistics expert, under him; John Terry, head of Public Relations, and his second-in-command, Duncan Moss; Recruiting was headed by Gordon Savory, with Harold Townly and Wetherby under him; Anthony Lines, the Home Secretary, to whom the whole of MI5 was ultimately responsible; and others too, any of whom could quite well qualify.

I had met many of them at a cricket match in which I had been invited to play. Invited, that is, in a manner not inconsistent with the manner in which I had been recruited into MI5. The British Secret Service is not a place where niceties, such as the option to refuse something, are a customary part of life; nor, in my limited experience, are they even an exception to the rule: they simply fail to exist.

It was in this sense of the word that the Home Secretary invited me to play in his team, in a curious match he was instigating that he hoped would become an annual event on the calendar: MI5 versus MI6. Two old enemies.

The invite greatly annoyed Scatliffe and not without reason, since I was far junior to everyone else who was going to be playing and I was an agent, and agents are meant, by policy, to be kept in the dark and not exposed to the gods that control them, except when it is vital, and in Scatliffe's view the shortage on the Home Secretary's team did not constitute something vital. But there was little he could do about it; it was a Friday afternoon during my year's hard labour for him, and Scatliffe was discussing with me a report I had made, when Lines strode into his office.

There was little doubt in anyone's mind in the whole country that Anthony Lines would be the next leader of the Conservative Party and that he would serve more than one term as Prime Minister. The media already took almost more notice of what he said and did than the Prime Minister, and he certainly shone through the media with a magnetic charisma. Serious but genial, incisive, tough, fair, ever on the ball, a brilliant fielder of awkward questions and a lethal bowler of challenges, a batsman who had had a long and striking innings, yet who gave the impression that his innings had only just begun; it wasn't surprising he wanted to organise this match.

He held out his hand towards me. It was warm, small, exquisitely manicured, a delicate white as if it had been sprinkled with talc, and had a softness about it which suggested that if ever during its 50-odd years of life it had held a spade, it had been wearing a kid glove at the time. This hand for sure had never held any rougher instrument of manual labour than the microphone of a dictating machine.

Like so many people in public life, he was smaller than I had imagined, no more than 5 foot 8, and his face was less assured, more nervous than that which I had seen on television and in the papers. It was a good-looking but basically weak face, with a boyish cut of fair hair, and blue eyes that squinted slightly, with heavy bags underneath. 'How do you do, Max!' he had said on being introduced by Scatliffe, using the American technique of jumping straight to the first name, and smiling a benign smile that had the warmth of an outdoor lavatory in January.

'Well, thank you, sir!' I buttered him up with the 'sir' bit and it earned me several more seconds of benign smile.

'Do you play cricket, Max?'

I hadn't played cricket for ten years and wasn't particularly good when I did. 'Yes, sir,' I said.

'We're having a little game this Sunday and I'm a man short in my team – perhaps you'd care to play?'

Scatliffe's face turned apopleptic: his most-hated

minion being invited to join the brass hats at play! 'I don't think it will be possible, Minister, for Flynn to play – I believe he's on an assignment over the weekend, aren't you, Flynn?' He gave me a hard stare.

'No, sir, I have a free weekend.'

'Good.' The Home Secretary handed me a photocopy of a map showing how to get to the cricket pitch near the village of Fulking in the Downs behind Brighton. 'Lucky for me you're here, Flynn – no chance of getting anyone else at this hour on a Friday.'

Scatliffe contained himself admirably, I thought.

So I turned up on a grey Sunday morning at the cricket pitch, to join 21 men who between them had the job of hunting out the subversives among Her Britannic Majesty's 1060-odd million Commonwealth subjects, and monitoring the rest of the world's attitudes and plans towards what remained of the British Empire.

As the umpire signalled the Chief of the Secret Intelligence Service, Sir John Hobart's third wide in succession, and Scatliffe wearily rubbed his hands in the slips as the rain drizzled forlornly down, I looked around this strange bunch of middle-aged men in their white flannels and college jumpers, among whom my destiny lay, little realising that one day not long after, one of them, with the bizarre code name of the Pink Envelope, would be playing a game with me considerably less amusing even than this.

Success or failure for me would depend on how deeply the Envelope had buried his tracks; I had one advantage, which was that with luck none of them except for Fifeshire and Jephcott knew I was here, but I didn't think that advantage would last very long.

I wondered about Wetherby; whether he was alive on the ocean waves and cursing blindly, or drowned by now, or on dry land, pacing the streets in search of me with a meat cleaver in his hand.

I was going to have to prove my case pretty damn quickly, because if time caught up on me and I didn't have the answers, I was going to have one great deal of explaining to do and I wasn't going to know where to begin. My having gone absent without leave from Intercontinental was, according to the rule book, a very serious no-no. I should have gone straight to Hagget, who was my chief there, and told him the facts, then waited for his instructions. There was a simple reason why I hadn't; it was a sincere belief that if I had, I would be dead by now. I knew that I had stumbled into a deadly game of hide and seek, and it was too late to try and stumble out.

I just managed to avoid solving everyone's problems, by halting two inches from the tail-overhang of an articulated lorry that didn't go in for brake lights. For the next couple of miles I actually concentrated on driving, before once again lapsing into my normal pattern of deep thought punctuated by occasional glances through the windscreen.

I found Wetherby's flat in a tatty building off Pembroke Square in Earl's Court. There wasn't even an entry-phone in the porch. I pushed the door and entered the building; it smelt, like many of London's conversion buildings, of boiled cabbage.

Wetherby's door was at the top of four steep flights, and there was no answer to my knocking; I hadn't figured what I was going to say if he himself answered it but the problem didn't arise. For an apparently insignificant flat it was remarkably well protected by locks; the custodians of the Bank of England would have eaten their hearts out if they could have seen the equipment he had securing that door to its frame. The door had enough ironmongery in it to keep a relay of safe-crackers busy for several weeks. It could have been used as the practical examination for the finals of a locksmith's apprenticeship course. Without the right crate of keys nothing short of gelignite was going to open that door. Wetherby had made damn sure that entry through this door was going to be on a strictly invitation-only basis. As I didn't happen to have an invitation I was going to have to find another entrance.

Wetherby's next-door neighbour's door was easier; it opened in about five seconds with my trusty AmEx card through the frame, tripping the latch. I let myself in and I found myself in a dim room which stank of joss sticks and burning hash, and was occupied by a hairy object, vaguely human, squatting on a threadbare carpet and jerking his head to the sound of a sitar coming from a portable cassette with nearly flat batteries. 'Hey, man,' it said, 'you might have knocked.'

I stood dumbfounded for a second. It hadn't actually occurred to me that this flat might be occupied. 'The door was open,' I said.

'Oh,' it said. It had almost lost interest in me.

'I've locked myself out – I live next door – mind if I use your window?'

'Use it, man, use it all.' It lapsed into a trance. Or maybe it was deep thought.

I lifted the window and leaned out. The next window, the start of Wetherby's flat, was less than an arm's length away. I wrapped my handkerchief around my wrist, leaned out and punched hard at the glass. It was double-glazed and exploded with a fiendishly loud bang, followed by a seemingly interminable series of smashings as chunks of glass fell down to the concrete basement. I ducked back smartly into the hairy's room and waited some moments before daring to look out, but the noise didn't seem to have attracted any attention.

I leaned right out and over, unscrewed the catch, and swung the window wide open. A few more chunks of glass fell out. I crawled out onto the ledge and heaved myself into Wetherby's abode.

It was a dreary place, sparsely furnished with

objects that were old without being of interest. Curtains and upholstery were in nasty cheap fabrics, in faded dull colours; lampshades were yellowing. There was an old record-player, an electric kettle sat on the drawing room floor beside the sofa, and on the far side of the room sat an old black-and-white television set that looked like it had been stolen from a 2-star hotel. And yet there were some objects of outstanding beauty among it all: there were a couple of fine oil paintings of ancestors on the walls, another oil depicted a Crimean war scene; a superb George III chiffonier stood against one wall, with a couple of fine Chinese vases on it. But mostly the flat looked the sort of place where second-hand furniture shops acquire their most miserable specimens.

It was clearly a bachelor flat, with bed unmade and the appearance of having been unmade for several weeks judging from the dust on the pillow, filthy crockery including a half-full cup of tea with mould growing out of it, socks and shoes and vests and dirty shirts piled around a bedroom chair. I worked my way carefully and thoroughly around. There was a small room that was his study; it had the only other decent piece of furniture in the flat – an Edwardian roll-top desk, but the appearance was spoilt by a complete absence of polish, and a nasty yellow anglepoise lamp plonked on the top.

I went through all his papers even opening his latest mail for him; judging from the postmarks it had been six weeks since he was last there. I pocketed the mail rather than leave it for him to discover opened, but it wasn't of much interest. There was an offer from a mail-order bakery in Texas, wondering if he could survive Christmas without having cakes from their world-famous bakeries delivered to all his friends. A note from the Brompton library to say that *These Old Shades* by Georgette Heyer would be held for him for 14 days, and an application for tickets to the Founder's Day dinner at Charterhouse were among the more exciting contents of the envelopes.

My visit looked as though it were going to turn out to be no more inspiring than my one to Scatliffe's house, when the thought struck me that the kitchen looked a great deal smaller than it should have been for a flat of this size. I looked around it carefully but for some minutes I couldn't figure out what was wrong. Then I realised; from its position in the flat it should have run the entire length of the dining room. But it didn't. It stopped, and yet the dining room didn't extend into the area where it stopped. There was an area of about 20 square feet completely missing.

I opened the kitchen cupboards that backed onto it and removed a stack of Heinz beans; then I put my hands through and felt the back wall. What my hands touched gave me a shock: instead of plaster, it was wood. I slid my hands round further and found a bolt, which slid easily; suddenly the entire cabinet came free. I pulled it out, revealing a door.

I went in through the door into a pitch-dark room. I lit my lighter and found a light switch, which I pushed; the room came to life in a dim orange glow. Looking around it gave me for the first time in the last few days more than just a little reassurance that I might after all not be completely and utterly mad: it was a very comprehensive photographic darkroom. In striking contrast to the rest of the flat this room was spotlessly clean and the equipment was up to date.

I searched every inch of the darkroom and went back out and searched every inch of the flat but nothing further of any interest yielded itself to me. I wished I could have found just one shred of evidence to put one more tiny piece of the puzzle into place. Whilst having a secret darkroom is distinctly odd there is nothing necessarily underhand about it; I knew damn well that it wasn't for processing snaps of Welsh valleys but I couldn't be sure exactly what it was for. If it was Wetherby's quirk to pass his leisure hours munching peanuts in a hidden darkroom, then he was fully entitled to, all the days of his life. He certainly swept up the shells all right.

CHAPTER 20

Trout and Trumbull would have looked more at home in a dusty gentleman's outfitters – probably the school clothing department of an old-fashioned provincial department store. They were pasty-faced men, both well into their fifties, Trout short and stocky, Trumbull short and thin, and both wore dark flannel suits, white shirts and grey-and-black patterned ties knotted very precisely.

They had clean hands, white, with a few veins showing, their shoes were brilliantly polished, and what hair remained to them was neatly lacquered to their heads. They smelt, ever so slightly, of a mixture of talcum powder and hair cream.

Trout and Trumbull ran the Playroom. This is the name given to the area of the underground offices at Hyde Park that houses the agents' weapons, or toys as they are better known. These two gentlemen were the agents' armourers; they doled out the weapons, cleaned the weapons, serviced the weapons, and spent much of their time trying to devise new weapons, some brilliant, some not so brilliant, but always weapons that could be trusted to work. Their reputation for reliability was legendary. Once, some years ago, a bullet had failed to go off; Trout and Trumbull were in tears for a week. The agent wasn't; he was dead. Now they packed every single bullet themselves.

Messrs Trout and Trumbull were not the world's liveliest people, nor did they have much of a sense of humour, or if they did they never made it apparent to me or to anybody else; but I had to take my hat off to them. 'I would take my hat off to any pair of grey-haired gentlemen who could hand me in all solemnity a packet of exploding parrot seeds without the faintest hint of a smile. They were showing me the latest they had to offer.

'Exploding parrot seeds?'

'Correct, Mr 4404,' said Trumbull. Due to regulations, they had to address everyone by their number only; but it was beyond their dignity not to place the correct title before the number. Accordingly my number was always prefixed by Mister.

'What do I do? Fill some poor parrot's food tray with these things and wait for him to explode?' I had visions of perplexed customs officials all over the world wondering why a small percentage of English businessmen and businesswomen had taken to carrying packets of parrot seed in their baggage.

'Mr Trout.' Trumbull indicated with a short movement of his hand.

Trout solemnly took a packet and held it up. It read: 'Oldham's sunflower seeds for parrots and other tropical cage birds.'

'Vacuum-packed,' said Trout, tapping the packet. 'No air inside. Open the top' – he proceeded to rip off the top – 'and the air reacts with the seeds, fuses them.' He took out a seed and held it up. 'Come, Mr 4404.' He walked over to the firing range and I followed. He pushed a button and a dummy man was automatically lowered down on a web of wires. The dummy was a complete life-size replica of a 200-pound human, authentic in every possible detail, including internally. Trout and Trumbull had invented this type of dummy, which were now produced in vast quantities for a great variety of testing purposes.

Trout tossed a parrot seed at the dummy and it landed at his feet; there followed an explosion which shattered the dummy completely, blowing him in forty different directions. I was impressed. Trout turned to me quite unemotionally. 'Don't leave an opened packet lying around. Best used for dealing with a crowd; throw the whole lot at once – don't want to go tripping over with an open packet.'

Trout could have spared his breath.

Trumbull handed me a cigarette lighter. 'Click one way and it lights cigarettes. Click another way and it takes pictures. Click another way and it records sound. Click another way and it's a radio receiver. Click another way' – he pointed it away from me, and a flame about 10 foot long seared out. 'Click another way,' this time he just pointed, 'and in ten seconds it blows to smithereens.' Trout and Trumbull were big licks on bangs this year.

'If you don't mind, gentlemen, I think I'll take a rain check on those two and stick to what I'm used to right now.' I handed them my Beretta and they gave me a shiny, stripped, repaired, oiled and tested replacement. Along with it they handed me a new pair of hand-made leather boots. I tugged my old ones off and pulled the new ones on. They were a good snug fit. One heel was packed with spare ammunition, the other contained a silencer.

Away down a corridor I heard the dull 'plunk' of a silenced gun, followed by the whang of the bullet hitting some metal target. The 'plunk' got louder at each shot until it became a loud 'crack'. It has always been a problem for the ballistics boys to produce an effective silencer. They were trying out a new lightweight silencer. From the sound of it, Trout and Trumbull had a long way to go.

In another direction a steady 'crack-whang-crack-whang-crack-whang' of target practice started up. Open-plan offices were all right in some places. Here it was downright mournful. Maybe if it wasn't for Trout and Trumbull it would be all the fun of the fair. Somehow I doubted it.

There was one specific item I wanted from Trout and Trumbull; I filled in a requisition form and Trumbull marched off into the racks of stores, moments later he returned, holding it with all the emotion of a man holding a replacement set of wiper blades; but it wasn't wiper blades in his hand. It was something that looked a good deal more innocent even than that: it was a slim object that to all outward appearances was one of a standard brand of slimline pocket calculators, complete with chimes. I slipped it inside my jacket pocket, left Trout and Trumbull to their devices, and look the elevator two floors up to Wotan's domain.

Arthur was white and shaking and looking very agitated when I went in. 'You're for the high jump!' he said.

'I know,' I said, 'which particular high jump are you referring to?'

'Your boss, Commander Scatliffe.'

'My boss is Fifeshire.'

'I know that and you know that,' he gave me a long warm smile, then shrugged his shoulders. 'It would appear that Commander Scatliffe isn't aware of that. Not that it's any of my business – and you can be sure I haven't told him a thing – but he's out for your blood.'

I refrained from telling him that that was more than a small hunch of my own. 'What do you mean?' I asked.

'He's left a message in no uncertain terms that the moment you turn up here I'm to tell you to go straight to Whitehall. He's really hopping mad, old boy.'

206

'What did he say?'

'Nothing very much at all; he just shouted down the phone at me, the same instructions about three times, then hung up. I damn near shouted back at him. Been rubbing him up the wrong way?' He smiled wryly.

'I don't have to try very hard with him.'

'Take a tip from me – it's not my business to be telling you this, but I think you should listen to me for a moment. I get to hear a lot; not everything, but a lot of what goes on in this outfit sooner or later ends up down here. I don't listen through keyholes but it's unavoidable, doing this job, that I should hear things. Scatliffe's going to the top. Whatever your view on him might be it's going to be better for you in the long term to stay on the right side of him. He's very good at rubbing people up the wrong way himself but he is going to the top, and he's a relatively young man so when he does get to the top he's going to remain there a long time. If you're going to stay in this game, really make this your career, your chances of promotion and getting into the plum jobs aren't going to be too clever if you remain on the wrong side of him.'

I nodded. 'Thank you; but it's not easy.'

'I'm sure it's not.'

'Will Fifeshire get the reins back?'

'Until the call I had from him yesterday I'm afraid I'd written him off. So had everyone else. Now I'm not so sure.' He shrugged. 'Commander

Scatliffe's got himself pretty well entrenched and he's got his hands on most things; if Fifeshire does come back, and please God he does, he's not going to have an easy task getting back to the real controls. That S.O.B., if you'll excuse my language, is making sure of that.'

I'd never before heard Arthur express a personal point of view. It indicated to me that he had very strong feelings indeed on the subject. 'Does Scatliffe know Fifeshire's coming back?'

'If he does he's kept damn quiet about it. Personally I shouldn't think so – I think he's written him off. And I shouldn't be saying all this to you.'

'So why are you?' I wanted to get as much out of him as I could and he seemed in the mood to talk.

He pulled out a bag of Turkish delight and proffered it to me. 'Without the likes of you,' he said, 'Wotan, all that clanking stuff out there, me, the rest of us, we'd all be bloody useless. There's nothing in Wotan's brain that hasn't been put there by the sweat of the likes of you. All my job consists of is filing it so I know where to find it. But in my time here I've seen a lot of good men on your side of the fence, youngsters like you, and there's damned few of them make it to their pensions. Too damned few.

'When you go out on a mission you have no idea what the truth of the situation is; only your chief knows and often he doesn't know that much, only has the vaguest of ideas – information given to him by other operatives, sometimes false information from double agents, sometimes he's just acting on a hunch. You and your fellow agents are unfortunately dispensible. Very dispensible. It costs the Government a lot less to train an agent than it does to build a Chieftain tank; to the British Government you people are very cheap indeed. I'm not saying this to demean you, I think you're one of the best that's ever come my way, and I want to make sure you keep on digging; but you have to look to your laurels. The next person that starts digging could easily be the chap in your village graveyard and the hole he'd be making could be for you.'

Arthur popped another sweet in his mouth and chewed for a few moments. 'What I'm saying to you is, don't antagonise someone like Commander Scatliffe; one day – it could be tomorrow, in a week, a month, or five years, but one day, as sure as the sun rises and sets every morning – he's going to have a job come up that he knows is going to get one of his agents killed; and when he's going through that list of those he could easiest spare you don't want to find your name is at the top. That's all.' He handed my plastic chip back to me. 'I've got the gen on this little fellow,' he said.

Arthur had made it clear that the subject was now closed. He tapped the chip a few times on his desk.

'What is it?' I asked.

'It's a booking clerk with a strange bias.' He went on to tell me exactly what I already knew about the chip. 'Where did you get it? And don't tell me it fell off the back of a lorry!'

'I dug it out of a hole in the ground.'

He smiled. 'You don't suppose,' he said, 'that there might be any connection in this chip between one Dr Yuri Orchnev and a certain Mr X, not unlikely to be one Charles Harrison, of Intercontinental Plastics Corporation in New York?'

I came close to falling off my chair. 'How the hell did you find that out?'

'Old Wotan's not too bad at digging either.' He smiled. 'Have another sweet?'

I thought in silence for some moments. Wotan wasn't a magician. It was a computer that could do no more than assemble, arrange and occasionally analyse facts that humans fed into it. If Wotan could figure out that Charlie Harrison was a mole, and I had figured it out myself pretty easily, then how, I wondered, did whoever originally hired him let him slip through the security nets? 'Who else other than you knows this?'

'Fifeshire. He ordered me to start running checks on all Intercontinental staff back in June. I sent him a memorandum of my view about Harrison on, er, let me see –' he tapped the keyboard – 'August 11th.'

I went very cold. 'How did you send it?'

'Courier. Security envelope. Usual procedure.'

'How did you find out about Orchnev?'

'It's logical: deputy chief of KGB computer technology; a mole in our own computer concern – this little chip might well be the link.' He paused and blushed; his beard twitched. 'To tell you the truth, I didn't much feel like facing my wife after I dropped you off,' he blushed more. 'So I came straight back here and set to work; I felt that if you'd brought it, it must be pretty interesting – but don't let that go to your head.'

Now I realised why Arthur had been sheet-white and shaking; it wasn't that he was about to be bumped off; it was simply lack of sleep. I also realised how he'd got to the position he held: he'd earned it.

'Surely this method of communication must now have been dropped by the Russians – they must know that Orchnev has defected and passed the information on to either the Americans or the British?'

'No, I don't think so at all; our information is that the wretched Orchnev was bumped off shortly after he arrived in the States and before he had a chance to make contact with anyone.'

'Where did you get that from?'

'By tuning in to Charlie Harrison; about an hour and a half ago.' He gave an extremely broad beam.

For sure, in spite of all that icing sugar that adorned him, there were no flies on Arthur.

'Who bumped him off?' I asked.

'Well – I only came in at the tail end of a message so I didn't get all the facts – but I would presume the Russians themselves; unless you know better?' He looked quizzically at me.

'I wish I did,' was all I decided to say.

I left Arthur's office and went out into the corridor; two extremely large men, about my age, nearly tripped over themselves in their hurry to get up from their chairs. They looked as though they had been constructed from a twin-pack Action Man kit. They succeeded in blocking my path in both directions at once. 'Mr Flynn?' they asked in stereo.

'He's in there,' I said.

'One moment, please.' One of them clamped his hand around my wrist. The other knocked on Arthur's door. I had taken an instant dislike to the one who held my wrist and I expressed this dislike by swinging my free fist, with all the force I could muster, into the area of his polyester-and-wool mixture, creaseproof, ready-to-wear suit trousers, about half an inch below where the zipper stopped; this caused him to start performing an action not unlike that of a Muslim saying his midday prayers, and I took advantage of the situation by bolting off down the corridor. I cut down through a couple of fire doors, up the back steps, past a couple of security guards, who nodded politely at me, and came out into the middle of a small, tatty barber shop in a basement off North Audley Street; this shop was one of the several camouflaged entrances to the complex. 'Afternoon, Henry,' I said.

The barber lifted his scissors from the short back and sides he was performing. 'Afternoon, sir.'

I was out into the street, doubled round into Park Lane, and managed to get straight into a taxi that was unloading a fare at an apartment building.

'Carlton House Terrace,' I said, '56.'

I got out at 56, flashed my security pass and, avoiding the excruciatingly slow lift, sprinted the four flights of stairs up to the Control floor.

There was the hawk-nosed, skinny, wrinkly tartar perched at the typewriter in the ante-room to Scatliffe's office; she lifted her bill to enquire the purpose of my visit and then promptly had to duck it under her desk in order to retrieve the pile of papers my slipstream had swept off it. I stormed straight into Scatliffe's office and caught him well and truly on the hop, one hand holding a telephone receiver to his ear, the other supporting a finger up his nose. The finger came out smartly and he snapped into the telephone, 'He's here now,' and replaced the receiver.

'I want to know what the hell's going on, Scatliffe. I'm just about through with you and everything else, I've had it up to here.' I swung my hand up under my chin. 'I've been kidnapped, shot at, my car's been blown up, my home's been destroyed. I'm mad and I'm fed up, Scatliffe, I'm fed up with the whole damn thing and I want some explanations.'

He stood in rock silence for a long time, his cold eyes colder than ever, his small frame cosseted inside his expensive and natty tweed suit, his pasty-white face shaking like a blancmange in a breeze. He clenched and opened his hands, pushing his white knuckles down on the leather top of his desk, and lifting them up again. Slowly he leaned forward; his lips curved into a circle and he began to spit out his words like a machine gun. 'I have been trying to get hold of you for eight days. You have gone absent without leave and I'm going to have you very severely disciplined. You have caused this department untold damage with your crazy recklessness, God alone knows what you have been up to but you must have taken complete and utter leave of your senses, running around like a chicken with its head cut off, breaking into my house, breaking into Mr Wetherby's flat, breaking your cover and returning to England, going here, going there, going bloody everywhere. Who the hell do you think you are? Have you gone completely and utterly mad? How much of the Secret Service do you intend to destroy before you've finished? Half of it? Three quarters of it? Or all of it? You're not above the law – who the hell gave you permission to start rummaging in my house? Who the hell gave you permission to beat up a member of staff less than ten minutes ago? I've got a million questions for you, Flynn, and I want every single one of them answered and answered thoroughly, and if you don't have some damn good answers, the consequences for you are going to be grave, very grave indeed. Do I make myself clear?'

I looked at him and with great restraint said, 'Yes. Perfectly clear.'

'You're removed from your assignment as from now. You'll work inside this building on your report and when you have finished it you will be suspended from this Service until we have decided what to do about you. You are not to leave London and you are to keep this office informed of your exact whereabouts, day and night. Is that also clear?'

'It is. And I want my house put back into order within half an hour.'

'What do you mean?'

'Don't tell me you don't know because I won't believe it. My house has been taken apart at the seams.'

'I don't know anything about your house; I didn't even know you had a house. Perhaps you've had burglars. You do get them in England, you know.'

'Burglars don't saw your radiators in half.'

'If you're accusing me I'd like it in writing.'

'You'll get it.' I stormed back out and sent the siren's pile scattering back onto the floor again.

I went down to the third floor to my office. It was just about an office, at any rate: it made the average changing room of a King's Road boutique look like the Mansion House banqueting hall. It had one chair, one desk and one light, and had to be entered sideways, and then by someone slim and agile. It was tucked away at the back of the accounts department; all agents' offices were tucked away in different parts of different buildings so that no one would know who were agents and who were lesser or greater minions. For all the accounts department knew, I could be a humble costings clerk; for all I knew, the entire accounts department could actually be field operatives in disguise – except that most of them didn't look as though they were capable of going to the bathroom unaided.

I filled in a requisition form and took it along to the filing clerk; he looked like he lived in a cosy little bed inside one of his filing cabinets. He was about 50, very short indeed, with an immaculate three-piece pin-stripe suit, watch chain, tie chain, chain-link sleeve bands and no doubt chain-link garters. His shirt was clean, his suit immaculately pressed, and every hair on his head perfectly and permanently ironed into place. Unfortunately the wretched man had filthy body odour and the rest of the staff permanently kept well clear of him.

Whilst accepting my requisition form with his usual dispassionate seriousness his face expressed the merest trace of excitement at the prospect of actually having a task to do. Without a word he scurried to a cabinet immediately behind him, pulled out a drawer about halfway up it, and had

216

to stand on tiptoe in order to see into it; he shovelled his two arms in over the top and gave the
impression from behind of an errant schoolboy
trying to peer into someone else's Christmas
stocking. He rummaged about for some while then
produced a sheath of papers. He came back over,
slipped them inside an envelope and handed them
to me.

'Thank you,' I said.

He nodded silently and I realised I had never in
all the time I had been here heard him speak. I
wondered if perhaps he was a mute. I turned to
go back to my office when behind me I heard him
suddenly and loudly say, 'High!'

I turned around thinking he must have discovered
his personal problem, but he was pointing at the
filing cabinet.

'Difficult for me to reach up there,' he said. 'But
it doesn't bother me,' he went on. 'Any time I can
oblige,' he said.

'Thank you.'

'Don't mention it.'

I decided the Department must have got him
cheap. I sat down at my desk and opened the
envelope. Inside was a wadge of phone bills
attached to massive breakdowns of times, zones
and units; these breakdowns had been instigated
by Scatliffe so that they could be analysed for
cost-effective use of the telephones. Even MI5 had
budget problems.

The wadge I held was all the telephone bills of

the Department for the past six months; it was a hefty wadge – the Department didn't scrimp on phone calls. I began with the April, May, June quarter and turned to May 1st, three and a half months before Fifeshire's shooting.

CHAPTER 21

The British telephone bill, as interpreted by Commander Clive Scatliffe, deserved to be in the Guinness Book of Records. The heading should be: 'Most unintelligible communication ever produced.' It was after eleven o'clock that night and I was just beginning to master those portions of it that it was in any way possible to master. I had sorted out inland call charges, peak rate, standard rate, cheap rate, direct dialled and operator dialled, exclusive of Value Added Tax, inclusive of Value Added Tax, analysed the lower operator charge calls and the normal operator charge calls, the international call charges, standard rate, cheap rate, reverse-charge call rate; even without Scatliffe's interference, I wondered how any normal human being could take such an unwise step as to have a telephone installed in his home without owning the latest data-processing equipment with which to decipher the bills.

But eventually I began to make headway and I was pleased because I hadn't really expected this particular avenue to turn up much. There was a distinct increase in the number of outgoing calls made from Scatliffe's office during the period immediately preceding the shooting of Fifeshire, continuing to peak for some while after, and then tailing away again. Whether it was coincidence, or whether it was part and parcel of that whole mystery, was something I had to try and find out. What the bills could not tell me was to whom these calls were actually made; from their charge-band rates it could have been to any of about 5,000 different places within a 100 to 7,000-mile radius of Whitehall. But working slowly and systematically at them, studying the charge-band rates and counting the units, I was able to establish that the calls were mostly made after 1.00 pm. Assuming they were made to another office rather than to a residence, an analysis of the time-zone charts eliminated half the working population of the world who would have either left their offices, or not yet arrived at 1.00 pm Greenwich Mean Time.

The most likely area, I came to the conclusion, was East Coast America, 5 hours behind: 2.00 pm English time would have been 9.00 am there. The East Coast of America contained both New York and Washington, the home of British Intelligence in the US and its main overseas base.

The offices were now very quiet; the cleaning staff, together with their security supervisors, had gone home. I took a walk around; apart from my own office, there were no lights on anywhere near; the only occupants of this floor were myself and the solitary night-security man who was seated in his cubby hole engrossed in a crossword. The other floors would be quiet too now except for the odd prowling security man.

I got up to Scatliffe's office on the fifth floor without being spotted and started searching it as best I could, using only a small torch. His files produced nothing of interest to me and I turned my attentions to a wall safe. It opened without much trouble and this time I struck lucky: there was a detailed memorandum from MI6, Washington, to Fifeshire. It was dated 3 July and concerned Battanga's proposed visit to London. It warned Fifeshire that there was a strong likelihood of an assassination attempt on Battanga while he was in London. It was marked Top Secret and was coded for Fifeshire's attention only. Clipped to it was a smaller sheet of notepaper with Washington Embassy heading. On it were the words: 'Please see this gets straight to Fifeshire.' it was signed 'G'.

There were two things that didn't make sense: why G, whoever he was, had sent it to Scatliffe and not to Fifeshire, and why it was locked in Scatliffe's safe. I removed the front casing of my watch to expose the camera lens beneath, another Trout and Trumbull patent, and photographed the documents before returning them to the safe.

All was still quiet and before leaving, I decided to have one further look around. Suddenly the floor-length curtains behind Scatliffe's desk moved

221

distinctly. I froze. They rocked a little, then stopped. I stayed still but the curtains didn't move again for several minutes, when they suddenly shot straight forwards. It was only the fact that I heard the sound of the wind gusting that saved me from a certain and fatal coronary arrest.

All the same I still made sure it was only the wind, by marching swiftly over and pulling them back; I wouldn't have been surprised if I'd discovered Scatliffe standing there brandishing a tomahawk, but all there was was a weak reflection of my own face in the dark glass and a small portion of the Whitehall skyline beyond. A tiny window high up had not been properly shut and the wind had caught it, pulling it open, I turned to Scatliffe's desk. Tucked in the edge of his blotter was a pile of messages which I had missed completely in my first look around. I sat down and read through them. None meant anything to me until I reached the one on the very bottom of the pile: It was dated with today's date and was taken at 4.15. It said, 'Mr Wetherby rang. Apologises for missing the meeting – says he went sailing instead (I think that's what he said – bad line). Please call him immediately. Very urgent.'

I went back down to my office. It was past two and I was once more dog tired. I didn't know whether I was glad or not to know Wetherby was alive. I didn't have any feelings about anything at this particular moment. The knowledge that I once more had Fifeshire at the back of me was the only

222

thing that kept up my morale; but if I was mistaken about him, or if anything happened to him before I had a chance to complete my current course of actions, I knew there was an extremely important part of my anatomy that Scatliffe would have delivered up on a golden platter; and if I was wrong with my hunches and my assumptions, and was misreading the still-flimsy evidence, it would be more than a little unfair to want to criticise him for such an action.

Scatliffe had told me to stay put, but as far as I was concerned I was now back under Fifeshire's instructions and I intended to be on a plane to New York at ten o'clock in the morning. Any further shouting Scatliffe wanted to do at me was going to have to be done from a range of 3½ thousand miles.

I set the alarm on my watch for half six and stretched myself out on the stone-hard heavy-duty carpet of my office. As I lay there trying to lapse into sleep with a continual cold blast shooting up my nose, I wondered if I would ever be able to get used to sleeping in a proper bed again. It didn't take me too long to decide that I would. Millions upon millions of people were sleeping tonight, as they did all the nights of their lives, in their soft warm beds, quite unaware of what utter luxury it was.

The girl at the airline ticket desk looked like a badly assembled robot. She had evidently studied and mastered the technique of passenger aggravation, and she did it all with the most remarkable economy of words. For the first several minutes in fact she said nothing at all, in spite of the absence of anyone else or any other task to occupy her. When she did finally speak she punctuated all her sentences with the phrase 'Do you?'

'I want a ticket on the 10.00 am flight to New York,' I said.

'Do you?' She remained motionless.

After a few more minutes had passed I asked, 'Are you selling tickets?'

'I don't see anyone else,' she said. 'Do you?'

I didn't rise to her bait. I had a cricked neck, a stiff arm, a running nose, a blinding migraine, a toenail that was on its way back into my toe and hurting like hell, and my hair felt like a vulture had thrown up onto it. I was tired out, my teeth felt like they were full of turkey from last year's Christmas dinner, and my stomach felt like it had a power drill inside it; all I wanted to do was to get my ticket and get my ass onto an airplane seat. '14B,' I asked for and to my surprise got. On a 707 it's not a particularly great seat but I felt I should keep in the spirit of things.

The plane was half an hour late boarding and nearly full. I sat in the blue nylon seat, hoped no one had booked 14A, and clipped my belt shut so that I didn't have to endure a brittle reprimand from another ill-assembled robot. I don't like airline seats in the upright position; I find them extremely uncomfortable. Being already stooped as a result of stiffness from my night's sleep on the floor I slouched in the seat, hanging forward, partly arrested in mid-slouch by the belt; I felt like a rather gormless marionette.

As I hung in this peculiar but not unrelaxing position a sporadic assortment of the jet-set division of humanity shuffled past, clutching their overstuffed hand baggage and their wafer-thin Samsonite briefcases; fat women in butterfly glasses and cream polyester trouser suits, glaring with menacing bewilderment at the seat numbers; businessmen in pin-striped suits wearing their 'I always go first class but they hadn't got any room on this flight' expressions; students, grandmothers and the rest, struggling through the folding of coats and the slamming of lockers while a motley assortment of hostesses and stewards battled to get them into their seats.

My thoughts turned to Sumpy; the fact that she would be there was about the only thing to look forward to when I got back to New York. Her temper had now had over a week to subside and I spent much of the flight thinking up a suitable explanation to give her for what had happened.

We landed at half one in the afternoon New York time. I took a cab straight to the Intercontinental building and took the lift up to my floor. Martha was sitting typing. She looked up and smiled at me as I entered the reception area. 'Is your cold better?' she asked.

'Not much,' I said. 'Is the world still going round?'

'If someone moved my desk to a window I'd be able to tell you. All your messages are on your desk and your mail too.'

'Is Hagget in?'

'No, he's been away on a trip for the last few days.'

I was relieved by that. Hagget was the president of Intercontinental, and the only person who could carry out any of Scatliffe's orders other than myself. I went into my office, which was considerably more spacious than the one in Whitehall.

I sat down, pushed the post to one side, buzzed Martha for a coffee, then attacked the pile of pink message slips. There wasn't a single one from Sumpy, which puzzled me – I thought there would have been half a dozen by now; there were more than half a dozen from Scatliffe, which didn't surprise me, although there were none from him today – as yet he didn't know where I was. There were three messages from a life insurance salesman; he evidently didn't know my profession; I could imagine his face when it came to putting my occupation down on the form: spy. That would go down a treat at Sun Life.

There was a mass of genuine business matters to be dealt with: I had to maintain my front and to do that I did from time to time actually have to do some proper work for Intercontinental. Right now, however, I wasn't in any mood for it and I didn't have any time to spare.

I picked up the telephone and stabbed out Sumpy's number. It rang on without being answered. I was worried, very worried, although at this hour in the afternoon she would almost certainly be out. I rang Werner, her boss at Parke Bernet but he hadn't seen her in over a week. I rang Sumpy's number again then I bashed the desk a few times with my hand; it didn't make Sumpy answer the phone and it didn't make the pile of work go away.

Outside the window it began to sleet. It was just over a week to Christmas; I wondered if I'd make it that far and where I'd be spending it if I did. Once upon a time I'd been excited by Christmas; I wondered how long ago that was.

Martha appeared with the coffee.

'I want a staff list of the British Embassy in Washington – any ideas where you could lay your hands on one?'

'Planning a party?' she asked.

'You could call it that.'

'Hope I get an invite.' There was a smile in her eye; it had the effect on me of half a dozen valium combined with a giant shot of adrenalin. I actually felt cheerful.

'It could be arranged,' I said.

She grinned. 'I've a friend in the consulate here – I'll see what I can do.'

'I need it right away.'

'It's a good friend,' she said and she swept out of the room. She was not the sort of girl one could call unattractive, not by a long stretch.

I allowed myself the luxury of a few glorious moments of contemplation of Martha and then returned to more serious thoughts. It couldn't be long before Scatliffe discovered that I had completely disregarded his orders and I was in no doubt that the moment he did, the proverbial shit would hit the fan in no uncertain terms. I intended to be well out of the range long before that happened. I picked up the Yellow Pages and turned to real estate agents.

A while later I went down to the computer room to find my friend Charlie Harrison, née Boris Karavenoff. I was relieved to see him sitting down – at least I hadn't done him any lasting damage in that direction.

He was alone and looked pleased to see me although he greeted me nervously. He opened a cupboard and unearthed a brown folder, which he handed to me. We didn't talk much and I made my way back to my office as quickly as I could.

It only took me a short while to be convinced that Boris Karavenoff had delivered the goods: inside the folder were print-outs of all messages that had passed through his hands during the past few days, both to and from Moscow. There was a confused flurry of reporting on the death of Orchnev, on the deaths of the gorillas who had hijacked me, on the deaths of the men in the basement of Sumpy's apartment. The Russians were very worried about a possible leak in the communications system. The mysterious G in Washington, who had sent the memo to Scatliffe about Battanga, was there affirming that there had been absolutely no leak that end. I was more than fascinated to read the report from the Pink Envelope in London that the situation was 'contained'.

I put the package through the office shredder. As I was feeding the last page in, Martha came up behind me. 'That last year's guest list?'

'Something like that,' I said.

She handed me a manila envelope. 'Here's this year's.'

'You must have friends in high places,' I said.

'Yes, and she'd like to come to the party too.'

At five I left Intercontinental and took a cab to East 56th and 1st, getting out the customary couple of blocks from Sumpy's apartment. I made myself a promise that one day I would be in a respectable job, one that would enable me to take a cab all the way up to someone's doorstep, a job that wouldn't require me to have to case every building I entered. A cab moves too quickly down the street, walking gives you a chance to take in what's going on; there wasn't much going on, right now, down 58th Street.

I rang the entry-phone buzzer but there was no reply; a couple of women walked out, and I grabbed the door before it could shut and went in. The two security men hardly looked up from their game of cards. I walked over to the elevators, went in and pushed the button for the forty-second floor. Sumpy could have been anywhere: out at work, out shopping, out copulating with a boat-load of Norwegian matelots; but I had a feeling she wasn't doing any of those, and I had a horrible feeling of apprehension as I left the elevator that I was going to find a very grim solution to her silence.

I stood outside her apartment door, braced myself, then slipped the catch and marched in.

A quarter of the way into the living room I stopped dead in my tracks. What I found wasn't what I was expecting at all; from the looks on their faces, they hadn't been expecting me either. They were quite an elderly couple: the man in his late sixties, with a huge pot-belly, the woman, not much younger, very long and skinny – both stretched out stark naked on a mink coat that was draped on the bare floorboards. In unison they both rammed their free hands over the most private of their parts and half sat up, blinking at me with expressions that seemed to be a mixture of embarrassment, guilt and sheer amazement.

I knew I wasn't in the wrong apartment; and yet the entire room had changed. There were no curtains, no carpets and not a trace of any of Sumpy's belongings. Apart from this couple, all that was in the room was a pile of packing cases, some sealed, some with their lids prised up. The man opened his mouth as if to say something, then shut it again. This action gave him the appearance of a particularly ugly breed of fish in an aquarium tank. I broke the silence: 'I'm looking for Mary-Ellen Joffe' – that was Sumpy's real name.

'I think you're in the wrong apartment,' the woman said coldly, not that I could expect her to have been suddenly flooded with cheer.

'I think it's you two who are in the wrong apartment,' I replied.

'What do you mean, the wrong apartment? It's ours; we bought it.'

There was a silence for a moment. I looked through the window at the spectacular view down onto the 59th Street Bridge and the East River, at the maze of lights that stood still and the maze of lights of the traffic that moved, like the greedy eyes of foraging insects.

'Bought it?' I echoed.

'Would you mind turning your eyes away, Mister,' the woman said.

'It's all right,' I said, 'I'm not bothered by your appearance.'

The man opened his mouth again. 'Look,' he said, then he appeared to forget what he was going to say next.

'Tell him to go away, Myron,' said the woman.

'When did you buy it?'

'Just get out of here,' the woman said.

'My wallet's in my jacket – over by that door,' the man said.

'I'm not a burglar; I'm a friend of Mary-Ellen Joffe. I'm her goddam boyfriend. Eight days ago she was here and now she's vanished, lock, stock and barrel; she never told me she was selling this apartment.'

'You want to see the fucking deeds?' yelled the woman, 'because I don't happen to have them on me.'

'I believe you,' I said. 'Did she leave a forwarding address?'

'No, she didn't leave a fucking forwarding address; she didn't even leave a fucking single light bulb in a socket.'

I retreated to the corridor. I double-checked the floor and the apartment number; there was no mistake. This was Sumpy's apartment. It didn't make any sense. I couldn't believe Sumpy could have up-sticked and vanished; and yet everything that was going on right now was bizarre, although this was one item that I didn't think needed to be on the agenda. I had to know whether she had really gone, or whether she had been killed and now someone was trying to stamp out all traces that she had ever existed.

I left the apartment, walked down the street and entered the first telephone booth I came to. There was a long list of Joffes in the directory and a corner smoke-shop grudgingly converted my five-dollar bill into a supply of dimes. On the eleventh

232

call I struck Sumpy's mother; a charmingsounding woman, with a strong, educated voice that came from several generations of money. She didn't know her daughter had sold her apartment and moved out and was a good deal more amazed at the news than I, since her husband had only bought Sumpy the apartment six months before. She suggested I came straight round if I didn't mind. I didn't mind; I didn't have anything else to do. Mrs Joffe gave me the directions; they lived a short way up town close to the Guggenheim.

I left the booth deep in thought and stumbled on the step; there was a sharp crackle by my left ear – unmistakable. It was a sound I had heard before, too many times for my liking, and one I could never forget. It's odd how being shot at can stick in the mind. I flung myself onto the sidewalk, rolling as I went, swivelling my head and trying to think logically at the same time, and work out which direction the bullet had come from.

The sound of clattering footsteps solved that problem for me; I could see the shape of a man sprinting off down the sidewalk. I made to reach for my gun then thought better of it. I'd already been to one Manhattan police station for shooting a man – Orchnev; if I ended up back there again it wouldn't look too good. It is, after all, the duty of law-abiding citizens in most civilised parts of the world to be able to accept being shot at without shooting back. A British agent arrested for a shoot-out in Manhattan wouldn't go down much of a

treat with the CIA; they wouldn't need to telephone Whitehall – the sound of their voices would
carry that far and it would be all Scatliffe needed
to have me spending the rest of my days searching
for enemy agents behind dustbins in John O'Groats.

So instead of going for my gun I started sprinting
too. The man turned the block looking over his
shoulder, and seemed to falter for a split second
when he saw I was following; he dived down an
alley and I followed. He was running very fast
indeed and I was stretched just to keep pace, let
alone catch up; he ran out of the alley, crossed a
sidewalk, and ran straight out across 1st Avenue.
As I reached the sidewalk there was a mighty crash
as I sent a Frankfurter stand and its operator
reeling; water, steam, buns, mustard and a stream
of oaths rolled around me.

I flung myself back onto my feet and tore out
into the road, cars and taxis and buses hooting
and screeching. He turned down the sidewalk on
the far side, sprinting and weaving in and out of
the pedestrians; I did likewise but was less adept
and side-swiped three pedestrians in a row before
I got the hang of things.

He carried on interminably down the sidewalk
and we covered at least a mile at full sprint; my
lungs were sore and bursting, my stomach pinched
in a vicious stitch, but I was going to get him, I
was going to get that bastard, I didn't care if
I had to run all night. He weaved straight back
over the road again. I followed. Blurs of shiny

metal, lights blazing in anger came at me from all directions and passed me, or I passed them, and somehow the deathly crunch didn't come. Back across the road again, the same dazzling nightmare, then off to the right, down a dim street, sprinting now off the sidewalk down the middle of the street itself. Over a junction, past a steaming subway vent, on down an even darker road, past offices deserted for the night, a few parked cars.

He stopped, turned around, brought two pieces of metal hastily together, stiffened his arms out at me. I crashed onto the ground a split second before a tiny spurt of flame shot out in front of his arms, then another spurt of flame and a small chunk of road flew up and struck my hand hard; and now he was hesitating, half-aiming, half-deciding whether to start running again. I made his mind up for him by scrambling to my feet and lunging forward; I was inches from him. He swivelled and tried to break into a run. I could almost grab the back of his jacket but not quite. He was very tall indeed, a good 6½-footer. He was trying to snap the gun in two again, evidently realising the lack of wisdom in sprinting down a New York street clutching a rifle. I hurled myself at him in a flying rugger tackle, clamping my arms around his knees, and he came down with a heavy crash. I thought he was stunned, until a clenched fist, heavy as a lifting weight, crashed onto the end of my nose.

As light alternately flooded into and ebbed out of my head I was vaguely conscious of my quarry wrenching out of my grasp; lurching to his feet, and starting to run once more. I dragged myself up onto my feet and stumbled on after him. I had lost all track of where we were; I was riveted to the back of the fur-collared anorak on the dark hulk in front of my eyes. I ran, increasing the pace as my head cleared. Already my nose was swelling and there was a clammy damp fluid running over my lips and down my chin. I was dimly conscious of the people we passed, some turning or half-turning out of a vague interest, but most ignoring us.

We ran in between garbage bags, in between lines of parked cars, sometimes on one side of the road, sometimes on the other, sometimes it seemed we ran down both sides. We crossed street after street, my legs moving mechanically now, all physical strength drained from my body; my brain had taken over, forcing the muscles to keep those legs moving forward, to keep shoving one leg out in front of the other. I wondered if he too was tiring, or whether he could go on for miles more. We were running past some warehouses then he turned down yet another alley. As we lumbered down towards the end I could see he had a choice of either turning left or right; as we got closer I realised he could only turn right – there was no left. As we got closer still to the end I realised there was no right turn either; all that there was at the end of this alley was a high wall linking two buildings.

He turned, desperately trying to jam the two halves of his gun back together. I hit him with the full force of my fist, backed by the full force of my momentum, straight in the solar plexus and then rammed my spare fist into the top of his throat, and with a long gasp followed by a hoarse, rasping croak he crumpled to the ground in a spent heap. I pushed my gun barrel hard against his temple. I was bursting for air, heaving great gulps into my lungs, but he seemed even worse and kept making as though to throw up although nothing actually came out.

'It would give me,' I gasped, 'great pleasure to lose you out here,' I puffed and inhaled and exhaled, 'so you'd better answer me straight.'

With his head jammed down onto the damp tarmac by my gun he wasn't in much of a position to start arguing. For the first time I took a good look at him: He was about 22, with fair, clean-cut hair, and quite handsome features. He was obviously a recent recruit and green to his job. He looked like an all-American football quarterback.

'Who are you working for?' I asked.

'Mickey Mouse.'

'I'm not joking, my friend; I don't like you one bit and I hardly even know you yet.'

'I work for the British Embassy in Washington.'

'Bit far north of your patch, aren't you?'

'Bit west of yours, aren't you?'

'Who's your boss?' I gave him a none-too-gentle

toecap in the groin to aid him with his memory; it seemed to work reasonably well.

'Unwin,' he spluttered. Sir Maurice Unwin was the head of MI6, Washington.

I repeated the toecap action. 'Unwin sent you out here?'

He retched then answered, 'Yes.'

My toecap swung again. 'I don't think Unwin sent you out here.'

'Okay; it wasn't Unwin himself.'

'Then who?'

'Hicks. Granville Hicks.'

I had discovered the mysterious G; the man who had signed the memorandum to Scatliffe. On the list Martha had brought me there were three people who could have signed themselves G. Granville Hicks was one.

'Hicks is going to be pleased with you when he finds you in jail on an attempted murder charge. Not going to be too good for your career, my friend. Or maybe you were off duty tonight, wandering around New York taking pot shots at casual passers-by.'

He looked at me curiously.

I removed his wallet and flicked out his driver's licence and a business card. The names on both tallied: Jules Irving, life insurance salesman. 'Have you thought about what your friends in Washington are going to tell the police when I've handed you in? I don't think you have: they're going to tell the police that they've never heard of you, that you must be some crank with delusions of grandeur, that's what they're going to tell the police. And do you know what the police are going to reckon? They're going to reckon that you're one of a million nutters in New York that likes to prowl the streets shooting people. And do you know who the police are going to believe? They're going to believe the British Embassy in Washington, and the more you try and convince them that you are really an agent working for them, the longer they're going to put you away. And while you're in your cell thinking what you're going to be doing for the next twenty years, someone'll come along quietly in the middle of the night and bump you off. Think about it; there's no hurry, we've got all evening.'

He thought about it. It didn't take much persuasion for him to accept the deal I offered him: that he came with me to the nearest telephone booth, called Hicks and told him he'd succeeded with his assignment.

Just to make sure it was Hicks who answered I dialled the number he gave me and waited until I heard the voice at the other end.

'Hicks here,' he said.

I handed the receiver over to my new friend. 'I'm calling you back about the car,' he said. 'I've decided to buy it. I'll be round in the morning with the money.'

I listened to Hicks's enthusiastic reply. 'Splendid! Thank you so much for letting me know. Good night!' I replaced the receiver and my friend turned his face towards me.

'What now?' he asked.

'You start praying I have a heart attack before tomorrow morning. Good night.' Holding firmly onto one half of his gun, which I thrust inside my jacket, I sprinted out into the road and grabbed a passing cab. As we drove off I turned and looked at MI6's dynamite hit man: he was busy scratching his head and trying to think at the same time. I settled back into my seat. It felt okay being dead.

CHAPTER 22

I stood outside the front door of Sumpy's parents' place, and I realised that the fifteen or so years that now separated me from the first time I'd stood on the doorstep of the parents of a girlfriend had in no way toughened me for such an ordeal. Apart from the fact that my features had now been beaten to hell and back by the ravages of time, booze, late nights, fists, and more than my fair share of grimaces, I didn't feel that anything much else had changed.

The door opened. She didn't need to introduce herself: she was Sumpy, albeit thirty years on, but the years had taken very little toll; if anything, the years had made her even more beautiful. Her hair was still fair, doubtless assisted by a careful hairdresser, and her face had all the vitality and sparkle to go with it. As she looked closer at me her expression began to drop alarmingly.

'Mrs Joffe?' I said, needlessly, but wanting to break the silence.

'Mr Flynn?' Her expression was now not far removed from sheer horror.

I suddenly remembered the blood I had felt

241

earlier running down my chin; I remembered that the clothes I was wearing were ripped and filthy from my recent encounter; I forgot about my two days of stubble. I decided to go for sympathy.

'I'm afraid I've just been mugged.'

'Oh my God,' she said, her voice plunging into sympathy. 'You poor boy, come in, come in.' She turned her head towards the interior of the apartment: 'Henry, quickly. Mr Flynn's been mugged.'

Henry was a 6 foot 2 inch photofit of a successful American businessman; he had a healthy, tanned face, a large frame, open-neck shirt, well-cut dog-tooth sports jacket, elegant grey slacks and the mandatory patent-leather Gucci loafers. In his concern to get me inside quickly he completely blocked the entrance.

I was swept across the floor and seated in a cavernous velvet ocelot-patterned Roche-Bobois chesterfield, a tumbler of Scotch on the rocks was thrust into my hand, and a damp towel started to dab my face. A nervous Puerto Rican maid was doing the dabbing. Among the Persian rugs, the original Canalettos and Fragonards and the Lalique bowls, I must have appeared to her to be a trifle out of place.

'You poor boy,' echoed Mrs Joffe. 'Look at him, Henry, he's all white and shaking like a leaf.'

I refrained from telling her that this was more due to the cumulative effect of lack of sleep during the last few days than to the events of the past hour. The maid finally stopped wiping my face and went away.

'Tell us what happened?' said Mrs Joffe.

I obliged with as lurid and heart-rending a tale of a mugging as I could muster. When I had finished I had to admit to myself that I hadn't done a bad job at all. My hosts were certainly impressed.

'I think we must call the police right away,' said Mrs Joffe.

'You can call but it's a waste of time,' said her husband. 'They'll drag you down to the station, mess you around for a couple of hours, take a statement if they can find someone who can read and write, then tell you there's nothing they can do about it and no way they're ever going to catch the guys. Better to save your breath and have some more whisky.'

I couldn't have agreed more. My first glass-full was already giving me a pleasant buzz. I remembered that on my time-clock it was now about half past two in the morning. I hadn't yet got anywhere to sleep the night – I didn't want to go near the Intercontinental apartment and I had been counting on staying with Sumpy.

As interest in the mugging subsided I brought the topic of conversation around to the purpose of my visit here: Sumpy. I was careful to remember to call her by her proper name, Mary-Ellen. Both parents were mystified by her sudden move. They were on good terms; they usually saw her about once a fortnight and spoke on the telephone every few days. They'd been away on holiday themselves for the past month and had only got back last night. Mrs Joffe had rung round all Sumpy's friends since my call but none of them knew that she had moved, and all were surprised by the fact; not even the famous lunchtime Lynn could throw any light on the mystery.

'I'm going to call the police,' said Mrs Joffe. She appeared to have a grossly misinformed opinion of the New York police force's interests and capabilities.

'Can you shed any light on it?' Henry Joffe stared pointedly at me.

'No, none,' I lied through my teeth; if I went a shade or two paler and shook a little more, they didn't notice. 'She knew I was going to be out of town for a few days and I'd told her I'd call her as soon as I got back.'

'Did you try Werner?' asked Mrs Joffe.

'No good. I spoke to him this afternoon; she's working on a project for him but he doesn't expect to hear anything from her for a couple of weeks.'

'There's probably a very simple explanation,' said Henry.

I could have told him how right I feared he was; but I didn't.

'What kind of simple explanation is it when a girl sells up her apartment and disappears without telling her parents and her best friends?' said her mother.

'When did you last speak to her?' I asked.

'Before we went off on holiday. She was fine; she told us she was going out with an Englishman working in computers, I guess that must be you, and that she was having a good time. She sounded very happy. I only hope she didn't discover some major art forgery and get . . . you know, it can be a pretty ruthless business.'

'She's been in it long enough to know the ropes, I would think.'

'No,' said Mrs Joffe emphatically. 'She hasn't been in it that long; she never used to be the least bit interested in art.'

That shook me.

'Not in the least. When she was at school she couldn't tell an oil painting from a print. She became interested at university.'

'She went to university?'

'Sure – didn't she ever tell you? She got a first at Princeton in sociology.'

'A first? No, she never told me.'

'Then she suddenly took a passionate interest in Impressionist paintings; she went to UCLA, studied fine arts and got another first. She joined Sotheby Parke Bernet here in New York, did a year with them, then left to become a freelance valuer.'

'Been a bright girl,' interrupted her father. 'Got me that on the wall.' He pointed to a small but brilliant Van Gogh. 'Forty-five bucks. It was framed facing inwards, with an oil of the Hudson river on the back.'

All this information about Sumpy was a shock to me. I knew she was no idiot but if she really was as bright as I had just been informed, and I had no reason to doubt her parents, then she had certainly done a good job of keeping it from me.

We talked on for a while but I gleaned nothing further of relevant interest, and as we talked and the effects of the Scotch sank deeper into my bloodstream I could feel myself becoming increasingly drowsy; words began to drift over my head, and it became a battle for me to concentrate on what was being said.

'You're staying here tonight,' Mrs Joffe suddenly informed me and the words jolted me wide awake.

'No, it's all right, thank you – I must be going.'

'You're not going anywhere; you're staying right here tonight. Rosita's made up the spare bedroom and you'll get a good night's sleep; we've spare wash things and everything. We're not having you going out and getting mugged again tonight.'

I didn't put up much resistance and besides I didn't have anywhere else to go; I didn't fancy traipsing around trying to get a hotel room looking the way I did.

Within half an hour I was between soft white sheets in a huge soft bed. I felt warm and comfortable and I fell into a much-needed and deep sleep.

In the morning I was given a massive breakfast and loaned a set of Mr Joffe's clothes that fitted me quite well. He'd already gone to the office, and

I sat and talked to Mrs Joffe. She was extremely worried, but rational, and I felt sorry for her.

'Mary-Ellen's a very independent girl,' she said. 'It could well be she's fine and there's a reason for all this that's very simple.'

'It's very likely,' I agreed.

She asked where she could get hold of me; I told her I had to go out of town again for a couple of days but I would call her that evening to see if there was any news. I persuaded her that there was no point in going to the police just yet; they wouldn't be interested: selling an apartment isn't a crime and a few days' absence doesn't constitute a disappearance.

I left Mrs Joffe just before ten, with a busy morning in front of me. My first visit was to a hairdressing salon, where I bought a straw-coloured moustache and a bushy beard to match.

'You'll have to have your hair dyed – look terrible otherwise,' said the hairdresser.

'It's all right, thank you, these are for a friend.'

He gave me the peculiar look I no doubt deserved.

My next call was to a drugstore to acquire brown dye and a bottle of peroxide. I hoped the peroxide would bring my dark brown hair down closer to the colour of the beard and moustache; I hadn't let the hairdresser do it, because I didn't want any witnesses to the disguise I was planning to adopt. From the drugstore I went and bought a coat, a tweed hat and a pair of silk-lined fabric gloves;

silk-lined to keep my hands warm; fabric so that I could use my fingers accurately. I also acquired a pair of sunglasses.

I went to a bank and cashed 2,500 dollars in traveller's cheques, then I set about looking for a suitably uninspired hotel; it didn't take long: it was called the Madison Park East. If you ever need somewhere cheap and nasty to stay the night, New York's the place to go; it does indeed have some of the best, but it specialises in having most of the worst.

The man behind the desk gave the impression that he had been sitting there long before the hotel had been built around him; he sat staring rigidly at a wall, an unlit, half-smoked cigarette gripped between his lips. He didn't look at me, nor move his torso one inch throughout the entire dialogue we exchanged; not that it was a particularly lengthy dialogue.

'Do you have a room?'

'Twenty-five bucks with shower, 30 with bath, 2 bucks a floor.'

'Two bucks a floor?'

'Each floor up, 2 bucks more.'

'Why?'

'For the view.'

I took the second floor. I looked out onto the second floor of another building across a short alley. I did a quick calculation: the building I was in was only fifteen storeys high; the building across the alley was at least forty; it didn't take me long to figure out that I hadn't missed much of a view.

The room was basic and frugal, and the management had laid on a couple of cockroaches on the bathroom floor to greet me. I wasn't too bothered; I'd paid in advance for a week but I didn't plan on spending much of that time there.

The peroxide was filthy stuff but it did the job. I now had whitey-yellow hair and straw beard and moustache. Behind the sunglasses, under the tweed hat and with the coat collar turned up, I had to admit I would have been hard pushed to have recognised myself.

I left the hotel, keeping my head turned well away from Quasimodo's grandson; he wouldn't have noticed me in any event – I walked well beyond the boundary of his vision. He was still utterly motionless, transfixed to the nicotine-stained wall that rose up to the nicotine-stained ceiling; maybe the wall was doing great things for him; maybe he saw wonderful visions, beautiful happenings, cosmic movies; maybe he just saw a wall.

I checked my watch; it was just gone midday and I was late for my first appointment. I felt apprehensive of my new disguise but no one gave me any peculiar looks and after a short while in the busy street I began to relax. I hailed a taxi and read him the address I had scribbled down on my notepad.

It was off Lexington, north of 96th Street, the

demarcation line of Harlem, where, within the space of less than 200 yards, the area turns from wealthy white-owned apartments to the start of the sprawl of the most infamous black ghetto in the world.

The estate agent was waiting impatiently outside; both his hands were full, one tackling an ear-load of wax, the other, a vicious itch on his backside. He was a large black man, and both his face and his suit were coated in a film of grease. He handed me a business card which was crumpled and stamped with a large and oily fingerprint; the name on it was Winston G. Desoto, Realtor. He shook my hand in a massive, crushing shake. He released the grip before I had the chance to squeeze back.

I followed Winston G. Desoto up three flights of stairs, past dirty children fighting in the corridors, and washing hanging on the banisters. The place was in no way right and I left quickly to pay my second call. During the next four hours I traversed the length and breadth of Manhattan without joy and was beginning to feel that maybe what I wanted didn't exist in this city.

On my last call of the afternoon I struck lucky; it was perfect: the building was eight storeys high, in the heart of Lower East Side on East 5th Street. The vacant office was on the eighth floor and had a clear view down the street on both sides of the entrance way. Apart from this office the entire building was derelict and in a bad state of repair;

it didn't look as though anyone had been in the building for years.

'If you want an office this is the best bargain in Manhattan,' said the agent, a white version of Desoto, who chewed a piece of gum which every now and then he would take out of his mouth, roll between his fingers, and then pop back into his mouth again.

'How long's it been vacant?'

'Only been on the market a few days,' he sniffed. 'Be gone quick, this one – a real mover.'

'What about the rest of the building?'

'Make hairdryers; gone down the tubes. Receiver will be putting it on the market soon. Going to do it all up. Be smart – new entrance, new lifts. Be a small version of the World Trade Centre.'

It was hard to imagine that this sad-looking pile might ever be transformed into anything remotely resembling the World Trade Centre. The building had what appeared to my untrained eye to be terminal subsidence. There were large cracks in the walls and ceiling on every floor; the window panes looked horribly contorted. The fire escape didn't look capable of supporting the weight of an undernourished cat. The place had never been built to last: it had probably been knocked up in a great hurry during the post-Depression years, and every conceivable cost had evidently been spared. The only thing that seemed in reasonable condition was the elevator and the agent sailed us up and down in it a few times to assure me of its good working order.

Since the building was empty the janitor had been laid off but there was a janitor at another building a few blocks away who did the cleaning and the such like, I was informed. From the amount of dust I was somewhat sceptical about the cleaning part but since I wasn't taking the place for the purpose of impressing any clients, I wasn't bothered.

For the sum of 1,100 dollars, being one quarter's rent in advance, and 100 dollars deposit, I had acquired myself a Manhattan office – not exactly in Wall Street, but not a million miles from it. Not that playing the stock market was at the forefront of my mind: it was the fact that the building was empty and most of the immediate neighbourhood was derelict that appealed most. There was a major redevelopment plan but nothing had been started.

I left the agent's office at about 5.00 and went straight back to begin a more detailed inspection of my new premises and their immediate environs. I went through the building room by room, floor by floor. The agent hadn't lied about the previous occupants manufacturing hairdryers, but he hadn't exactly given a truthful account of the length of time since their demise; he'd described it as though it had happened only a week or two back: looking at the equipment and the dates on odd bits of paper, I reckoned the best part of a decade had passed since the last dryer had been bolted together and dropped into its cardboard box.

For the best part of ten years the place had been left alone to the roaches and rats and vandals to vie for supremacy. Most of the windows had been broken and boarded up; everything worth stealing had been stolen and everything worth breaking had been broken.

I took a slow and careful walk around the neighbourhood, my gun in my jacket pocket, safety catch off and my hand firmly clasped around it; not that I reckoned there would have been enough meat down here for any intelligent mugger to make it his pitch. There was a hideous atmosphere to the whole area, dirty, desolate, looted, with a few abandoned cars literally smashed to pieces – stripped of their wheels and engines, and every bit of glass smashed, and every inch of their bodywork hammered and bashed almost out of recognisable shape. Most of the shops were boarded up, where the owners had evidently eked out ever-diminishing existences until they'd gone out of business and gone away. The occasional black kid wandered around, and a couple of blocks down was a stark empty supermarket. It was the sort of area where students make films of decaying Manhattan; if there were more people it could have been called a ghetto. There was almost no life at all down here. It was ideal.

I walked back up to Wall Street and hailed a cab to West Greenwich Village. I checked in at a nondescript hotel called the Hotel Kilgour, that could have been the sister to the Madison Park East, and again paid a week's rent in advance. I left, found a call box and telephoned Mrs Joffe. She still had no news and invited me over; I told her I was in Washington and would call her in a couple of days when I got back to New York. Then I went and found the best-looking restaurant in the area and allowed the British taxpayer to treat me to a not-inexpensive meal.

CHAPTER 23

I awoke early in the morning to the interminable wailing of sirens that punctuates the Manhattan air almost every minute of the day and night. In no other city is the cry so mournful and so penetrating; it sounds at times as though the city herself is weeping over the loss of something dear and treasured, and purging herself for being in some way responsible for this loss.

The siren was receding into the distance to the newly discovered body of a murder victim, or a bloody car smash, or a coronary thrombosis, or a leaking nuclear plant. Whatever it was that it was going to would doubtless be some area of human suffering, and that siren made sure all Manhattan shared in a small part of that suffering.

It was hot in the room and I opened the window a little, letting in a blast of bitterly cold air. I looked out over the wide ledge at the street down below; sleet was falling and columns of steam rose from the vents all the way up the road like smoke signals to some far-off planet.

Today was the day I was going to set in motion a chain of reactions which, if I was right, would bring everything out into the daylight. It was a chain of events in which I would get my revenge for the attempts on my life and on Fifeshire's life, in which I would get to the bottom of Sumpy's disappearance, the Pink Envelope's identity and solve the riddle of Orchnev's suicide. In short, it was a chain of events in which I would find out just what the hell had been going on. I sincerely hoped I was right.

Staring at the cold grey New York morning did nothing to reassure me that I was right; nothing at all. The cold grey New York morning told me to be sensible, go back to England, make out the report to Scatliffe and let him make the decisions on what should be done. Or, more sensible still, go to Fifeshire, tell him the latest news, and let him deal with it. But no, I didn't believe that would work. Instinct told me either of those could be disastrous. This whole damn thing was too big, too complex to be solved by any normal remedy that was open to me. Scatliffe was in this up to his neck, I was absolutely certain. Fifeshire was innocent, I was equally certain. I didn't know how big Scatliffe's web might be and unless I took the course of action I had in mind I was certain I wouldn't have the chance to live long enough to find out. I had somehow stumbled into this and now I had to see it through. The consequences would be ghastly but in all probability a lot less ghastly than if I didn't go ahead with my plans, and at least this way gave me a sporting chance of increasing my immediate life expectancy. I started to wash quite enthusiastically.

I checked my face for tell-tale black strands of hair around the edges of the moustache and beard, but couldn't see any in the badly lit mirror. The glued-on fungus wasn't comfortable but I was going to have to live with it for a while longer. I hoped to hell Boris Karavenoff could be trusted, that Jules Irving, life insurance salesman and second-rate hit man, hadn't been lying, and that I wasn't gravely mistaken about Fifeshire.

I was worried about Sumpy, worried for her safety, and yet . . . somehow there was something distinctly odd rather than worrying about the whole thing. I was certain that she had not come to any harm and yet her disappearance made no sense at all, none whatever. Perhaps she was wound up in this whole business; but if so I couldn't for the life of me figure out how.

It was 8.15, Friday morning in downtown Manhattan. A traffic-reporter helicopter clattered overhead, and the cab drivers had started their daily cacophony of hooting as the morning traffic was building to a peak. I walked briskly through the tart cold of the morning gloom and entered a glaringly lit cafe, where I ordered a hefty plate of scrambled eggs and some coffee.

I looked at my watch. It would be 1.21 in the afternoon in London: allowing enough time for things to sink in, a brief discussion and sufficient leeway for basic delays, but not allowing enough time for any complex plot to be hatched. I was happy that my choice of Sunday was right. With the weekend looming up people would be hard to get hold of, harder still to assemble together. The only course of action was likely to be hastily thought out and ill-conceived. Perfect.

I finished my breakfast and read the *New York Times*; if there was anything much happening in England it hadn't rated news in this paper. The only article on England stated that there were more strikes brewing. That was news? My watch showed five past nine. I left the cafe and made my way to the nearest call box.

The girl on the switchboard at the British Embassy in Washington put me through to Sir Maurice Unwin's secretary. I told her I was calling on a confidential matter and it was imperative she put me through. There was a pause then she came back to me: Britain's top spook in the US of A was busy, could he call me back?

'No,' I said. 'It's an SIA priority.' The SIA was a code that members of the Secret Intelligence Service were permitted to use in dire emergencies.

Within seconds a voice said, 'Unwin here. Who's speaking?'

'I have information about a British double agent who is known as the Pink Envelope and unless you pay me 100,000 dollars in cash I intend making this information known to a major American newspaper.'

'Can you elaborate?'

'I can elaborate plenty when we meet. I want you to come to New York on Sunday morning to a telephone booth at the junction of 10th Street and Greenwich Avenue. I will telephone at exactly twelve o'clock. You are to answer with the words: "Good morning, Digger," and I will then give you the address of where we are to meet. My lawyer, who is somewhere in America, has a letter in his possession which contains the same facts that I shall tell you: this letter is addressed to the newspaper. If he is not telexed by a certain bank at 9.15 on Monday morning to state that the sum of 100,000 dollars has been deposited into his client account then he will immediately deliver this letter to the editor of the newspaper.'

'Just wait a moment,' he said.

'I will repeat the instructions once and then I have to go.' I repeated it all clearly, once, then hung up and left the call box. It was one of five booths in a row – a precaution I took against the particular one I had chosen becoming out of order.

I had started.

I took a cab and got out several blocks away and went into another call box. I telephoned the Intercontinental offices and asked for Charlie Harrison.

'This is Harrison here,' said Karavenoff.

'I'm confirming our drink this evening.'

'Grand,' he said. 'Seven o'clock?'

'Make it five past, okay?'

'Okay.'

259

'See you.'

I left the booth. In our brief and innocuous-sounding exchange I had given him the go-ahead to send a message down the 14B wires that was going to ruin a number of people's whole day for them. However, the rendezvous we had made for later was genuine; Karavenoff was going to hand me a transcript of all the day's communications. I had a feeling it would make interesting reading.

I had a small amount of shopping to do and then several hours to kill. I went first to a stationer's and then to an electrician. After that I wondered if there was any further point in trying to trace Sumpy; my nerves could have done with a soft, warm companion for the next couple of days. But I didn't feel I would get very far. I thought about Martha but I couldn't do anything about her right now – it would have been far too big a risk to take. I went off and whiled away the day at the Frick Gallery, the Metropolitan and the Museum of Modern Art. I enjoyed myself. After all, even a spy's entitled to a bit of culture now and then.

Karavenoff was already at the bar when I got there, a bourbon on the rocks cupped in his hands as he sat on a stool, elbows on the table, looking nervous and pensive. Neither of us acknowledged the other as I took up the stool next to him, not that there appeared to be anyone around to take any notice of us.

It was a barn of a place with a long bar at one

end and an extraordinarily good jazz band playing at the far end, with everyone's attentions on them. I ordered a bourbon on the rocks also; the barman gave it to me quickly then went back to watching the band. It seemed safe enough to talk.

'You've earned yourself a colour,' said Harrison suddenly. 'Mark of extreme importance. You'll see when you read it. Been a busy day. Seems to be a lot of interest in your message.'

'Good man,' I said.

'I'm scared.'

'There's nothing to connect you with any of it,' I said.

'Go tell that to Moscow.'

'As far as they're concerned you're doing your job and doing it well. They've no axe to grind in your direction.'

'But when this finally blows up they're going to have to close down this whole system and I'll be called back to Moscow.'

'It might not all blow up,' I said, not sounding terribly convincing. 'And if it does, why should they want you back in Moscow. They're going to need a new system; it's bound to involve electronics – unless they plan to go back to the dark ages – and who better to set it up than you?'

'Well, we'll see.' He didn't sound happy. 'They don't like failure.'

'There's no failure on your part. This has all sprung from one of their own side defecting. There's no evidence to suppose it's a conspiracy.'

'Maybe not,' he said solemnly. He called the barman for his cheque. I asked for mine at the same time. We both pulled our wallets out; a large wadge of papers came out of his pocket with his; it went back into my pocket.

'If I get recalled, you know,' he said, 'to Moscow, can I, er, come to England?'

'Sure. I'll fix that for you. No problem.'

He seemed relieved. I didn't feel inclined to tell him that if this lot went wrong on me I wasn't going to be capable of fixing anything; not even a nail to a piece of wood.

Karavenoff left the bar; I stayed on and had another drink; the bourbon tasted pleasant, the music wasn't bad, and I didn't have any other plans for the evening.

I read through the transcript when I got back to the Hotel Kilgour. Karavenoff hadn't been exaggerating about it being a busy day. I wasn't surprised that it had been busy; Moscow had been informed by the message that Karavenoff had sent off on my instructions that the facts about the entire airline communication system were about to be blown.

Livid communications had been hurled around the wires and a torrent of abuse was flung in the direction of the Pink Envelope, who was given the job of tracking down and halting the squealer before any damage could be done. It was clear from the messages that Unwin was not a Russian agent, which enabled me to tick one name off my list. What Karavenoff had said about my having earned a colour became apparent to me in a short exchange between G in Washington and the Pink Envelope.

G's message was, 'The Blue Bow is dead.'

The reply was, 'Are you sure?'

I didn't require a university degree to figure out who they were talking about.

CHAPTER 24

The newspaper headline was loud and clear: Embassy suicide mystery. It didn't mean much to me. A couple of blocks further down the street another headline sold a copy of the *Washington Post* to me: British Diplomat in Death Plunge.

I read the entire article motionless by the news stand. Sir Maurice Unwin had jumped to his death from his fifteenth-floor office window. He was happily married, with three children, had no financial worries and was a popular figure in Washington. The *Post* hadn't yet discovered that he happened to be the US head of MI6; but they would. In time.

The article stated that no one could give any immediate reason for his suicide. I wasn't surprised. Suicide didn't come into it.

It was Saturday morning and I was walking down Houston towards my new office. I let myself in and again made a careful search of the whole building. It was eerily dead, unwanted, unwelcoming. Nobody had been there since yesterday and it was unlikely that anyone would come uninvited.

When I reached my own office suite I pressed the button for the elevator. I listened to it whine and bump its way up and then come to a halt at my floor with a definite clunk. Its metal door slid open unsteadily and in short jerking movements. I pressed the stop-watch start button on my watch, and stepped in, pushing the button for the ground floor. I rode the thing up and down a couple of dozen times, carefully recording the timing for each stage. The variations were to within a second on each run, which was fine.

Next I set to work on the brains of the machine, if brains was the right description for the frayed and battered box of wiring that carried the instructions from the various buttons inside the elevator to the various electric circuits and motors and switches that made it go to the fifth floor when button 5 was depressed and to the first floor when button 1 was depressed, and the such like.

Because of having to run up and down to the basement power switch to test every stage of my tricky operation, it took me much longer than I had expected, and it was not until late into the afternoon that I finished.

I went and sent an overnight cable to Fifeshire. I sent it to his home address in the country, reckoning he'd be back there by now. The cable would reach him about 8.00 or 9.00 in the morning, English time – it would put him on alert and he would know the significance immediately the deed was done. I worded the cable simply: 'Check the elevator operator's private bank account. You'll know what I mean. If I have been right, place advertisement in *Times* personal column, Tuesday or Wednesday, saying: All forgiven, Charlie. If I have been wrong, place ad saying: Goodbye.' I signed it 'Sam Spade'.

Saturday night passed slowly. I was worried about the following day, very worried. If I was wrong not even all the power Fifeshire might be able to muster was going to be able to get me out of it, but I had made no real contingency plan: I was gambling everything on being right. Whilst bits of evidence had gathered with each day, I knew that the horrific gamble I was about to make was still mainly on my hunch and the odds were not too attractive.

I went over and over everything late into the night, pacing the hotel room until the facts blurred into an unfathomable mess inside my mind and I slept a fitful sleep. Rain lashed through the night and a howling wind shook the windows, and I had repeatedly to get out of bed and ram wedges of paper down the sides of the frames in an attempt to stop the rattling. I awoke finally at 7.00 feeling in need of a good night's sleep.

I checked the room thoroughly to ensure there was nothing through which I could be traced. At least there were no fingerprints to worry about: I had worn either my fabric gloves or my surgical gloves all the time I had been in the room. I left the various wash things, and everything except what I needed today, in the room, although it was unlikely that I would be coming back.

It was bitterly cold outside; the rain had gone but the wind remained, gusting in great sweeps down the corridors formed by the skyscraper buildings. I had breakfast in a cafe then walked to the office. I unlocked the front door and left it unlocked. I switched on the power for the elevator then again made a thorough search of the building. Each time I walked through the rooms of that building they looked worse.

I sat down in my own suite; it was eleven o'clock. I took from my pocket the calculator I had been given by Trout and Trumbull: it was an innocuous-looking thing and had emblazoned in gold lettering on the outside the model-name: Vatiplier. I also took from my pocket a large pink envelope, a black marker pen and a strip of blue ribbon. On the outside of the envelope I wrote with the pen the word Goodbye.

I was craving for a cigarette and realised I had forgotten to buy a new packet. I went over to the window and looked out. Bits of paper and other garbage swirled down the street. There was nothing else in sight, not a person nor a car; it was desolate.

Twelve o'clock finally came. I lifted the receiver and dialled the number of the call box: I hoped to hell it hadn't been vandalised during the night.

The number was answered before it even had a chance to ring.

'Good morning, Digger,' said a heavily disguised voice. There was no mistaking whose voice it was: Scatliffe's. I gave him the directions, repeated them once, then hung up.

Then I clapped my hands together; I'd done it, I knew I'd bloody done it! He'd taken the bait, hook, line and sinker, and now I was reeling him in. I looked at my watch. I reckoned it should take him about twelve minutes by taxi; allow him a couple of minutes on top to hail one. Fourteen minutes.

The taxi arrived in thirteen minutes and pulled up outside. I didn't stretch over too much as I didn't want to risk being seen, but I could see only one person emerge, a figure in a trilby hat and blue Crombie coat. I pulled on my coat, turned up the collar, put my dark glasses on, pulled my hat down over my forehead; my own mother wouldn't have recognised me. A sharp buzz from the alarm system I had rigged up told me he'd pushed the button for the elevator.

At the top of the calculator was a plastic lid, which I slid aside, revealing a small pin-shaped object. I pulled the pin out and pocketed it. In exactly ninety seconds the calculator would explode with, Trout and Trumbull had assured me, considerably more force than a conventional hand grenade.

I stepped inside the elevator, pushed the down

button, and we started our descent. I sealed the calculator inside the pink envelope, tied the ribbon in a neat bow around it, and then taped it to the inside panel of the sliding door. When the door was open it would be invisible and it would only appear as the door slid shut again. By then it would be too late because the next time the door shut it would stay shut and the elevator would automatically rise to between the second and third floor; there it would stop, and there it would stay.

Thirty of the ninety seconds had ticked away by the time we reached the bottom. As the door slid open I bowed my head slightly to sink further into the upturned collar, watching out of the corner of my eye the envelope neatly disappear from view.

From the way I had arranged the lighting panel on the ground floor it would have appeared to Scatliffe that I was coming from the third floor, not the eighth floor where I had actually come from, so he would not have any reason to connect me with the purpose of his visit. I swept out of the elevator as the figure in the trilby hat and the blue Crombie coat entered. He gave me only a cursory glance, his mind evidently preoccupied with other matters, but there was nonetheless the vaguest hint of recognition in his glance, a moment of uncertainty, as if he knew that he had once somewhere met me before but he couldn't think where.

As the door shut, gratingly, unremittingly, upon him I knew that if he was thinking he had seen me once before he was right. He'd bowled me out. The man in the trilby hat and blue Crombie coat who had just entered that elevator wasn't Scatliffe at all. He was Anthony Lines, the Home Secretary.

I walked swiftly down the road. Ninety seconds came up on my watch when I was about a hundred yards down. I was in a state of shock. I heard a faint muffled noise through the wind, very faint. A moment later there was the sound of crashing glass; it was followed by more crashing glass: it was a huge noise. I turned and looked back at the office building. In a random succession, one after another, windows dropped out and crashed down to the ground. I stared in amazement, watching the frames twist, then buckle, flinging great chunks of glass out, away and down.

Suddenly one entire side of the building sagged; bricks, plaster, wood, glass rained down, then the entire building leaned over and collapsed like a pack of cards into a vast irregular pyramid of rubble that spewed right out into the street.

This time, I thought, Trout and Trumbull had really gone over the top.

CHAPTER 25

Life has a nasty habit of creeping up behind you and clipping you on the ear when you least expect it. As you lift your hand up to your ear the great iron fist of life strikes out full into the area some six inches below your belt. For a long time after, you feel weak as hell and sick as a dog. That's how I felt standing over the wash-basin back in the Madison Park East Hotel.

The brown dye was revolting and streamed down my face as I attempted to restore my hair back to its usual colour. The moustache and beard came painfully away, ripping out three days growth of hair in the process, and I flushed them down the lavatory. I didn't think it would take even the New York police too long to figure out there might be a connection between a collapsed building on 3rd Street, the dead body inside it, and a blonde-haired man with a beard and moustache.

The hotel hadn't changed in the last few days since I had last stayed. Quasimodo's grandson downstairs still seemed to be enjoying his movie show on the blank wall; the cockroaches still seemed to be enjoying themselves in the bathroom.

The one person who was definitely not enjoying himself was me.

I was busy figuring out hard how having murdered the Home Secretary was going to help my future career. I didn't think it was going to help it too much. Nor, probably, did he. What had happened was still only just beginning to sink home. The further it sank, the less I liked it. And this was the least of my worries. I tried to think clearly and it was difficult. It all pointed to Anthony Lines and yet it couldn't have been him. His role in this was crystal clear to me: he had discovered exactly what I had; he'd intercepted the message to the Pink Envelope and had come out himself in order to get to the bottom of the matter.

But it had been Scatliffe's voice on the telephone. I was absolutely certain of that. Lines's voice was nothing like Scatliffe's. Either Scatliffe had been with him or he had done a remarkable job of mimicking Scatliffe's voice. It didn't make sense that he would have mimicked Scatliffe's voice. But it was possible that there was a reason; anything was possible. Too many things were possible and only one thing was absolutely certain: that I was up shit creek, in a barbed wire canoe with no paddle. By what I had done to Lines I had probably pulled the bung out as well.

I had been certain that Scatliffe was the Pink Envelope. When his voice had come on the telephone I knew that the agony and risks I had put myself through during the past days had paid off.

And now I was holed up in this wretched room with my career destroyed, a murder hunt about to begin for me, and not the first idea what to do next. If I had been right about Scatliffe then I seemed to have walked into an extremely clever trap. If I was wrong, I could expect no mercy and he would gleefully have me put behind bars for the rest of my days. My only saving grace right now was that everyone except two men, Irving and Karavenoff, thought I was dead. It was in Irving's interests that I remained so but Karavenoff worried me; he was on the fence and would come down on whatever side suited him best. If I was going to make a run for it then I should kill him first to protect my back.

But I knew that idea was crazy. I didn't want to spend the rest of my life as a criminal on the run. There had to be a solution to this whole damn mess. If I thought long enough and hard enough maybe it would come. I wasn't convinced but I had to give it a go.

I sat long into the night, stubbing out cigarette end after cigarette end. It was a slow night and a lonely night and as grey dawn came up I dozed a little and woke a little. Finally I couldn't stand it any more. I put my coat on and went out into the freezing cold air.

New York is a confusing place. It never really sleeps; while one half goes to bed, the other half gets up to work. At five o'clock in the morning you can buy a second-hand car, or a new suit, or

273

the week's groceries; not as easily perhaps as at five o'clock in the afternoon but easily enough.

I walked down the streets; less than one week to Christmas, and tinsel and fairy lights and glittering packages shone out at me from the windows. I felt tired and sad and a million other things, and I didn't want to be here doing this at all. I thought back on what I had done yesterday and wondered if it really was me that had done that and, if it really was me, how I could now be walking casually along, looking in these windows, thinking about Christmas in childhood, without any remorse, any feeling of guilt about the man who had gone to his death in a crummy elevator in a crummy building, yesterday afternoon.

It was a long time since I had gone Christmas shopping, trailing round the London stores with my mother, sitting on Santa Claus's knees in Harrods, Swan & Edgar, D H Evans. I thought about all the long, sometimes happy, sometimes wretched process, of growing up, becoming a man, and now I was a man, and had been a man for a long time, and I was alone, wandering down this cold Manhattan street,

feeling like an old toy that had been chucked into a waste bin.

I spent the day shuffling the streets, drinking eternal cups of black coffee and smoking eternal cigarettes in the cafes that came my way and I came no closer to any solution. Finally in the early evening I hailed a cab, went to Kennedy Airport and bought a ticket on the 10 pm TWA flight to London. The flight was a little under seven hours and, depending on the strength of the tail wind, we were scheduled to arrive at Heathrow Airport at about 9.40 in the morning.

The stewardess brought me the *New York Times*. The front page headline read, 'British politician dead in New York Building collapse mystery.' The article stated that no cause for the collapse was yet known but there was evidence of an explosion. The IRA was mentioned as possibly being involved but they had not claimed responsibility and there was as yet no clear evidence of any foul play. The article went on to state that the building had been scheduled for demolition under a redevelopment scheme.

It normally drizzles most of the week before Christmas and this Tuesday morning was no exception. If you ever feel gloomy and despondent, avoid flying into England on a wet day. Not that to have been greeted by blazing sunshine, a temperature of 95 degrees, and a host of naked dancing girls would have made much difference to my mood.

No one arrested me at the passport control and I walked out into the arrival lounge. I hired a car and drove off onto the M4 and the West Country. The plane had had engine trouble and the tail wind was weak; I switched on the radio to catch the one o'clock news. Not surprisingly the late

Anthony Lines MP featured prominently. Considerable advances had been made since the *New York Times* had gone to press. Lines had definitely been killed by an explosion, which in turn had brought on the collapse of the building, the explosion apparently having taken place in the elevator. The IRA had denied responsibility and none of the other Irish terrorist organisations had as yet claimed any part in it. But whilst his death was given great prominence in the report, what was given even more prominence was the fact of Lines's being in New York at all; that was a complete mystery to everyone.

He appeared to have told his wife late on Friday that he had to go to an emergency conference with the Prime Minister and wouldn't be back until Monday. But the Prime Minister denied all knowledge of this conference and had been seen by numerous people out Christmas shopping all that Saturday. Had Lines gone to a secret meeting with a terrorist group? Why hadn't the Americans any knowledge that he was coming? Under what name had he flown over since no passenger of his name had been carried by any of the airlines over that weekend? The speculation was well and truly rife. Already the death of Sir Maurice Unwin was being linked with Lines's by the reporters. The Prime Minister had not yet issued any statement but was expected to later that day. In a strange way it all cheered me up.

*　　*　　*

Fifeshire's country house was deep in the Cotswold hills, on the outskirts of two minute hamlets, and I found it with some considerable difficulty. There were two impressive stone gateposts topped by handsome gargoyles; the gates were open and looked as though they hadn't been shut in years. Inside the gates the drive dropped sharply down to the right, and as I drove down, the house came into view some way below me. It was a massive Elizabethan manor, sunk deep in the hollow on one side, but looking down over hundreds of acres of rolling fields and hills in the distance on the other. It was a rich man's house but sufficient parts of the facade, the driveway and the gardens looked in need of some care, not a great deal, but just enough to give it the feel of a private home rather than a National Trust set piece. It was the kind of house that told you, whatever else you might be feeling, that all was all right in the world.

I rang the doorbell and a rather matronly housekeeper opened the huge oak door.

'I've come to see Sir Charles,' I said.

She looked at me, surprised. 'But he's not here,' she said, 'he's in town.'

'I thought he wasn't working up there at the moment.'

'Not usually, he isn't – at present; he's still convalescing from his, er,' she couldn't bring herself to say the word. 'But some telegram came over the weekend and he drove up very early on Monday morning; we don't expect him back for a few days.'

'Oh. I had an appointment with him,' I lied, 'three o'clock this afternoon.'

'If you like, I'll ring and tell him you're here.'

'I'd be most grateful if you would.'

'May I have your name, please?'

'Spade,' I said.

She left me on the doorstep and went off inside. After a few minutes she returned:

'Sir Charles is terribly sorry, sir; he says he completely forgot about your appointment. He asks if you will come in and make yourself at home; he will be back down just as soon as he can get away from his office.'

It didn't sound to me like the message of an angry man but then Fifeshire never had given much away. I accepted the housekeeper's offer of tea and biscuits, then fell into a deep sleep in the armchair in front of the roaring inglenook fireplace in the drawing room.

I awoke with a bolt of cold fear to the unmistakable clattering of a helicopter overhead. My immediate reaction was that the bastard had sent the army to get me. Then I looked at my watch: it was past seven. If he'd wanted me arrested, he'd have done it several hours ago. The huge door opened and in strode a beaming Fifeshire, limping a little, but looking fitter than ever, with attaché case in one hand and newspaper in the other; he dropped them both onto a chair.

'Well, well, good evening, Mr Digger!' he gave me a firm, warm handshake.

'So you're still speaking to me,' I said.

There was a grin on his face from ear to ear. 'I purloined a chopper to get down here as quickly as I could; damn traffic's dreadful otherwise. Look like you've been to hell and back – you probably know the way by now.' He gave me another big grin; he was looking pleased as punch, like some child that's just got up to some mischief and is waiting for the results of its handiwork to take effect. He picked up the newspaper, the *Evening Standard*, and thrust it at me. 'Have you been watching the news on television?'

'No, haven't heard anything since one o'clock; I'm afraid I fell asleep.'

He nodded at me to look at the *Standard*. The thick black type across the top of the front page blazed out the legend: Was Lines a Russian spy? I looked quizzically at Fifeshire.

'Go on,' he said, 'read it.'

'On Friday evening in Washington Sir Maurice Unwin, Britain's attaché to the United States, apparently committed suicide. It is not widely known that Sir Maurice was the Head of MI6 in the US.

'On Sunday afternoon in New York the Home Secretary, Anthony Lines, was murdered by a bomb.

'It has today been learned that Commander Clive Scatliffe, deputy head of MI5, has been

279

missing since Friday night. Intelligence sources report that he boarded an Aeroflot flight in New York, bound for Moscow, late on Sunday. Commander Scatliffe was acting head of MI5 since the hospitalisation of Sir Charles Cunningham-Hope, who was seriously wounded by gunfire when President Battanga was assassinated in his car in August of this year.'

I read through the rest of the article. It dragged up a number of left-wing remarks made by Lines during the course of his career, analysed his Cambridge education and the left-wing society with which he mixed at the time, and attempted to link the situation with the Philby/Blunt affair of 1980 but without actually producing any concrete evidence. I looked up at Fifeshire.

'There's more to come,' he said.

'Tell me.'

'Whisky?'

I nodded assent and we sat down with hefty tumblers of Scotch: Glenfiddich, what else?

'I received a telephone call from a gentleman with whom you are familiar,' he said, 'one Harold Wetherby. He's involved in this whole thing up to his neck and wants to bargain a lot of knowledge he claims to have in return for a pardon. He's terrified he's about to be bumped off at any moment. I've had a word with the Prime Minister; no one's happy about granting any pardons since all the flak of that business of the Blunt affair, and I've told him so. Anyhow, he's flying over to

London tonight to tell all and to throw himself at our mercy.

'This is really the most extraordinary affair. The one man I just do not understand is Unwin: I can't believe he's mixed up in this but the way the muck's going to hit the fan during the next few days we're all going to have to brace ourselves for a lot more shocks yet.'

'Unwin's innocent,' I said. 'He was murdered. I'm certain of that; and I'm responsible. I knew there was at least one mole in Washington but I didn't know who for sure. I suspected both Wetherby and Hicks. I telephoned Unwin and gave him a message that wouldn't have made much sense to him. I told him I was going to reveal the identity of the Pink Envelope to the press unless I was paid 100,000 dollars in cash at a secret rendezvous. I figured that Unwin would be bound to discuss this message with Hicks and Wetherby, along with the other members of his senior staff. To make sure, I leaked the news of my message to Moscow. I knew that the mole in Washington was in regular communication with the Pink Envelope and I was sure that in the light of everything that had been going on, the Pink Envelope wouldn't leave it to anyone else to deal with the matter this time, but would come over himself. The Envelope obviously instructed someone at Washington to bump off Unwin before he could have a chance to talk too much and to ensure he didn't show up in New York himself. I was certain

that the Envelope was Scatliffe and I don't understand what Lines was doing in New York.'

'Lines and Scatliffe went over together. They took
different flights but met up when they got there.
Both were scared witless and wouldn't let the other
out of sight any more. Wetherby told me. You'll also
be interested to learn that Hicks has disappeared.
Scatliffe, Wetherby and Lines went to a call box
together to call the blackmailer – presumably you –
and then Lines insisted on going off to the meeting
with the blackmailer alone. When Lines didn't
return, Scatliffe got scared and bolted.' He paused.
'Why did you kill Lines?'

'I thought he was Scatliffe. I set the trap for
Scatliffe and Lines walked into it. I could have
stopped him but I'd gone so far I felt I had to go
on.'

'I don't follow,' said Fifeshire.

'Somebody's tried to kill me most days for the
past couple of weeks – I told you that when we met
in the Clinic. I was certain that Scatliffe was at the
back of it but I had no evidence. I was certain too
that Wetherby was involved, and others, possibly
many others, but I didn't know who. After I left you
I found out more evidence; you were the only person
I could trust to tell it to but if I'd gone back to you,
your next step would have been to have reported
the matter to your superior: and that would have
been Lines, and you and I would be 6 feet under
right now – unless Lines was innocent.'

'Both Scatliffe and Lines have the sterling

equivalent of 50,000 dollars each missing from their bank accounts. Both withdrawals were made on Friday. Lines wasn't innocent. Go on.'

'Right, the only thing I could do was to try and flush out the Pink Envelope, get him to turn up with some evidence to implicate him. Having done that, I would have to kill him if I was to have any chance of ever getting back alive to tell the tale. And in my heart of hearts I felt that by killing him I might just start off a chain reaction.'

'That you have certainly done. But you took one hell of a risk.'

'You don't have to tell me, sir,' I smiled – for the first time in a long time.

'The next few days are going to be interesting, very interesting,' said Fifeshire.

'There are two mysteries I want to resolve: the first concerns Orchnev; and the second, the girl I was going out with who just suddenly disappeared off the face of the earth.'

'Could her name be Mary-Ellen Joffe?' Fifeshire grinned.

'How the hell do you know?'

'I'll tell you in a minute. Tell me what you want to know about Orchnev; he started this whole damn thing off, or so it seems.'

'He did, certainly. What I haven't told you accurately, sir, is how he died.'

'I understand you shot him – thought he was an intruder – that's what you told the New York police at any rate.'

'Right. But I didn't shoot him. He shot himself.'

Fifeshire looked puzzled and I told him the story of exactly what did happen. At the end of it he nodded his head. 'It makes sense,' he said.

'I'm glad it does to someone,' I replied, 'because it's been baffling the hell out of me. He came to see me because someone must have told him to come and see me – but that's as far as I can get. Going back historically, Orchnev originally wrote to you. Scatliffe, Hicks and Wetherby between them intercepted these letters and they never reached you. They didn't want you to know Orchnev wanted to defect because they didn't want him spilling any beans and blowing open the whole communications system between the KGB and the US. So they tried to kill you to get you out of the way; they didn't succeed in killing you but they disabled you sufficiently so that you were no longer a threat. But why did they send Orchnev along to me and why did he kill himself in front of me?'

'Orchnev was in New York eighteen months ago. He went over on a holiday; being a senior Party member he was trusted enough to be allowed to holiday alone. He had access to information vital to an operation MI6 were planning so they thought they'd have a go at him while he was in the States. They set a girl up as bait and he went for her. They dated a few times, she seduced him, but instead of her getting anything out of him, he went and fell madly in love with her. The only thing that stopped him defecting in order to live with her right there and then was his wife and three children in Russia. So very reluctantly he returned to Russia.

'Six months later his wife and children were wiped out in a car crash. It appears to have been a genuine accident – we don't think he fixed it. A couple of months passed, then this girl started to receive passionate love letters from him. She was instructed to respond equally passionately. She did. Her letters prompted Orchnev to make his decision to defect. He had nothing to live for in Russia any more; he had this gorgeous girl who was head-over-heels in love with him in New York. So he wrote to the head of the Soviet division of the CIA and sent the letter via a courier friend at the British Embassy, who passed it to MI6.

'Having got their hands on the letter, MI6, who wanted Orchnev themselves, faked a reply to Orchnev from the CIA telling him that the CIA were not interested in his deal because they were scared of damaging some delicate negotiations they were having with Moscow, but said they had discussed the matter with the British who would be prepared to accept him, subject to being satisfied that he could and would provide worthwhile information. He agreed to this on the proviso that he could firstly come to New York and that there was some hope that at a later date the US might permit him residency. So MI6 wrote him a fairly standard letter offering him a new life in exchange

285

for worthwhile information and agreeing to his visiting New York prior to coming to England. It was at this point that the Home Secretary was informed, since when Orchnev arrived in England he would be placed in the hands of MI5. Lines should of course have then immediately instructed me to handle the matter. Lines and Scatliffe should have told the Russians what was happening so that the Russians could prevent Orchnev from leaving, but this would have given the game away that there was a leak our end. It would be much easier for them if I was out of the way and they saw this as a good time to get rid of me. They would let Orchnev reach New York then bump him off before he had a chance to talk to anyone.

'Then they had an even better idea: rather than have the problems of a dead Russian at all, they would try and get him to return to Russia of his own free will. They thought that if between the last love letter she wrote and the time he arrived in New York the girl had acquired a new lover and was no longer interested in him, he might decide there was no point in defecting after all and return to Russia.

'So his defection was arranged as an innocent holiday to the States to get away from the bad memories of his wife and family for a while – all perfectly plausible. He was to be met in New York when he arrived by a Russian expatriate who was an old friend, who worked, incidentally, as a double agent for Wetherby. The Russian was to take him round to the girl's flat. Orchnev was to go in and surprise her late at night but to his horror he would find her in bed with her new lover. He would leave in disgust and his friend waiting outside would persuade him that the most sensible thing he could do would be to go straight back to the airport and take the first plane he could back to Russia.

'They agreed on this plan and set it in motion. Unfortunately it backfired horribly on them. Orchnev had a gun and instead of leaving the girl's flat, he was so shocked by what he saw that, on top of all the tragedy of his wife and children and the strain of all the planning he had done, his mind became unbalanced and he shot himself. The girl was the one you called Sumpy and you were the lover. Have another Scotch.'

I couldn't see any point in refusing.